YOU'RE FAMILY NOW

JACK STAINTON

ALSO BY JACK STAINTON

A Guest to Die For

This novel is entirely a work of fiction and any resemblance to actual persons, living or dead, is purely coincidental.

An imprint of Windmill Streams *Publishers*

You're Family Now

For Alex & Jared

AUTHOR'S NOTE

Thank you for reading 'You're Family Now'

This is part one of 'The Family' Trilogy - three novels based around the central character, Matthew Walker.

They can either be read as individual stand-alone books, or in chronological order.

Either way, I hope you enjoy!

PROLOGUE

RUNNING. Running as fast as he can. Tripping and stumbling over the tree roots that protrude from the ill-defined footpath; a footpath that is rarely, if ever, used.

He's deep in the woods, deeper than he's ever ventured before. Following his instincts, believing this route must take him closer to the village, he drifts further into the undergrowth. But the light is fading fast. He wanted to wait until after dark, but then he would have to use a torch, a light that would tell them his whereabouts. Dusk would be his best chance.

Slowing down, catching his breath, he looks around. He turns full circle as he walks, straining his neck and making himself feel giddy as he admires the tops of the impossibly tall trees. The last glimmer of light silhouettes the branches, giving them the appearance of long spindly arms, each one reaching out, trying to touch him, to grab him. He shivers and pulls the zip on his sweatshirt up to his chin, before continuing his abscondment; and then he hears the snap.

A twig, a tiny branch, a splinter underfoot. He freezes to the spot, eyes darting from left to right. He edges backwards, watching, listening. Without looking where he's stepping, he trips over a tree root and falls awkwardly onto his back. Keeping as calm as he can,

I

he crawls backwards, using his hands and feet in tandem, scrambling for grip amongst the soft pine needles which carpet the woods. Finally, he pushes himself upright again, eyes straining through the rapidly fading light. At first, he isn't sure if his mind is playing tricks, but there they are. He sees shadows in the distance, darting in and out of view. They've followed him. Although he knew they'd soon discover he'd gone, the speed they have been able to track him down astounds him.

Turning and breaking into a jog, he keeps glancing behind, praying that nobody is there. A bird escapes from a nearby bush, flapping its wings frantically, making him gasp. He follows the flight of the panic-stricken bird as it heads to the top of the trees and beyond. He wishes so much he could do the same; escape forever.

Another branch snapping pulls him back to the present. Then another, and another. Footsteps to his right, running parallel with him. Next, more steps from the left, closer than those on the other side. He picks up his speed, although he's moving up a slight incline. He knows the village must be close now, within his reach.

But the footsteps in the trees are keeping up with him, mocking him. Each time he increases his speed, the pursuers increase theirs too.

How is it possible when they are amongst the dense vegetation whilst I'm on the path?

He can just make out the brow of the hill, less than fifty metres ahead. Breaking into a sprint, his heart pumping and his legs screaming, he inadvertently reaches out his hands, trying to drag the top of the rise towards him. Laughter from his right, quickly followed by laughter from his left. He feels sick, petrified by what's happening to him, by what might *happen to him.*

Eventually, he's at the summit. He stops momentarily and allows himself a split second of elation. The trees ahead are much more sporadically spaced, and he can make out the street lamps and house lights from the village below. It's less than half a mile away, down a steep incline; he can be there in only two minutes, at the most. *The path is better defined from here, even in the rapidly fading light.*

And then the footsteps behind, walking along the same path to which he just ran. He spins around, fists clenched, expecting an attack from his tormentors who have mocked him throughout the attempted escape. They stop less than ten paces from where he stands, both grinning. Those hideous grins that he's learned to detest over the past few months.

He's caught in two minds. Does he fight or does he run? As soon as they take a step forward, their faces contorting from mocking laughter to desperate hatred, his mind is made up. He turns to run.

But he hadn't heard the third person creep up from behind. Somebody else is blocking the footpath and his hopes of reaching the village. The game is over now.

As his adversaries move in for the kill, he spots her in the distance, deep amongst the trees.

He smiles and holds out his hands. It's sheer desperation for one last chance of reprieve.

But the little girl, in the oversized white dress, just stands and stares.

PART I

1

EIGHTEEN MONTHS AGO

My hands were sweating; so annoying that it only happened when nerves got the better of me. Normally, I'd be confident, but that day wasn't normal; it was the final interview for a job I *had* to get. The chance to take my career to the next level, but more importantly, an opportunity to get my life sorted.

After I'd signed the visitors' book, the receptionist phoned someone to inform them I'd arrived. She instructed me, rather than politely asked, to take a seat in the spacious foyer. Sitting on one of four bright orange sofas which circled a large smoked glass table, I heard an indoor water feature trickling from somewhere behind. The sound didn't have its desired effect and invoke calmness within me; instead, it just caused me to want to visit the bathroom.

Discreetly rubbing my hands along my trousers to try to keep my palms dry before the inevitable handshakes, I attempted to block out the need for the toilet. The shrill ring made me jump.

"Mr Walker?"

The receptionist held my gaze. Her stern face gave the impression that she derived no job satisfaction at all.

"Mr Whelan will see you now. Just take the lift to the fourth floor, somebody will meet you there."

With a slight nod towards the back of the foyer, she returned her attention to a magazine and a nail file.

Thinking it strange that I could walk around a building unaccompanied, my initial thoughts were soon scuppered as I stepped out of the lift. There were two choices. I either needed a security pass to open the tinted sliding glass doors in front of me or I must step back into the lift.

And that's when I first noticed her, walking towards me along the aisle which split the open-plan office into two. Most people sat behind their computer terminals, whilst a few gathered in small groups; talking, laughing. But I ignored everybody else; I only had eyes for her.

Her long black hair was the first thing I noticed. Shiny, like in the television adverts for shampoo or conditioner. It was jet black, long, at least halfway down her back as far as I could tell. As she got closer, I began to make out her features. Such a pretty face, her cheekbones prominent and a mouth enhanced by deep crimson lipstick. Her eyes drew me in as she approached the glass doors. Dark brown, the brownest eyes I'd ever seen. She looked roughly five and a half feet tall – although I'd always been an awful judge of such things – and the belt on her knee-length pencil skirt pulled her waist in; her figure accentuated by her tight black jumper. She glided across the room as though she were on a catwalk. I noticed a few of the male occupants stare after her whilst two women looked up for a couple of seconds, before whispering to each other behind cupped hands.

She held her security pass to a keypad and the glass doors glided effortlessly open. She looked me up and down before extending her hand to greet me.

"Mr Walker? Matthew Walker?" Her voice matched her demeanour, professional yet somehow sultry.

Reaching out to shake her hand in return, I couldn't help but notice the stares from over her shoulder, looking at us in unison. It seemed strange that the staff, who must see her every day, would pay so much attention. The feel of her skin on mine brought me back to the present.

"Hi, yes, I'm Matthew. Matthew Walker."

"Nice to meet you. I'm Amelia. Amelia Reid. I'll be interviewing you with Mr Whelan. Follow me."

The handshake lasted a few seconds longer than I would consider normal. She held my gaze. I felt momentarily mesmerised. Close up, in my mind at least, she looked even more beautiful than I'd originally thought.

Amelia walked a few paces ahead of me, fleetingly glancing over her shoulder to ensure I was keeping up. I felt eyes bore into me, but I didn't look at anybody else. As we approached a row of glass cubicles, I saw a large gentleman stand up from behind a table in the second meeting room along. I needed to concentrate on the task ahead and pushed all thoughts of Amelia to the back of my mind. At least for the present.

An hour later, as I sat lightly drumming on the steering wheel of my car, I let out an enormous sigh of relief. Immediately I felt myself relax, back to the real Matt Walker and not the pretend, need to make an impression, formal Matthew Walker.

Taking deep breaths, I allowed myself a smile. The interview had gone well, very well in fact. Mr Whelan, Mike, turned out to be a down-to-earth guy, which defied my original perception of the stiff, middle-management, corporate type person I despised. As soon as I'd walked into the glass cubicle, the first thing I'd noticed had been his old-fashioned suit, blue and shiny – not something I'd associate with a modern, forward-thinking company, hell-bent on being the market leader in a commercial property operation. His greased back hair, which belonged more in the nineteen seventies than the twenty-first century, aged him considerably. However, he oozed knowledge about commercial property and I already knew I would learn much from him; if I got the job of course.

Then there was Amelia. During the interview, I knew my eyes kept drifting from Mike to her. And every time they did, I caught her staring directly back towards me. Mike must have noticed, and diplomatically informed me that if they offered me the role, then Amelia would be my personal secretary, or *executive secretary*, as the company liked to call them. A thought shot through my mind – it would mean we would have to talk to each other every day, see each other most days and even attend appointments and conferences together.

My light drumming of the steering wheel became more of a joyful banging as I realised I'd have to liaise with Amelia Reid every working day for the rest of my life. Well, at least until one of us was no longer required.

Then there was the money – far more than I'd ever earned before – with added monthly and annual bonuses. Mike had mentioned a company car. My choice within reason. It was everything I'd wanted. At thirty-six years of age, my career, and life, had stagnated. I lived alone in a tiny rented flat in North London and drove around in a fifteen-year-old car, which contained as much rust as paint.

If it hadn't been for that chance meeting at the bar, I'd have never even known the job existed and I'd have never been put forward for the interview.

The next day I paced up and down in my flat, continually picking up my phone, somehow thinking that might make it ring. Earlier, I had called in sick to my current employer, feigning a migraine. It wasn't entirely untrue. I'd made my way through one and a half bottles of red wine the night before, half in anticipation that landing the job would be a formality. However, doubt replaced the certainty as the day wore on. Finally, I convinced myself that I'd blown it altogether. I played the interview over and over in my head – where had I messed up?

Eventually, just as I'd given up any last lingering hope of success, my phone rang. I hauled myself from my old leather sofa – the arms of which were completely worn through, and the seats sagged so much you had to lever yourself out – and picked up my mobile from the adjoining kitchen work surface. The caller ID informed me it was the employment agency. My heart skipped several beats before I hit the accept button.

"Hi. Matt Walker speaking."

I immediately realised my voice sounded uneven.

"Hello, Matt. It's Greig from Hammond Appointments. Are you well?"

Cut to the fucking chase, mate.

My professional head kicked in.

"Yes, fine thanks. You?"

Just fucking tell me.

"Yeah, I'm very well thank you."

Oh, I am pleased. And your wife, kids? How's your fucking cat?
"That's good."
A pause.
"Anyway. I have some splendid news for you…"
Yes, yes, yes!

"… Opacy Property Management wants to make you an offer. Obviously, I can't decide for you, but I genuinely believe that if you don't take it, you'll regret this decision for the rest of your life."

2

Following the call from Grieg at Hammond Appointments, the next month passed by in a whirlwind. I'd really wanted to take a holiday; escape somewhere warm for a week or two, but my old company insisted I see out my four-week notice period, and I only had three days leave to take at the end. I couldn't argue because I needed the money and, just as important, a good reference before Opacy would grant me a contract. I spent the final three days between the two jobs shopping in London. Two new suits, five extra shirts and two fresh pairs of shoes, the combination of which had almost maxed out my credit card.

My first morning nerves soon dissipated as everybody made me feel welcome. The only disappointment was that Amelia wasn't due in until lunchtime because of some pre-arranged appointment. Mike did the introductions and gave me a full tour of the office.

Apart from Amelia Reid, there were two other executive secretaries, each working directly with a senior port-folio manager. First, Mike introduced me to Tracy. Although I would find out later that she was thirty-seven, Tracy gave the appearance of somebody much older. Around five foot seven, she had wavy brown hair – just over shoulder length, and set in an old-fashioned perm – and a face that reminded me of my strict, old head-mistress; drawn and sombre. She wore a brown tweed jacket and a free-flowing ankle-length brown skirt. Her blue eyes were her best feature, although somewhat let down by a pair of glasses perched towards the end of her nose. They were half-moon shaped, and instantly reminded me of the days when my teacher would look at me from over the top of her own spectacles, before launching into a tirade of criticism at my inept attitude towards my work. Tracy's firm handshake caught me by surprise, and so did her voice. She spoke cheerfully, undermining her stony-faced appearance, and wished me a long and happy stay with the company. Tracy had been with the company for several years, and her particular portfolio manager, Don Clark, was the most senior member of staff, after Mike. Don wasn't in the office that day, instead out visiting a potential client. Tracy explained that Don's portfolio included the majority of the top ten customers, and his vast experience meant he was the person to ask if I encountered any problems. Even though I hadn't met him yet, I'd already taken a dislike to Don.

The other secretary was Lisa Ingram. In complete contrast to Tracy, Lisa was in her mid-forties, yet could easily have passed as ten years her junior. She was attrac-tive, medium height and medium build. I think *curvy* would be the most accurate description, which is meant as a huge compliment. Her straight blonde hair just covered her neckline, and like Amelia, she had dark brown eyes.

Lisa's portfolio manager was Chris Forde, a quiet guy in his late fifties who looked as though he was going through the motions until he could afford early retirement. Lisa made me feel the most comfortable of all the staff they had introduced me to. She came across as funny and gave the impression she was very confident, both in a professional and personal manner. She was also flirty, in a good-natured way. I immediately took to Lisa.

Just before lunch, as I eventually began to understand how to use my brand new MacBook Pro – somewhat different to the shabby Windows XP laptop my old company had provided me with – the office fell silent. A few people continued with their phone calls, but the majority had stopped the murmur of conversation and the tapping of keyboards. Looking up, the first thing I noticed was Lisa peering over at me from behind her desk. She smiled and turned her head to follow the stares of everybody else. I followed her gaze.

Exactly as when I had walked out of the lift on the day of my interview, it seemed most people had stopped in their tracks to follow Amelia as she walked along the length of the office.

Why is everybody so fascinated with her?

And just as on my interview day, Amelia looked stunning. A tight yellow jumper hugged her body and a tight pair of black jeans stretched the length of her long legs. I noticed her black nail varnish and matching eyelashes, emphasised by her long black hair.

Lisa looked over towards me again, the smile returning to her face. I tried to look neutral, uninterested, but deep down I knew it was futile. Amelia said good morning to a few people who reciprocated with a friendly nod and 'good morning' in return. It struck me she wasn't unpopular, but I couldn't understand why she drew so many looks. Yes, she was attractive − to me at least − but it wasn't as though everybody in the office would have seen her that way.

She put her laptop and handbag onto her desk and walked directly over to me. I stood, now aware that most of the office was watching our reunion. I forced myself to stay professional and not to blush or clam up. The very worst thing I could have done was show any kind of weakness. I was the new portfolio manager on the block, and I needed to exude confidence if I were to be taken seriously and become a success. I noticed Lisa turn her attention back to her laptop; I couldn't be sure, but it looked like a flash of envy that shot across her face.

Amelia extended her hand, to which I reciprocated. She continued to shake my hand as she spoke.

"Good morning, Matthew. So happy to welcome you aboard."

"Hello again. It's great to be here at last. But please, call me Matt."

Well aware we were still shaking hands, and also conscious that those in our proximity were still watching us, I pulled my hand away. Amelia held on a moment longer before releasing her grip and letting her fingertips slide along my palm. I could feel an instant connection between us, and I knew Amelia felt it too.

Mike offered to take me to a local pub for lunch, which I gladly accepted. During the meal, he told me of his plans for the company over the coming months and years. He had big ambitions to make the firm one of the biggest property management companies in the southeast of

England, and he said I could be a huge part of that success. Although it was only my first day, I couldn't hide my excitement at joining Opacy. It felt as though I had a wonderful future ahead of me if I got my head down and worked hard, something I was determined to do this time.

The afternoon went by in a flash. I sat with Amelia for an hour and she talked me through the first two clients that Mike had put me in charge of. One was in central London, almost within walking distance of the office, whilst the other was in Brighton, on the south coast. Driving to customers would be a pleasure, given that I had chosen my company car three weeks previously. They had sent me a comprehensive choice of vehicles along with my job offer. They would deliver the car before the end of my first week.

The final two hours I spent reading up on my two clients; their purchasing history and properties they had shown an interest in. I became impatient to get started.

Just after five o'clock, the office emptied. A few people made their way over to say goodbye or jokingly comment on how well I'd done to stay all day. Everybody made me feel part of the team.

Chris and Mike left together, leaving only myself and the three secretaries, Tracy, Lisa and Amelia. I'd wanted to leave as late as possible to set a good impression but was surprised at the trio's reluctance to go home. They had made it quite clear at the interview that it wasn't necessary to work long hours unless there was an emergency that couldn't wait until morning. Mike had said that they wanted to create a happy culture and not a 'work, work, work' scenario. It had been one benefit that had stood out to me before I accepted.

Eventually, Tracy left, leaving just the three of us.

"You go ahead, Lisa," said Amelia, "I'll see Matt out tonight."

Lisa smiled, somewhat sarcastically, before switching off her laptop and packing it away. She collected her jacket and swished past Amelia with a nonchalant 'good-bye' before turning to me.

"Great to have you working with us. I hope you enjoy it here."

Just as I was going to respond, Lisa looked over towards Amelia who was busy tidying her desk and getting her coat and bags together. Lisa bent down, and not taking her eyes off Amelia, whispered in my ear.

"Just be careful, okay?"

I opened my mouth to reply, but Lisa had spun away and walked across the office. I stared after her, somewhat bemused by what she had just said. I'd wanted to say, 'Don't worry, Lisa. I know exactly what I'm doing'. Amelia's voice brought me back to the present.

"You ready?" She was standing beside me, following my gaze at the disappearing figure of Lisa.

"Er, yeah. You go ahead…"

"Nonsense. Now, which hotel did I book you into this week?"

"The Thistle, I checked-in last night."

"That's right. Great. I'll walk you there."

3

DURING THE NEXT TWO MONTHS, my feet barely touched the ground. I'd struck up my first big deal with the company in Brighton and made progress with my other client in London. I had impressed Mike with my start, so much so he trusted me with two more customers, both in London. The company car had arrived at the beginning of my second week, I'd paid off a significant chunk of my credit card with my first two pay cheques, and I'd even sold my fifteen-year-old rusty car to a neighbour. Things were certainly looking up.

At thirty-six years of age, I knew the job could be make or break for me. Following university – where I'd studied economics – I had let life drift by; always promising myself that next year would be the year that I finally did something with myself.

I moved from job to job, mostly estate agent work; property was the one thing that seemed to stir some kind of passion within me. Each move to a larger agent spurred me on, but within months, sometimes just weeks, I became bored again. My entire life revolved around living for the weekend. Work was just an inconvenience that paid for rent, beer and holidays – in no particular order.

Two or three trips abroad with friends each year were always the highlights. However, the older I'd become, the fewer mates there were, either single or wanting to go on a lad's holiday. I had a couple of short-term relationships, but I just wasn't ready to settle down. Attracting women had never been difficult, especially in London. It may sound arrogant, but I'd always seemed to find someone of the opposite sex who found me attractive enough in return but the one-night stands were happening far too frequently. I was fast becoming the kid who never grew up.

When I was in my early thirties, I landed a job with a modest property management company in North London. I would be the only account manager there, and so I finally tried to settle down. I rented a cramped flat, which still cost a small fortune, on the outskirts of the city. I invested in my first ever car too. The holidays with friends were replaced by city breaks around Europe – sometimes alone, and sometimes with my latest girlfriend. None of these relationships ever lasted though; I just couldn't meet the right woman – it felt as though I never would.

Then, shortly after I turned thirty-four, my parents were involved in a car accident and both were tragically killed. They had lived in Scotland; somewhere they'd called home for the past fifteen years. Once I'd finished university, I'd informed them I wouldn't be returning home. They sold their house and moved north within six months. As far as I could tell, they were both heartbroken and delighted in equal measure. Their only child had left home for good, but it also gave them the opportunity to move to a part of the world they had fallen in love with over the years.

Following the funeral, the next few months had been a struggle. I managed to just about do enough in my job to keep my head above water, but I knew it wasn't a company to hold my interest for much longer. I applied for a couple of other roles, both in property management, but the agent advised me to stay patient. Life drifted by me and I recognised I needed a new challenge. Yet again, I found myself in danger of wallowing in self-pity.

My darkest time coincided with the chance meeting that would finally get my life on track – the very reason I applied for the position at Opacy and subsequently landed the job.

I'd met Julia in a bar in central London. It had followed a particularly hectic day at a property trade show in the city. The conference was the only one my current employer permitted me to visit. Money had been tight for them, and the boss saw exhibitions as a bit of a luxury, and somewhat a 'skive off work'. He was unusually old-fashioned in his approach and couldn't see the bigger picture of mingling with so many prospective clients.

Although I didn't find Julia particularly attractive, we had an instant connection. Probably down to being in the same line of work – she worked in property too, although for a company I'd never heard of – plus the fact that we were both staying in the same hotel after the conference.

Sharing several drinks, she listened to the woes of me losing my parents and needing to find some focus in my life. After I'd finished outpouring my problems, she suggested that I applied for a role at a central London company called Opacy. She said she'd heard good things about them and they were hiring a new portfolio manager. It sounded ideal, albeit after a few drinks, and she wrote the name of the agency that was dealing with the vacancy – Hammond Appointments – on a piece of paper she'd found in her handbag.

We had a lot more to drink, before inevitably spending the night together in the hotel. I'm not convinced that either of us had wanted it to happen, but one thing had led to another.

The following morning, Julia told me she was married, and it was probably best if we didn't see each other again. She told me a bit about her husband and left me under no illusions that spending the night together had been a mistake. It was the predictable conclusion to another drunken one-night stand. We said our goodbyes and I watched her as she left my room. She briefly turned around once she reached the door and smiled before wishing me good luck with the job application. That was the last I saw of her.

Later that day, I found the piece of paper Julia had written the details on, and, after staring at it for a while, I forced myself to pluck up the courage to call the agency. They were positive and made all the appropriate phone calls. As a result, later the same day, they put my application forward. I researched the company address and discovered they were right near Covent Garden. It all sounded very positive until I received a message informing me they had put recruitment on hold for a few weeks until they shored up a large deal. Grieg at Hammond Appointments told me they were very keen to see me though and recommended that I waited for the call. It would be six weeks later when Opacy Property Management eventually got back in touch, but thanks to my chance encounter with Julia, it had been worth the wait. Finally, my life was taking shape. My parents would have been so proud.

. . .

It was a cold, cloudy Tuesday morning in December when I arrived in the office. It had been several weeks since I'd started, and I still felt positive and eager to learn. The overwhelming feeling of boredom I'd always had in previous jobs hadn't materialised at all. Maybe things were on the up. I had a spring in my step and work was something I looked forward to. Besides, seeing Amelia every day was enough to get me out of bed and hurry into work on its own. She always made a genuine effort with her appearance, and she wore expensive clothes that complimented her every move. We were forming a bond; purely professional of course.

As soon as I sat down and booted up my laptop, Chris wandered over from his desk and asked if I'd like to visit a client with him.

"It's a company out near Heathrow Airport. They're called Jayavant Packaging. I've been talking with Lisa, and she thinks they would be a good fit for you."

Lisa looked up and smiled.

"Is that a good or bad thing?" I joked, returning Lisa's smile.

"Oh, all good," she replied. "They've kind of stagnated lately, but we believe they could be expanding. A new face from our company could help them go with us."

As I opened my mouth to reply, a voice from behind interrupted my train of thought.

"In that case, we accept."

Lisa's smile turned to a frown, and I spun around on my chair to see Amelia standing only a few feet behind me. I had no idea how long she'd been there, or that she'd even listened in to our conversation. It irritated me she spoke on my behalf, but I guessed she was only doing her job. Besides, it would be her who would have to liaise with the client once I'd been through the initial meetings.

"Okay, sounds great." I turned back to Chris. "When shall we go?"

"We set my meeting up for twelve o'clock. Er, Lisa, do you think you could call them and ask if they'd like to make it a lunch appointment instead?"

"Great idea. I'll get onto them now."

Chris stood next to me whilst Lisa made the call. I wondered why he didn't mind giving up a potential customer so easily. Meanwhile, Amelia had resumed her duties back at her desk. As soon as she sat down, she looked up and smiled at me. It wasn't an ordinary smile; one I'd ordinarily associate between two work colleagues. No, it felt flirtier, the look two strangers might exchange across a crowded pub. My heart momentarily fluttered. I'd been attracted to Amelia ever since I first set eyes on her, but that moment was the first time that I felt something inside. Just as I'd hoped, I knew there was something between us.

"Done!" exclaimed Lisa, immediately taking my mind back to the present. "Lunch at twelve thirty at The Wheatsheaf. I've booked us a table for four. You know it, don't you, Chris?"

"Yeah, friendly pub. Thanks, Lisa—"

"Sorry, Lisa? Did you say, 'table for four'?" Amelia stood again.

"Yes, that's right. I thought it would be a good idea if I went along. I know the client well, and I hoped it would help smooth over any transition between Chris and Matt." It was Lisa's turn to smile, directed towards me and Chris, obviously trying to keep Amelia out of the conversation.

"But, if they're to be Matt's new client, surely I should

go along? After all, I'll be the one working with Matt with them from now on."

Although there was obvious acrimony between Amelia and Lisa, it was right that if anybody should come along, then it should be Amelia. Chris rolled his eyes towards me, a *'you're on your own, buddy'* kind of look, and walked back to his desk. I attempted to defuse the growing tension within the room.

"How about Amelia comes along to lunch, but before we leave, I sit with you, Lisa, and you can give me all the information and background on the client? That way I'll be going in well prepared."

My suggestion appeared to placate Lisa. She knew it was Amelia's role if it was my client, but she'd given the impression of wanting to accompany me to the lunch. It disappointed me she couldn't come along too.

"Okay, good idea." A thought sprang into her head. "In fact, I'll book us a meeting room for the rest of the morning." She looked over to Amelia before speaking again. "That way, it will be just us two."

The smile disappeared from Amelia's face as quickly as it had arrived. She looked to me for moral support. I acknowledged her, hoping she could read my mind that it was all okay, just a work meeting. She then looked over towards Tracy. Until then, I hadn't noticed how intently she had been following the conversation too. I watched as Tracy nodded towards Amelia in return.

A few minutes later, I stood with my laptop and followed Lisa to the meeting room. Amelia called after us, stopping us in our tracks. Everybody in the immediate vicinity waited for Amelia to speak again. She spoke slowly and clearly.

"By the way. I've booked your first conference. It's in

Harrogate, Yorkshire. Two days, three nights. There's a dinner after the second day, great for mingling."

I knew which conference she was referring to. The biggest property conference in the UK, and one I'd always wanted to attend; something my previous company never permitted. Unfortunately, they'd never had the budget, or inclination, to put in an appearance.

"Sounds great. It's in a few weeks, isn't it?"

"Yes, first week of the new year."

She smiled again before Lisa and I turned back to our meeting.

"Oh, and Matt." I stopped again, but this time I noticed that Lisa didn't. Instead, she hastened her pace and strode across the office without looking back.

"Yes?"

"I've arranged to come along too. It will be a good experience for me."

Aware people were listening, I nodded my approval before pacing after Lisa. Amelia hadn't quite finished, and this time Lisa baulked.

"Oh, and Matt? I've booked us into a lovely hotel."

4

THE LUNCH near Heathrow Airport had gone very well, and I'd immediately found common ground with the owner, Sumit Jayavant, an Indian businessman who was looking to expand his business around West London. It was the first time I'd been in front of a client with Chris and, although we're all different, I couldn't understand how he did any business at all if that was how he acted. He was quiet, essentially shy, and after the initial introductions, he said little else during the two-hour meeting. He appeared disinterested throughout, almost as if he'd given up.

In stark contrast, Amelia was a natural. Charming, professional, and very knowledgeable. Sumit took to her straight away, and I knew we could do business with this guy soon. My preparation with Lisa had also helped immeasurably, something I thanked her for later that day in the office.

Two weeks later, on the eve of the conference in Harrogate, Mr Jayavant called Amelia to arrange a meeting with me to look at some properties. I'd sourced five or six, which were local to him, and I knew they would be an excellent investment, especially long term.

Mike took me to one side later that day and told me he may have to take more clients off Chris. He'd asked if I'd be interested in any of them. It felt awkward. I'd been with the company less than three months and didn't want to upset any of my colleagues; it wasn't my style. I said I'd think about it, stalling until I got away and spoke with Amelia about it.

After my impromptu meeting with Mike, we set off on the drive north to Harrogate. Apart from my first day when Amelia walked with me back to my hotel, we had spent no time alone. We'd had meetings in the office, and occasionally worked late to discuss clients, but we had never been together in a non-business environment. As we walked to my car, I felt kind of nervous, wondering what we would talk about and how we would connect. I needn't have worried.

It was a four-hour drive, and we'd deliberately left London mid-afternoon to avoid the rush hour. We planned on arriving around seven o'clock – time to freshen up and eat in the hotel restaurant.

Once we left the city skyline behind, we were soon on our way north, along the M11. After the initial chit-chat about the upcoming conference, I asked Amelia about taking on more of Chris's clients. I conveyed my concerns about standing on people's toes, but she dismissed it and advised me not to worry. She admitted she'd had words with Mike and told him to give me a chance to prove myself. "Chris and Lisa can look after themselves," she said, bringing a swift conclusion to that conversation.

We sat in silence for several more miles, both deep in our own thoughts. Eventually, Amelia spoke, this time going straight for the jugular.

"So, tell me, has there ever been a Mrs Walker?"

I glanced over, momentarily taking my eyes off the busy motorway. She smiled, giving the impression it was just light-hearted conversation, and not prying in the slightest.

"Well, no. I guess I've never met the right person."

I looked at her again, trying to gauge her reaction. She was looking straight ahead, but still wore the same smile on her face. The sun was setting in the sky behind her, making its final journey west that day. It exaggerated her bone structure and shape of her face. I noticed her eyelashes flickering when she blinked; her cute small nose and those lips, full and slightly pursed. She was a good-looking woman. It was my turn to break the silence, and now I had the perfect opportunity to ask her the same question.

"And you? Has there ever been a Mr Amelia?"

She let a brief gasp escape, more of a 'ha', before replying. Her voice changed marginally, taking on a more heartfelt tone.

"No, there hasn't. Maybe I haven't met Mr Right yet. Well, until…"

She left it hanging. I caught a glimpse of her, still looking directly ahead, still smiling. I dropped it there, mainly because I just didn't know what else to say, but also because I didn't want to ruin the thoughts going through my head. I hoped that I hadn't misheard her, or misunderstood her.

Amelia had been right; she had booked us into a lovely hotel. It was central to town, only a few minutes' walk from the conference hall. I parked the car nearby, and we strolled, carrying our luggage, to check in.

The receptionist was young; early twenties. She was attractive, wearing a tight white blouse complete with hotel motif just above the chest. As we walked through the lobby, Amelia noticed me ogling. She fixed a smile for the girl behind the desk and spoke through her teeth, almost ventriloquist like.

"Put your tongue away, Matt, you're old enough to be her dad."

"Eh? What did you—"

"Good evening," she interrupted me, still strolling confidently towards reception. "We're here to check in. Three nights, under the company name, Opacy."

Joining Amelia, I stood my case upright and leaned forward onto the wooden counter. Amelia felt her pockets, patting them individually.

"Oh, damn it. Matt. Would you be so kind, but I've left my phone in the car."

The receptionist looked up and smiled at me before I turned on my heels.

"Meet you back here in five minutes. I'll check in for both of us. That okay?"

I waved my arm nonchalantly over my shoulder. "Yeah, whatever," I replied playfully.

Amelia was waiting at the lift when I returned with her phone. She'd left it on the front seat.

"I've never seen you leave your phone anywhere before. Even in the office, you don't leave it on your desk."

"Oh, it must have dropped out of my pocket or some-thing. Anyway…" The lift arrived, and we stepped inside. "…anyway, we're on the fourth floor. Rooms four-one-six and four-one-seven."

Once we'd made our way to our respective suites, we agreed to meet in the restaurant thirty minutes later. I felt shattered and just wanted to sleep, but my stomach growled, reminding me I hadn't eaten since lunchtime.

Unpacking my clothes, I unfolded my suit and walked over towards the wardrobe. I noticed an extra door in the far corner of the room. I'd already taken my wash gear into the bathroom so couldn't understand where the additional doorway could lead to. Then it hit me.

Shit! She's booked adjoining rooms.

I checked my phone for the original booking. There was no indication of neighbouring rooms, just two executive en suite doubles.

Deciding not to mention the room arrangements – I thought acting innocent would be the best option – I joined Amelia for dinner in the restaurant. She had changed into a tight-fitting blouse and equally tight jeans. Just like the young girl on reception, she had left an extra button undone. She had a body to die for. I felt inadequate, having changed into jeans and a loose-fitting checked shirt, which I hadn't even tucked in.

Once we'd ordered food, I realised that it hadn't registered with me before that Amelia was a vegetarian. She explained over dinner that animal cruelty had always upset her, even as a child.

We both had mushroom starters, but when the main course arrived, I wished that the ground could have opened up and swallowed me whole. They had cooked my steak medium rare, and a small amount of blood leaked across my plate.

"I'm so sorry. I didn't think."

Fortunately, she laughed. Her hand reached across the table and rested on the back of mine. A shot of electricity ran up my arm, jolting my heart as it arrived at its ultimate destination.

"Don't be silly, Matthew." She hadn't called me Matthew since my first day. She slid her hand off mine and picked up her cutlery again. Just before she ate, she added, "I'll just have to teach you what that poor creature went through before ending up on your plate."

She put a forkful of food into her mouth, looked up at me and smiled. "Come along, eat up."

I didn't understand if she was joking or not. I'd dated a couple of vegetarians in the past and, although I'd always respected their beliefs, I'd found both girls intrusive with their ideologies. I hoped Amelia wasn't the same.

Soon, the conversation flowed again. We ordered a second bottle of wine. Maybe not very professional on the eve of a conference, but it felt right. I became relaxed in Amelia's company. It was like dinner with a best friend rather than a colleague from work.

The conference went very well. We were a great team, bouncing off each other in front of client after client. We talked business, how we could help them, and put them at ease or made them laugh. After the second day, we had enough new contacts to keep us busy for weeks ahead. It had been a great success. I'd always wanted to attend the Harrogate conference with my previous company, as I knew the business opportunities could be massive. It's a biennial event, and I sincerely hoped I'd be returning in two years' time; preferably with Amelia again.

And to complete the business trip, we spent the final evening at the gala dinner. A black tie and evening dress party. Amelia looked lovely in her full-length red outfit.

During the evening I noticed many of the men look at me in envy, especially once we took to the dance floor together as midnight approached.

It would be after the gala dinner that Amelia and I took our friendship to a whole new level.

5

"YOU LIAR!" I teased Amelia as we left Harrogate and began the journey back south along the A1.

"I swear, I didn't know." She was giggling, hardly able to form a coherent sentence.

"I knew the night we checked in that you'd arranged adjoining rooms. You left your phone in the car on purpose. One thing I didn't know was that you had the key." I was laughing too. She squeezed my leg to stop me talking.

"Stop it. I promise it was pure coincidence."

Once the laughing and joking stopped, Amelia rested her hand on my leg.

"You don't regret what we did, do you?"

Glancing over at her to gauge her mood, it surprised me at how serious she looked.

"What? Hell, no. Why would you say that?"

The smile immediately returned to her face.

. . .

One day, during the following week, Amelia asked if I could stay behind after work to discuss something. She wasn't exactly discreet about it, asking me across the office, ensuring she had an audience. Lisa and Tracy looked up from their desks and I noticed Tracy wink at Lisa. Lisa glanced over at me, measuring my reaction before returning to her work. Her expression remained non-committal.

Did they know something was going on?

Although I was secretly elated that we were – how should I put it? – seeing each other, I wasn't ready for all and sundry to know our private business. To begin with, I did not know how Mike would react, and if they would frown upon it at work.

The weekend before, two days after Harrogate, Amelia had spent both days – and nights – at my flat. To be more precise, we spent both days and nights in bed at my flat, only surfacing for food or calls of nature. We couldn't keep our hands off each other, and when we weren't making love, we kissed and talked and laughed. It was one of the best, yet simplest, weekends of my life. Everything had felt just perfect.

As promised, I stayed behind after work that night. We waited until everybody within earshot had gone home. I'd noticed Tracy look over at Amelia and smile as she left. Even Mike gave me a wink on his way out.

Shit, they know.

It turned out to be exactly what I'd wanted. Amelia asked if I'd like to meet her family. Although it was unexpected – we'd only been seeing each other for around a week – I was happy that she was so keen to introduce me. It meant she must have totally fallen for me too; why else would she ask me to make that kind of commitment so early in our relationship?

"I'd be delighted. Are they ready to meet me though?"

"They'll love you, I know they will. Besides, it will be nice for you to be around people. It can't be easy for you without your parents, or any other family for that matter."

Her comment left me feeling uneasy.

"What do you mean? How do you know about my parents or what family I have?"

Amelia had an instant response.

"You told me your parents had been killed in that dreadful accident when we had dinner on our first night in Harrogate. Remember, silly?"

We had spoken about many things that evening, but I couldn't recall telling her that. However, we'd drunk a lot of wine and I didn't want to fall out with her. It wasn't as though it was a secret, anyway.

"Hmm, fair enough. Besides, I don't mind you knowing. Where were we? Oh yeah, I'd love to meet your parents."

"Parent, Matt, singular. My father left home when I was four years old. I can't even remember him."

"Oh, I'm sorry. I didn't know."

She remained upbeat.

"It's fine. We're all okay with it."

"'All', did you say? Who else will I be meeting?"

"Wait and see," she said, before kissing me on the lips, "it will be a pleasant surprise."

The following Friday after work, I drove myself and Amelia out of London and towards Epsom Downs in Surrey. She'd previously told me it took her around an hour on the train each day to get into work but never informed me of where she lived exactly. After the city, it was so refreshing to be out in the green and stunning landscape of leafy England. I also knew it was a very expensive part of the world to live in.

Eventually, we made our way down a narrow country lane. I'd noticed a handful of properties at the start before the road gave way to a combination of tarmac and loose gravel. It was more of a track by the time we reached our destination and I became conscious that grass was growing in the centre of the lane; an obvious sign of few vehicles using it. Amelia directed me around the last corner before instructing me where to park the car. There was nowhere else to go anyway, as the track disappeared upwards and deep into dense woodland. The house stood directly in front of us.

An imposing structure, set at the bottom of the hill. It was not a conventional-looking property, the front of which housed a bay window downstairs and a sash window above. To the right, set back from the principal part of the building, was a further bay window, smaller this time, but above it stood a turret type structure which sprung upwards towards the sky. Arched windows circled the perimeter, and the building appeared to stretch backwards, encompassing further rooms. I noticed a few slates missing from the tower, and at least two sash windows in the house had cracked panes. The property looked as though it was in a state of disrepair. Painted white, but peeling in several places, it exposed red bricks beneath. A faded red front door completed the scene where the door knocker hung at an odd angle. The garden was overgrown; long grass had clumped together and weeds climbed from the base of the house, clinging to the walls as if trying to peer into the downstairs windows. At the front was a rusting garden bench, looking as though it hadn't been sat on in years. On two sides of the property, to the right and the rear, the garden gave way to huge trees, the woodland slowly meandering upwards, as far as the eye could see. A vast expanse of land stood to the other side of the house, laid to lawn yet resembling a farmer's field rather than a pleasant garden to sit in.

Climbing out of the car, trying to take it all in, I jumped when I felt a tap on my shoulder. Amelia stood beside me. I hadn't even heard her creep up behind.

"Well, what do you think?"

She said it as though expecting a tremendous compliment. Such a stunning property to take my breath away, complete with landscaped gardens. I looked at her and then back at the house, aware my mouth was open but no words were forming.

"It's, erm, it's an amazing property. Really, quite amazing."

"Isn't it?" she responded in glee. "It just needs some cosmetic work and it will soon be back to its former glory. Come on, let's go."

Just some cosmetic work? Could she see something different to me?

She kissed me on the cheek and skipped along the cracked concrete slabs that made up the footpath. I couldn't see one step that remained intact. I followed, somewhat slower, still staring at every nook and cranny that the house offered. As I approached the front door where Amelia patiently waited, I noticed an old swing in the overgrown garden to my left. It stood at the brow of a small hill, nothing behind it but the grey skyline. The breeze caught the swing, slowly sending it backwards and forwards. Each time it began its forward motion, the rusted chain squeaked. It sent a shiver up my spine and I was relieved when I finally caught up with Amelia. She squeezed my hand, and I turned my back on the swing, consciously trying to block out the sound too.

Amelia wiggled the key in the front door and twisted the old wooden handle at the same time. It gave with a creak and she pushed her way in. If I'd felt a chill outside, it didn't dissipate once indoors. Confronted by a long hallway, I could see my breath in the air each time I exhaled. The next thing I noticed was the yellowing walls and ceiling, like an old London pub before they'd banned indoor smoking. A single light bulb hung from above; it had no lampshade attached and, even though it was on, it gave off the dimmest beam, barely illuminating the room. A small table on the right-hand side was the only piece of furniture in the entire hallway. There was an old-fashioned dial-up telephone perched on top, but I noticed the wire was threadbare and hung nonchalantly next to the socket. The amount of dust the phone had collected made me realise it hadn't been in use for many years. A wide staircase took up the left-hand side of the hallway, and I could just make out the bannister of the landing in the gloom above. A narrow, crimson coloured carpet ran up the centre of the stairs, held into place by brass stair rods. It looked new compared to everything else I could see.

The sound of a floorboard creaking above made me jump. I looked around and realised Amelia had disappeared. Not sure what to do, I stood still, waiting, listening. The footsteps grew louder, and I noticed a shadow form and stretch along the landing at the top of the stairwell. Wishing Amelia was with me, I suddenly felt alone and a little frightened. The house was giving me the creeps.

Then the figure appeared. Slowly turning the corner from the landing and onto the top step. I involuntarily took a step backwards. An elderly lady bent her head to see below. Once she'd spotted me, she stood upright again, staring at me, fixated by my presence rather than alarmed. Although she was short in stature, her lofty position gave her the advantage of dominance over me. Her mouth sat in a straight line until she eventually spoke.

"Yes. Who are you?" she asked, slowly and calmly.

I desperately looked around for Amelia, but there was no sign, no sound.

"I'm... I mean... I am Matt. I mean, Matthew. I'm a friend of—"

Her demeanour changed like the flick of a light switch, and an enormous smile spread across her face.

"Matthew!" she beamed, and began a steady descent down the stairs, her hand maintaining her balance on the rail but not taking her eyes off me.

Once she reached me, she hugged me and kissed me on both cheeks before putting her hands on my shoulders and taking a step back.

"Let's have a good look at you, young man. My Amelia never stops talking about you."

"You're her mum?" I asked, somewhat relieved.

"Mother," she corrected me. She continued to look me up and down. I found it all disconcerting, even though she acted like a long-lost grandmother rather than somebody deliberately trying to unsettle me.

Amelia's mum, mother – Melissa, as I found out later – was in her late sixties. Although shorter than Amelia, she had the same dark hair, albeit rapidly turning grey from the temples back, and a pretty face, complete with those dark brown eyes. She had also kept herself trim, and I could tell she must have been quite a catch back in her day.

The sound of Amelia walking swiftly along the hallway eventually made Melissa let go of me.

"Where have you been hiding this one?"

Amelia looked sheepish before joining me and interlocking her arm through mine.

"Mother! Don't embarrass poor Matthew."

That's the second time she's used my full name.

"He's not embarrassed, are you, Matthew?"

The sound of someone clearing their throat at the end of the hallway stopped me from replying. We all looked.

A colossal figure was silhouetted by the doorframe.

"And do I get introduced?" he asked gruffly, stepping forward towards us.

"Of course you do! Matthew, this is my brother-in-law, Graham."

Offering my hand, he took it and pulled me towards him, almost squeezing my lungs empty with a bear hug.

"Anybody who takes on my Amelia needs a huge embrace."

Amelia punched him on the arm. It must have felt like a fly had landed on him.

"Don't you start," Amelia quipped.

Graham was over six foot tall and heavily built. Although I'd describe him as slightly overweight, he easily carried it off with huge broad shoulders, arms that looked like he worked out and hands that could smash a coconut with a single squeeze.

However, the thing that struck me most about Graham was his hair. It was a ginger, rusty colour, matched by a long untrimmed beard. His blue eyes shone out in the gloom of the hallway. I heard further footsteps behind him, but his vast frame hid whoever was there.

"Aha, there she is," beamed Melissa. "Matthew, I believe you've already met."

Graham stood aside, and I immediately recognised the woman in the doorway.

"Tracy! What are you doing…?"

Amelia squeezed my arm before answering my unfinished question.

"Tracy is my older sister, Matt."

6

THAT EVENING, I joined the Reid family for dinner. It would be the time when I made my first faux pas.

Melissa had instructed me and Graham to relax in the lounge, whilst she, Tracy and Amelia prepared the food. The front room of the house contained a three-seater sofa and a mismatch of chairs. They all sagged in the middle, and after Graham had invited me to sit where I wanted, I chose the largest chair tucked into the bay window. I could see my car from there, which somehow made me feel less vulnerable. As soon as I sat, I sank into the cushion and felt myself clinging to the shiny arms for support. Inadvertently, I let out an audible shriek. Feeling embarrassed, I watched Graham, hoping I hadn't offended him. He appeared not to have heard me, or selected not to, and eased himself gently into another chair on the opposite side of the open fireplace.

"So, Matthew——"

"Please call me Matt," I interrupted.

"Okay. So, Matt. Amelia tells me you're making quite a name for yourself at Opacy."

43

"Well, just doing my job I suppose," I replied modestly.

"No, you carry on. You'll have that Chris fellow out on his ear before you know it."

Graham chuckled. I tried to join in but felt very uncomfortable. What had Amelia been telling him?

"No, I don't want anybody to lose their job or anything, I'm just—"

"Don't apologise. From what I hear, he's useless anyway. That company needs young blood. The dead wood has to go. It's life, no hard feelings."

Feeling uneasy, I tried to steer the conversation somewhere more neutral.

"Are you and Tracy married, Graham?"

He chortled heartily. He'd seen the funny side of the question, even though one hadn't been intended.

"No, no. My wife is away."

He leaned forward, and for the first time, attempted to keep his voice lower. Graham didn't succeed, though; his vocals only seeming to have one volume level.

"Tracy's husband left us a few years ago now. Tragic it was. Tracy took it terribly."

"Oh God, I'm so sorry. I had no—"

"Don't worry. How were you to know?"

Well, Amelia might have fucking told me for a start.

Thinking it best, I steered the subject away from Tracy and her absent husband.

"Can I ask what you do for a living?"

"Yes, I'm a solicitor. I work freelance, pick and choose, if you know what I mean?"

"That's great. Keep yourself busy?"

Before Graham could react, Amelia and her mum entered the room.

"Dinner's about ten minutes. Do you guys want a drink?" Amelia asked.

I looked at Graham, hoping he'd take the lead so I could have the same as him. Even though I was driving, I secretly prayed he'd have a beer. His reply put me on the spot.

"Guests first. You choose, Matt."

"Well, okay. I'll have a beer if that's alright?"

The room fell silent. The three of them stared at one another. You'd have thought I'd asked for drugs. Graham and Melissa looked towards Amelia, hoping she would speak on their behalf.

"The thing is, we don't, well, we don't drink."

I couldn't help but laugh. I pulled myself forward in my chair, sitting on the edge, the only part that felt sturdy enough to hold me in place.

"You don't drink? What about...?"

Amelia shot me a look that could kill. I felt myself redden. I looked at the three of them, hoping one would crack and this was just a prank they played on new guests. The seriousness nature of their expressions soon dispelled that theory.

"What about what?" Graham said, now standing. He looked like a giant, towering over everybody else. I felt exposed, all eyes on me. Amelia mouthed something under her breath. It looked uncannily like 'Don't you dare'.

"Well, I was going to say, what about a soft drink? Lemonade or something."

Amelia's expression changed from looking as though she would be sick to one of sheer relief. She laughed, the other two soon joining in.

"Oh yes," said Melissa, "great idea. I'll make a jug of my infamous *Reid organic lemonade.*" With that, she turned to go. Graham followed her into the kitchen to join Tracy, whilst Amelia stayed behind. As soon as the coast was clear, I hurried over to her.

"What the fuck was that about?" I whispered. "You drank enough red wine in Harrogate to float a battleship."

She looked nervously over her shoulder before grabbing my arm and pulling me back towards the bay window.

"Keep your voice down, will you? I only did that with you. Please, just play along whilst you're here."

"Okay, but why didn't you say? And why didn't you tell me that Tracy is your sister? And I've just heard from Graham, her husband left her. And…"

I recalled the look that Amelia and Tracy had given each other across the office the day we tried to keep the peace between Amelia and Lisa. A brief nod of approval. It made sense now.

I wanted to say more, but her innocent little face made me putty in her hands. I nodded my consent as Graham shouted out that dinner was being served. Amelia stood on tiptoe and kissed me on the lips, lingering a few seconds longer than a peck.

"Don't ruin it. We get on great together."

Dinner was delicious, albeit not the food I would normally eat. Amelia had led me through to the dining room, another huge, scantily furnished space, lacking both pictures on the walls or ornaments on the sideboard. The table had six wooden chairs spaced equally around it, each with a placemat and cutlery laid out.

Taking my seat, Melissa must have noticed me observing the extra settings.

"I always set the table for six, Matthew, it keeps things easy."

"Ah, okay. Thought we were being joined by others," I quipped, trying to keep it light-hearted.

Graham spoke next, as he scooped a huge dollop of vegetarian moussaka onto his plate.

"Yeah, we like to get together as a family as regularly as we can. I come around as often as possible…"

Graham gestured for me to pass him my plate.

"Oh, I thought you lived here."

Melissa, Tracy, and Amelia laughed.

"Oh no, Graham just comes round for the company, don't you, darling?" Melissa reached out her hand and squeezed Graham's arm.

"Yeah, they keep me fed, while the wife's away," he sniggered.

The conversation fell silent for a few moments before Graham cleared his throat. He seemed to look at his in-laws for approval to carry on. I noticed Melissa give a slight nod of her head.

"My wife works for a charity. She spends months abroad at a time, around Africa, you know, dealing with orphaned kids and other stuff."

"Okay, that's very commendable," I replied.

"Yes, and the other dinner place is always set for Tracy's daughter."

How many more surprises are they going to throw at me?

Nobody volunteered to elaborate on this, so I took it as my cue to ask more. I directed my question to Tracy.

"Oh, okay. How old is she, Tracy?"

"She's fourteen." For some unknown reason, that was the total amount of information she appeared to want to divulge. Melissa took up the baton.

"Yes," she said, somewhat abruptly. "She's fourteen

and lives with us here." She took a few seconds to compose herself before finishing her sentence. "She's a little different, shall we say?"

Amelia took over from her mother.

"Yes, Katrina is fairly quiet."

"And does she go to a local school?" I asked, just trying to keep the conversation flowing more than anything else.

It was Graham's turn to answer. He lay his cutlery down before he spoke.

"No. The thing is, well, Katrina has some learning difficulties. Nothing major, just that she has trouble communicating with people. It's why she's upstairs in her room now. She would have found this awkward and quite overwhelming."

I know how she feels.

I didn't know how to respond. Fortunately, Amelia spoke brightly, undoing the melancholy atmosphere that had descended around the table. I found Tracy's silence particularly disconcerting.

"But you'll love her when you meet her. She can be hilarious, can't she, Tracy?"

"Oh yes, quite the entertainer when she gets going," Tracy added, completely lacking enthusiasm.

The laughter that ensued felt remarkably forced.

"Are you all vegetarians then?" I walked arm in arm to my car with Amelia. The rest of the meal had gone off without incident. The conversation had flowed, and I felt as though I'd made a decent impression. I'd made Graham, Tracy and Melissa smile with tales of how good Amelia was with clients and how well she'd interacted with them at Harrogate. Her mother had beamed with pride.

"Yes, and thanks for pretending you are too. I'd told them you didn't eat meat either. Mother hates the way we exploit animals for human consumption."

"Well, the look you gave me about the alcohol, I wouldn't dare cross you about being a meat eater too."

She looked over her shoulder again.

"Yes, well, sometimes it's just much easier to pretend, only to keep the peace. Don't you agree?"

We reached my car, and I leant against the driver's door, turning to face her. She took both of my hands in hers and kissed me. A long, passionate kiss. I pulled away after several seconds, looking up at the house. Amelia laughed.

"Don't worry, they don't mind kissing. In fact, Mother told me in the kitchen she thinks you are very dishy. Told me you're one to keep."

"Oh, did she now? And what did you say?"

"I said I have no intention of letting you escape."

She kissed me again before saying goodnight. She promised to spend the following weekend at my place again.

"We can spend both days in bed, just like last time. This time, I'll bring the wine. I can't wait."

I watched her walk back up the makeshift path and into the house. She blew me a kiss before going inside. I blew her a kiss back and climbed into my car.

Starting the ignition and adjusting the mirror, I caught myself smiling. Despite one or two awkward moments, it had been a successful introduction to her family. Graham wasn't my kind of guy, quite the opposite actually, but he had been friendly and made me feel welcome. Melissa might have been set in her ways, but she was approaching seventy and I had to make allowances. I put the car into reverse.

Then something caught my eye. Looking over to my right, past the house, at first, all I could see was dense woodland. The light was fading fast so I could easily have been mistaken. I strained, searching for what I thought I'd seen. There it was again.

Somebody was standing in the shadows, on the edge of the woods. Whoever it was, they were looking in my direction. A chill ran down the length of my spine.

She stood motionless, but her flowing, full-length white dress made her distinguishable against the ever-increasing gloom.

7

AMELIA DIDN'T JUST SPEND the following Saturday and Sunday at my flat, she spent the next six weekends there. To begin with, I took her back to her family home on the Sunday afternoons, and I would stay for a cup of tea and a slice of homemade cake with her, Tracy and her mother. Graham was there too, every time, doing odd jobs around the house; to be fair, there was plenty to keep him going. It would be weekend number seven when Melissa invited me to stay over at their home instead. At first, it disappointed me, as I wanted Amelia to myself, but I also knew I was being selfish and I had to mix with her family at some point.

After my initial visit, I'd mentioned to Amelia that I thought I'd seen someone standing on the edge of the trees. She'd joked that I must be seeing things.

"I've never seen anybody near the woods and I played there every day when I was a child. Tracy and I were forever playing hide-and-seek in there, but I must admit, I haven't been in for years."

"Who do they belong to?"

"I'm not sure. I'll ask Mother if you're interested? As far as I recall, they go on up a hill for quite a way. I always remember Tracy used to tease me and say if you went to the top of the hill, the world ended and you fell off the other side."

She shivered, adding effect.

"But you're sure nobody lives in there, there're no houses or anything?"

"No way. The trees are so dense, it wouldn't be possible to build a house. Honestly, you must have imagined it. Anyway, wasn't it getting dark when you left that day?"

She was right. It had passed dusk, and the shadows could have played tricks on my mind. I let it go, thinking I wouldn't be going anywhere near the trees myself anyway.

During those following six weeks, we got along great and built a strong relationship. It was becoming obvious I was falling in love and I felt emotionally sick at the end of each weekend when she had to go home.

"Why can't you just stay at my place all the time?" I asked one Sunday during the drive around the M25.

"I'd love to, believe me. It's just I feel guilty leaving Tracy with Mother all the while. Don't forget she has Katrina too."

"But Graham's always there."

"Only at weekends, when I'm not around," she corrected me, rather abruptly.

"Sorry for wanting to be with you." My reply dripped with sarcasm.

Amelia put her hand on my knee and squeezed it

gently. She followed by slowly sliding her palm up my thigh, sending a tingling sensation right through my body.

"Well, then you'll have to make an honest woman out of me."

I kept my eyes on the road ahead, but inside my heart was doing somersaults.

The weekend we were due to stay at Amelia's house soon came around, and I drove us both there straight after work on the Friday evening. As soon as we pulled up outside the house, I saw Graham in the garden. He was chopping wood with an axe. I recalled the house had two open fireplaces I knew of. I waved as I went to collect my overnight bag from the boot of my car and he mopped his brow and nodded in reply, without appearing over-friendly.

Amelia joined me, having watched our somewhat uncomfortable greeting.

"Why don't you help him?"

"What? Well, I don't really—"

"Go on, please." She stood on tiptoe and kissed my cheek. "For me."

"Okay, just for you," I said, and handed her my bag. "See you inside."

Walking over to Graham and the pile of wood, I couldn't help but notice how much he was sweating. He continued to place logs in front of him and bring the axe down with some force. He didn't look up to acknowledge me at all.

"Evening, Graham. Need a hand?" I did my best to drum up interest in my voice. Again, he didn't take his eyes off the task at hand.

"To what do we owe the pleasure? I thought you two lovebirds would be shacked up in North London again."

Taken aback, I again tried my best to remain cheerful.

"Not today, no. Amelia's mum, I mean, mother, invited me to stay over this weekend. I thought I—"

Graham immediately stopped what he was doing and stood upright to face me. He already towered above me, but with the slight incline of the hill in his favour, he looked like a giant. A giant wielding an axe.

"Listen. We only want what's best for Amelia and the family." He took a step closer, lowering his voice whilst swinging the axe back and forth in his right hand. He continued before I could reply.

"We keep ourselves to ourselves and have always got along just fine. If you're getting serious with my sister-in-law, I need to know you will not hurt her."

What the fuck is this all about?

"I, yes, of course."

"She's only ever had one other boyfriend. Right twat he was." It was the first time I'd ever heard Graham swear. It sounded alien coming from his mouth.

"Okay. She's never mentioned him to me—"

"She wouldn't, would she?" Graham interrupted me again. "But put it this way, once he messed her around, I had to make sure he never did it again."

I looked at the axe in his hand. He was spinning it round and round. On each cycle, the sharp blade caught the descending sun. I couldn't take my eyes off it, desperately trying to think of something positive to say. I didn't even see his other hand reach up and grab my shoulder. I flinched, hoping he couldn't feel me shaking.

"Hell, that's enough wood for now. Can't give me a hand and carry it up to the bunker, can you, mate? It's just around the back of the house."

Graham's manner had changed like the flick of a light switch. I looked up at him and he was beaming. A bead of sweat trickled down his forehead. I thought it was going to go in his eye, but he wiped it away at the last second.

"Come on, I'll load the barrow. Meet you up there." He pointed behind the far side of the house; the side closest to the woods. "It's around the back."

Making my way up the path, Graham called after me. I was aware I hadn't spoken for some time.

"Oh, and, Matt."

"Yeah?" I said, turning to face him.

"There might be a little treat in the house for you once we've cleared this lot up."

"Oh, right, thanks."

"Don't you want to know what it is?"

I was too scared to even ask. Graham's little 'pep talk' had shaken me to the core. I shrugged my shoulders.

"I've sneaked you a cold beer in, but don't tell the others, okay?"

He smiled and winked. You'd have thought he'd just offered to go halves on a huge lottery win. I turned back to walk around the house.

"Big fucking deal," I whispered under my breath.

Once Graham tipped the last load of wood onto the ground next to the bunker, he asked if I minded stacking it away whilst he went inside and showered. I didn't mind at all; it gave me the opportunity to be on my own for a few minutes. I wanted to gather my thoughts.

The wood stacking proved therapeutic, and I soon rationalised Graham's odd behaviour. He was just protecting his family. They were a close-knit unit, looking out for each other. I also felt a little guilty at my initial reaction to his offer. I craved that cold beer more than anything else in the world.

As I walked around the back of the house, I turned and looked into the woods behind me, trying to recall the spot where I thought I'd seen someone a few weeks before. My eyes scanned up and down, but it was relentless row after row of identical-looking trees. Amelia had been right. It didn't look at all habitable. It was dense woodland, gently making its way up a long and gradual incline. The trees reached as far as the eye could see – right to the end of the world.

Smiling to myself, I turned to make my way to the back door of the house. Then I froze, my heart feeling as though it would burst out of my chest, and the hair on the back of my neck standing on end. Sitting on the swing, directly in front of me, was a girl. She stared straight at me.

"Why are you looking in the woods?"

She spoke slowly, high pitched, and like a child well below her teenage years. Taking deep breaths, I tried to calm myself. She had startled me, and a child sitting on a swing drummed up a multitude of spooky images in my mind.

"Er, sorry?"

"Why are you looking in the woods?" she repeated.

I turned to look at the trees as if to remind myself of where she was talking about. The woods looked even more forbidding than they had seconds earlier. Shadows flickered across my eyes and I heard noises that hadn't been there before.

"I wasn't, no. I was looking around, that's all."

"Are you, Matthew?"

"Yes. Yes, I am. May I ask who you are?"

Even though I asked, I instinctively knew who it was. She had the same black hair and the same dark brown eyes as her aunt and grandmother. However, her eyes were sunken, somewhat blackened around the edges. Her hair grew wild, sticking up in all directions. It looked wiry; putting a hairbrush through it would be a task for at least two people. Even though she had inherited the pretty features of Melissa's side of the family, she looked gaunt, scrawny even. She stopped staring at me and instead focused all her attention on the back door.

"You have to go in now," she said. I turned to follow her gaze, and a split second later, the door swung open and Graham stepped outside.

How the fuck did she know that?

"Aha, you've met Katrina, I see. All okay?"

"Yeah, fine." I was relieved to see someone familiar. "She was just telling me…"

I looked around, but Katrina was no longer there. The swing squeaked in her absence, now propelled by its own momentum. Stepping sideways to get a better look around the house, my eyes scanned everywhere for her, but she was nowhere to be seen. Where was she? I turned to Graham. Maybe for some explanation. But he just smiled.

"Just leave her. Katrina loves her own company. Sometimes it's best to let her go."

His hand gripped the door handle, holding it ajar for me to join him inside. But his eyes still scanned the rocking swing and the field beyond.

"She'll come in soon, once she's hungry."

8

KATRINA DIDN'T JOIN us for dinner that night. In fact, I didn't see Katrina again until several weeks later.

Once she had disappeared from the swing, Graham had held the door open, waiting impatiently for me to go inside.

"You alright? You look a bit pasty." He attempted to joke, although I noticed concern etched across his face too.

Deciding to let it go, I sighed and made a conscious effort to join in with his strained humour.

"Yeah, I'm fine thanks. By the way, is that beer still good?" I nudged his arm. He instantaneously went rigid and stared down at the very spot where I'd just touched him. His tone returned to the threatening voice he'd used outside when I'd first arrived.

"Hey, be careful. Okay?" Without another word, he turned away and walked off.

I felt like putting my shoes back on and going straight home. I didn't need an idiot like him treating me like some child. As I contemplated my next move, the voices of Amelia, Tracy and Melissa drifted through the house. Just hearing Amelia speak lightened my mood, and I followed the sound. As I stepped forward to open the door and join them in the dining room, Graham sprang out from the kitchen. He put his arm around my shoulder and walked with me side by side. We entered the room where the females were chatting. They stopped their conversation and looked up, all three smiling in unison. Graham spoke for both of us.

"Look who I've just found wandering around the house." Incredibly, he was grinning from ear to ear.

"Matthew, so nice to see you again," said Melissa. "Did he do well, Graham?"

"Yep, he did fine. We'll make a man of him yet," he added, nudging my arm in exactly the same manner I'd just done to him at the back door. I so wanted to tell him to be careful.

"Follow me, Matthew." Melissa beckoned me into the kitchen. I noticed the broad smile on Amelia's face as she nodded her approval for me to follow her mother. I joined Melissa in the kitchen and she immediately closed the door behind me. She stood so close it left me feeling awkward.

"I was watching you outside, working so hard."

I didn't know what to say. It brought back memories of my dad telling me I'd done well after I'd washed his car or mowed the lawn. However, Melissa was still a virtual stranger to me, though her comment felt just as personal as my father's. She walked across the kitchen and opened the fridge door. Reaching inside, she grabbed a cold bottle of beer and held it out towards me. Just as I was going to thank her and take it from her grasp, she pulled her arm back, keeping it out of my reach.

"Now, this is a little treat. We don't normally allow

alcohol here, but I could see you deserved it. You also make my Amelia very happy." With that, she passed me the beer.

"Thank you," I said, taking the bottle somewhat shakily. The entire event felt so surreal.

"As I say, I watched you stacking the wood from the window. You seem very strong, Matthew." She held out her hand, just inches from my bicep. "Do you mind?"

What the fuck is this?

"What, erm, no," I replied, bemused.

Melissa held my upper arm, squeezing it in and out. I tensed.

"Hmm," she said, "nice and firm. Just as I imagined."

And then she walked away, opening the door as she went. Just before she left the kitchen, she turned to face me.

"The bottle opener is in the drawer." She pointed somewhere behind me.

Later that night, after dinner – more vegetables – we retired to one of two reception rooms within the house. The fire had already been lit by Graham and four seats were equally positioned around it. Melissa sat behind us at a small table. I still couldn't get her little performance out of my mind. I watched her take a pile of papers out of a large envelope before spreading them out in front of her. One dropped to the floor, next to my seat.

"I'll get it," I said, trying to be helpful. It wasn't as though I was interrupting any conversation.

Picking up the single sheet, I noticed a sequence of square printed boxes on it, all joined by an array of lines. It looked like a giant spider's web. Before I could take in any more, Graham snatched the paper from my hand and returned it to Melissa.

"Sorry," I said. "Is it top secret?"

Before he could reply, Melissa spoke for him, trying to keep the mood light.

"Oh no, Matthew. It's just that they're all in order, that's all. Graham didn't mean to snatch, did you, darling?"

"No, no. Didn't mean anything at all, mate."

Amelia held my hand, reading my mind.

"Mother loves her puzzles. It's her hobby, isn't it, Mother?"

"Oh, yes. But we don't own a computer here, so a friend has to print them off for me."

No computer, no alcohol and, I found out later that evening from Amelia, that they didn't even own a television. It was like stepping back in time.

An hour later, Graham made his excuses and said he was going home. I asked where he lived, but he was non-committal in his response, saying it was just down the road. I overheard him speaking to someone on his way out and I mouthed to Amelia, asking if it was Katrina. She nodded.

Melissa made her excuses shortly after and collected her papers together. She had been busy writing on several of the sheets, so engrossed in her hobby she had left me and Amelia to discuss work with no interruption. Tracy, who had sat quietly reading a book all evening, said she needed to attend to Katrina and wished us both good-night. She looked as though she had the weight of the world on her shoulders where Katrina was concerned.

Finally, we were alone. Amelia left her chair and sat on my knee, snuggling herself as close to me as she could. At first, I felt uncomfortable, believing that Melissa would walk in anytime soon. But then I heard noises above and knew her family were being diplomatic and giving us some space. I relaxed, and we spent the next hour kissing and talking and kissing some more. The sound of the fire crackling in the background made it feel even more romantic.

At one point, Amelia tiptoed out of the room, only to appear a few minutes later with a bottle of wine. I couldn't help but smile.

"What the...?"

She poured two glasses.

"Shh, our little secret," she whispered.

The wine made us both even more amorous, and we let our inhibitions run wild. The kissing became much more passionate and our hands explored underneath each other's tops. Just as I unclipped her bra, a creak on the floorboards above stopped us both in our tracks.

"Stop," Amelia said in my ear. We froze in our positions, like a game of musical statues, waiting for the beat to start back up. It was silent, only the sound of the fire in front of us.

Amelia stood up, fastening her bra as she did. I pulled her hand, trying to get her to sit back down.

"No. We must stop. Someone is around."

"Oh, come on. Five more minutes."

It was pointless trying to persuade her. We soon lost the moment as she collected the bottle and glasses and left the room to 'dispose' of them somewhere secret. When she came back, she said she was tired and wanted to go to bed. My face lit up until she reminded me we would be in separate rooms, something she had mentioned to me on the drive over. Although disappointed, I also respected her mother and knew it would only be on the odd occasion that we stayed over.

Upstairs was in worse decorative order than downstairs. I noticed wallpaper peeling on the landing and more lightbulbs hanging without lampshades. Everywhere looked bare and uninviting. It didn't feel like a home or a house that was loved.

"You're in here," Amelia said, grabbing my attention. I followed her into the bedroom at the end of the landing, to the left of the staircase. As far as I could see in the gloom, it was the last room along. The opposite end of the corridor appeared to turn a corner, just after the stairs. I thought it must lead to the other part of the house, the side of the turret.

She kissed me goodnight and told me to sleep well. She explained that the bathroom was next door to me and she would be in the next bedroom along after that.

Once I'd brushed my teeth and changed into a pair of shorts – I normally slept naked, but thought I'd make an effort in case of an emergency – I crawled into bed.

It was freezing in my room and the sheets felt slightly damp as I climbed in. There was no duvet, but a few layers of thick blankets instead. The top one felt rough, itchy against my skin, so I peeled it back. The bed was like a rock, bumpy in places and uncomfortable. How the hell was I going to sleep?

But somehow, I did. A night full of dreams, or nightmares to be more precise. And no matter how many times I awoke, damp with perspiration, wondering where the hell I was, I still heard the same noise.

The squeaking sound of the swing. Back and forth, back and forth.

9

—————

It was now three and a half months since Amelia and I had spent our first night together at the conference in Yorkshire. By this stage, the entire office knew we were an item; people had even stopped gawping at Amelia whenever she walked around the workplace. I could only describe our relationship as a whirlwind romance. We spent every spare minute together, mostly at my flat. We'd also been away for a long weekend in Cornwall, staying in a secluded cottage overlooking the wild Atlantic Ocean. I think that was the weekend when I knew I wanted to spend the rest of my life with her.

Graham had been more accepting of me, although occasionally, there were little digs, but nothing untoward. I always let them go; besides, it was Amelia who I was seeing, not him. Melissa had been her usual self, and although there had been no more asking to feel my muscles, she had continued to show a great deal of interest in my life. I put it down to being polite – conversation could be stilted – and just wanting the best for her girl. An overprotective mother, nothing more. Tracy remained quiet, often attending to her daughter some-where upstairs. We spent as little time at Amelia's house as possible; mostly at my request, I must admit.

Work went from strength to strength too. I'd found commercial properties all around the southeast for many of the prospective customers who we'd met at Harrogate. Don, of course, picked the genuine quality for himself – with the help of Tracy – but they had left me with more than my fair share of high calibre clients. Only Chris had failed to make the most of the opportunity, something that hadn't gone unnoticed by Lisa. Mike hadn't offered Chris many of the prospective leads, which surprised me; he seemed to get the ones that Amelia and Tracy hadn't grabbed for me and Don.

It was Friday morning, and I'd arrived in the office early. I'd been unable to sleep, mostly from excitement but also from uncontrollable nerves. Today would be the day. Upon reaching my desk, I noticed that Lisa was the only other person in.

"Somebody looks cheerful," she said, as I booted up my laptop, so far unaware that I had been smiling to myself.

"Yeah, I'm good thanks. Everything is going well. How about you, Lisa?"

She looked worried. Something was amiss. I attempted to cheer her up.

"Listen, do you want to grab a coffee around the corner? My treat."

Lisa reluctantly agreed. As I stood to leave, I instinc-tively looked around at Amelia's desk.

"Don't worry, she's not in yet," Lisa teased. "In fact, she's left a message. Her train's delayed, she'll be in after ten o'clock."

Feeling myself blush, I slipped my jacket back on and

followed Lisa outside and to the coffeehouse, just along the busy street from the office.

As usual, it was crowded with early morning clients, most of whom were grabbing a takeaway. Lisa ushered me to a table near the back before joining the queue to order our drinks; she'd insisted on buying. I studied her as she waited. Although she was a little larger than she'd ideally like to be, Lisa was still a very attractive woman. She had curves in all the right places and a lovely smile that complemented her pretty facial features. When she returned with the drinks, I noticed that she wasn't wearing her wedding ring. She followed my eyes, before sliding my white Americano across the table, and squeezed into the seat opposite.

"Divorced," she said, opening a sugar sachet, before pouring it into her drink. I reddened for the second time that morning.

"What was that? Sorry?" I stumbled.

"Yep, finally came through. But I haven't worn my ring for weeks. Oh, but silly me, why would you notice that when you only have eyes for one woman?"

Lisa laughed, but it was so ridiculously put on. I tried to get off the subject of me and Amelia. I knew Lisa didn't approve – although I did not understand why – and focused on her instead.

"I'm sorry you're divorced. Was it all amicable?"

"As amicable as it could be. We don't have kids, which is a blessing I suppose." She silently stared into her coffee as she continued to stir the already dissolved sugar.

"And? Anybody else on the horizon?" It was her turn to blush slightly. Finally, she looked up from her drink.

"Ha! No. There's somebody, but he's taken." She looked directly into my eyes. I picked up two sugar sachets myself and rolled them around in my fingers. Lisa broke the silence.

"So, you and Amelia. Serious is it?"

I felt uncomfortable discussing it with her. She'd always appeared distant to Amelia in the office, and I knew she wouldn't be throwing too many compliments in my direction.

"Well, yeah. We get on great."

"It seems that way. You make a perfect couple."

Her comment dripped with sarcasm, but I didn't want her to spoil my good mood. I'd been building up to that evening all week.

"We think so." I glanced around the café before leaning in closer. I wanted to know why she acted as she did. "Can I ask? What is it about her you don't like?"

She looked taken aback, but couldn't have been surprised by my question. It had been brewing since my first day.

"What makes you ask that?"

I gave her an 'oh, come on' look, leaving it open for her to speak.

"It's something and nothing." She stalled, not wanting to say anything out of turn. "It's like she never looked so nice, so sexy even, until you applied for the job…" She stopped herself from saying more. Eventually, she placed the small wooden coffee stirrer onto the table.

"Ah, just forget me. If you like her that much, you go get her. I'm pleased for you, I genuinely am."

"Thank you. I like you, and I respect your opinion."

"I like you too." She looked around the café, miles away with her thoughts before her attention eventually refocused on me.

"Come on, you. Let's get you back to your lover." She smiled, but under the exterior, I could tell she was laden with sadness. I'd never met her husband, but he'd left some scars.

That evening I drove me and Amelia around the M25 and back to my tiny flat in North London.

As soon as we were inside, I grabbed us a cold beer each from the fridge. The flat was made up of just three separate rooms. The main reception area combined the living space and kitchenette, with a door leading to the bathroom at one end, and another door to the bedroom at the other. It was a good job we got on so well as there was nowhere to escape.

Sitting next to Amelia on the two-seater couch, I passed her a beer and kissed her on the lips. She kissed me back, this time longer and with a lot more passion than I'd just managed. Eventually, I pulled myself away, albeit reluctantly.

"Something wrong?" she asked.

"Nothing at all. In fact, I couldn't be happier, and it's all down to you coming into my life."

I knew it sounded slushy, something I'd never been with any previous girlfriend. At that precise moment, I didn't care.

"Wait there…" I added and sprang to my feet to fetch something from the bedroom. I returned with one hand behind my back. Amelia looked inquisitive, her dark eyes scrutinising me.

"What are you hiding?"

I thought about what my old mates would say if they could see me now. Cocky Matthew Walker turning into Mr Sentimental. I bent down on one knee. Amelia gasped.

"Would you, Amelia Reid, do me the greatest honour of my life and agree to—"

"Yes, yes!" she squealed before I'd even finished. We stood in unison and hugged each other tightly. Once we'd finished the next passionate kiss, she stood back whilst I undid the little velvet box in my hand.

"Oh, my..." was all she could manage, as I slowly removed the ring from the box. Her hand trembled as I slowly slid it onto her finger.

Then she stopped me.

"What's wrong. Don't you like it?" Amelia stood perplexed, holding the ring but her mind miles away from the room.

"Mother," she whispered.

What the fuck?

"Mother? What about Mother?" Inside, I was furious, but I hoped nothing would ruin the moment. I did my utmost to hide my emotions.

"Er, well, I'm not sure how she will react." She looked up at me, still holding the ring. "And I don't need your sarcasm. What's with all this 'mother', 'mother' thing?"

This was not going to plan. It was supposed to be the most romantic thing I'd ever done. Here I was with the woman I wanted to commit the rest of my life to, and I'd been sure she did with me. Surely she wouldn't let her mum come between us. I wanted us to get back to where we'd been a few moments earlier when I thought she was going to explode with delight.

"Listen, I'm sure your mum will be fine about it. She loves you and she seems to like me—"

"Oh, she does, she does. It's just, it's just such a shock, that's all. Yes, Mother will be thrilled. I'm sure she will approve."

Approve? I want your fucking approval, not hers. Shall we ask Graham too?

"Please, try it on." I nodded at the ring. She looked overwhelmed again. Sliding the ring to the end of her finger, she held her arm at full length, wiggling her hand so the diamond kept catching the light.

"It's beautiful," she eventually said. A solitary tear rolled down her cheek, which I wiped away with my thumb. I held her tightly in my arms and spoke into her ear. I was barely audible, not sure if I wanted to know the answer or not.

"Are you happy, Amelia? Truly happy?"

She loosened my grip and kissed me, long and hard. It was maybe the most passionate kiss we'd ever had, and I didn't want it to end. Finally, we broke free.

"I'm delighted. It's a dream come true." She held my hand and led me into the bedroom.

Once inside, she turned back to me and rested her arms on my shoulders, kissing me intermittently between talking.

"I knew you were the one," she whispered. "I always knew there was a special connection between us."

Just as I relaxed and fell deeper into her embrace, she murmured something else. I'm sure it came out louder than she had intended, and I hadn't been supposed to hear.

'And Mother knew it too'.

10

WE SPENT the early evening in bed, only surfacing because the pizza delivery guy turned up.

"Leave it outside!" I shouted as he impatiently knocked on the door. Amelia giggled, trying to pin me down, not letting me escape.

"Please," I squirmed out of her grasp. "I'm starving."

We sat on the sofa to eat, me in my shorts and Amelia in one of my T-shirts she'd helped herself to from my wardrobe. I opened a bottle of wine, and half an hour later I opened a second. We were celebrating, both overjoyed with our news. Before going back to bed, we'd agreed we wanted to get married soon, not hang around. I had no family and Amelia only had her immediate family, who all lived in the house, plus Graham. We weren't sure if Graham's wife could make it, and we settled on a small registry office wedding. We planned to follow it up with a slap-up meal at a country hotel near Epsom. We decided to additionally invite a few people from work, plus a couple of my close friends from years gone by. The arrangements suited us both perfectly.

Amelia had agreed to make all the preparations as soon as possible.

I awoke in the early hours with a start. The wine had sent me into a deep sleep, accompanied by a vivid nightmare. As soon as I woke, I realised I was damp with perspiration and my heart was pounding. Sitting upright, I reached for my phone on the bedside table. Two fifteen. I lay back down and turned my head to look at Amelia, secretly hoping she was awake too. But she wasn't there. My hand instinctively stretched to her side of the bed. The sheets were cold. Then I heard her voice; it was coming from the far side of the closed bedroom door, so faint I couldn't make out anything she was saying. However, she was definitely talking to someone.

Crawling to the end of the bed to get as close to the door as possible, I saw my T-shirt discarded on the floor. It was the same one that Amelia had worn earlier. Was she in the living room naked? I shivered on her behalf, both because of the cold flat and still recoiling from my graphic dream.

The swing.

It was no use; I couldn't make out a word she was saying. I presumed she must be on the phone, but who on earth could she be talking to at this time of night?

Unsure if I should wander out and confront her, or lie down in bed and pretend to be asleep, I heard a distinct 'goodbye' from the lounge. Quickly, I threw myself back, pulled the quilt up to my neck and closed my eyes, convinced she would walk back into the bedroom within seconds.

But she didn't come back into the bedroom. I lay there for several more minutes, my eyes now fully accustomed to the dark as I deliberated what my next move should be. To begin with, she must be freezing cold, sat out there with nothing on. Why wasn't she coming back to bed?

Deciding I could wait no longer, I purposefully climbed out of bed making as much noise as I could. I heard Amelia move around, standing up maybe, followed by footsteps on the laminate flooring.

Pulling on my shorts, I clicked open the bedroom door and feigned a yawn. Amelia stood directly in front of me, making no attempt to cover her nakedness.

"Amelia?"

She was shivering.

"I just got up to get a glass of water," she lied.

I walked over to her and pulled her to me. Her skin was freezing and I noticed goosebumps covering her bare back.

"How long have you been up?"

She lied again.

"Oh, only two or three minutes. I couldn't find my way in the dark."

"Are you okay——?"

Amelia stopped me in my tracks, whispered for me to be quiet, and slowly ran her fingernails down my back; her gesture spoke much louder than words. I became immediately lost in the moment. The feeling of her naked body next to mine had already aroused me, but Amelia's actions were taking it to a whole new level. She kissed me, her tongue darting around inside my mouth. I wanted to ask her so many questions, but her attentions completely absorbed me. We walked together, kissing, back into the bedroom and spent the next half an hour making more passionate love than we'd ever made before.

"I'll get you that glass of water you wanted," I said,

once we'd eventually let go of each other. We were both lying on our backs, staring at the ceiling, smiling. I purposefully ignored her phone call earlier; that could wait.

"Thank you, darling," she mustered, and she let her hand rest on mine until I dragged myself from the bed.

As I walked to the kitchen, I noticed Amelia's mobile phone on the arm of the sofa. I looked back into the bedroom to make sure she hadn't got up to follow me. It was dark, but I could make out the distinct silhouette of her body lying motionless on her back. I couldn't tell if her eyes were open or closed.

Instead of walking to my left and into the kitchen, I took a long sideways step to my right, trying to keep my number of footsteps to a minimum. One more and I could reach her phone. I stood still, listening for movement from the bedroom. Nothing.

As I took the final stride, my foot made a sticky sound underneath as it left the laminate flooring. I had begun to perspire, suddenly aware that I wasn't so sure I wanted to know who she had been on the phone with. Again I paused, and again no sound.

Picking up her mobile, the screen immediately lit up. It was searching for face recognition to unlock itself. I couldn't believe the entire room could become so illuminated by such a small device.

Shit!

I covered the screen with the palm of my hand, suddenly feeling very self-conscious that it was past three o'clock in the morning, and I was walking around my flat naked and holding my girlfriend's mobile phone trying to work out who she'd been calling. It felt so surreal.

Keeping the phone covered, I made my way to the bathroom and locked the door behind me. The first thing

I did was let out a vast sigh. It felt as though I'd been holding my breath for several minutes.

Holding the phone in front of me, it again attempted to unlock itself with face recognition and then displayed the keypad to unlock it manually.

Think, Matt, think.

Her date of birth. No. My date of birth. No.

Shit, shit, shit. It could be anything.

I tried her date of birth backwards, to no avail. It was no use. Begrudgingly, I flushed the chain and left the bathroom before carefully placing the phone back on the sofa then went to the kitchen and poured a glass of water from the tap. I guzzled down the first one before refilling it and returning to the bedroom.

Amelia was lying on her side, with her back to me. Her deep breathing gave away that she had fallen asleep. Placing the glass of water on my side table, I rescued the quilt from the floor and dragged it up and over us both, before climbing back into bed. I hardly slept at all. As I listened to Amelia's shallow breathing, I tried to work out who she could have been speaking to.

The smell of frying bacon awoke me. It was late morning; I'd eventually slept, fortunately nightmare free this time. The bedroom door opened gently, letting in bright sunshine and the outline of Amelia. She had my T-shirt back on.

"Morning, sleepy." She walked over with a mug of steaming hot coffee and put it on the bedside table. Nudging me across, she perched herself onto the edge of the bed and pecked me on the cheek.

"Hey, sorry. I must have drifted off."

"Yes, it was a late night, shall we say?" Amelia was

grinning. I held her waist, pulling her closer, but she resisted.

"That will do, Mr Walker. Your breakfast is almost ready. I've even cooked bacon," she turned up her nose, "disgusting as it is." She stood to walk back into the kitchen. Once she reached the door, she turned to face me, this time looking a lot more serious.

"Matt?"

"Hmm?"

"Once you've eaten, I want to talk."

It sounded ominous. Was it connected to the late-night phone call?

Amelia watched me eat, willing me to finish. She sat on the sofa and as soon as I'd put my dirty dishes in the kitchen sink, she patted the space next to her. Reluctantly, I joined her. I decided to pre-empt the conversation.

"What's wrong?" She looked taken aback.

"Why would you say that? Nothing's wrong, I just want to talk, that's all."

"Okay. Is it about us getting married? You don't want to, do you?"

"Hey, steady on. Stop being so negative." I held up my arms and showed her the palms of my hands.

"Okay, I apologise. Go on."

"Thank you. Right, please hear me out before you go flying off the handle or anything."

I sat in silence, not agreeing to any such thing until I'd heard what she had to say.

"I've been thinking, thinking a lot, actually. This place…"

She stalled whilst looking around my small flat.

"…this place is tiny. I find it so claustrophobic—"

"Thanks," I butted in.

"Shh, let me finish. Please." I nodded.

"I want us to live in our own place; buy somewhere on the outskirts of the city. If you agree." Again, I nodded. It was impossible to argue that we could live in this tiny flat. It was a bachelor pad, not a couples, or dare I say it, a family home. She continued.

"I'm so glad you agree. It will be perfect, our own little home." She looked sheepish.

"So, what's wrong?" I asked, taking her hand in mine.

"The thing is, I've only got about ten thousand pounds in savings. We would need to save a lot more for a deposit."

"Yes, we would. A lot more."

We both fell silent for a few seconds before I spoke again.

"Listen, I've got a bit in a savings account, you know, from after my parents died. Still, it's nowhere near enough." I did the sums quickly in my head. "We're about thirty grand short to put down a deposit on a decent house."

Amelia turned and took hold of both of my hands. She smiled as she spoke, her eyelashes fluttering. I knew she had an idea. This was what she'd been building up to.

"Matt, I know you will not want to, but I think I've got the perfect solution."

I can't believe I didn't work out exactly where the conversation was heading.

"We could move in with Mother and—"

I let go of her hands and stood up. I paced over to the window before turning back to face her.

"No. It would take months, years even, to save that kind of money."

"But it wouldn't. You just said yourself we're about

thirty thousand pounds short. We could save that in no time. How much is the rent on this flat?"

She looked at me, waiting impatiently for me to reply.

"Nearly fifteen hundred a month."

"There you go," she was becoming animated, buoyed on by her plans. "Fifteen hundred plus bills. That's at least two thousand, meaning half of the thirty saved in six months. Plus food, and not to mention the cost of getting to the office from North London compared to where I live."

"But we'd still have to pay your mum."

"Mother would give us great rates. I hardly pay anything now. With both our salaries combined, plus what you'd save here, we could put away at least five thousand a month. That's only six months, absolute maximum."

She stood to join me and reached out for my hands again. "What do you say? Come on, please. Imagine our dream home, in only a few months."

The money side made complete sense. It would take twice as long to save enough for a deposit if I kept the flat on. Living with her mother wouldn't be ideal, but they had tried to connect with me, and six months would pass in no time. I decided quietly that I could immerse myself in work if the strain of the in-laws became too much to bear.

"Okay…" She hugged me, kissing me over and over, "…but on one condition."

"Yes, yes, anything." She kept kissing me.

"It's an absolute maximum of six months."

Finally, she broke away.

"Six months. That's the deal," she agreed, then walked towards the bedroom, smiling.

There was still one thing we hadn't cleared up.

"Er, Amelia?"

"Yes?"

"But what about your mum? Don't we have to run it by her first?"

She picked her phone up from the arm of the sofa, instantly taking my mind back to the early hours of the morning.

"Mother's fine with it. I've already asked her."

PART II

11

IT HAD ONLY TAKEN ten weeks from proposal to marriage. During that period, I had turned thirty-seven and Amelia's birthday had fallen ten days later – she was thirty-three just before our wedding day.

We'd chosen Leatherhead Registry Office, some five miles from the Reids' family home – *my* family home for the next six months. As previously agreed, we kept it to close family and a couple of my friends and their respective partners. Lisa and Chris from work also attended, and Mike and Don who acted as witnesses. Katrina hadn't been well enough to put in an appearance, or at least that was the family line. And Graham's wife still hadn't returned from her latest trip abroad.

The wedding was on a Friday afternoon, and we had a week's honeymoon booked in Corfu, leaving the following day. The actual ceremony went off well. We'd been blessed with the weather, and the lack of a huge occasion suited us both fine – it was exactly what we'd wanted.

We held the reception above a pub in Epsom. I had

put my foot down after getting quotes for the country hotel. I'd persuaded Amelia that it would be a waste of money, especially as we were now on a tight budget. Melissa and Graham were reluctant, saying they didn't want Amelia's special day ruined by people getting drunk. I'd politely reminded them it was my special day too, and they begrudgingly agreed.

Whilst Amelia and I stood chatting at the bar – it must have been around ten o'clock – Melissa, Tracy and Graham approached us. I had a pint of bitter in my hand, which Melissa looked at disparagingly. It hadn't gone unnoticed by me that Amelia had stuck to soft drinks all night, keeping in line with the rest of the family.

"We're going now, darling." Melissa addressed her daughter, turning her body at an angle to me so she was almost sideways on. Graham stood behind his mother-in-law, towering above her and avoiding all eye contact with me too. Only Tracy acknowledged me, albeit with only a courteous nod of her head.

Amelia kissed her mother on both cheeks before giving Graham and Tracy an enormous hug.

"Thank you all so much for a wonderful day," she said. It felt as though I'd become invisible. Suddenly I felt vulnerable, and a wave of anger rode over me. I knew I'd had a bit too much to drink, so I tried to bottle up my feelings.

They turned to leave, without speaking to me at all. I wasn't prepared to let it go.

"Goodnight, you three," I shouted after them, the alcohol boosting my confidence.

They spun in unison. Melissa looked me up and down whilst Graham just stared into my face. Melissa spoke on their behalf.

"I think you've had enough to drink now, Matthew. Don't you?"

As I tried to think of a quick retort, Amelia squeezed my hand. It was a 'don't you dare say anything' squeeze, even though she'd fixed a grin on her face for her family's benefit.

"Don't worry, Mother, that's his last one."

With an exaggerated tut of disapproval from Melissa, they turned on their heels and marched across the room to the exit. I couldn't resist a snide remark.

"Yeah, I'll need to perform—"

Amelia yanked on my arm, spilling beer from the top of my glass. She stood on tiptoe, so we were face to face, only inches apart and spoke through gritted teeth.

"Don't you dare ruin this for me. I've not married a drunk, and my family doesn't want an alcoholic living in their house."

"What the fuck are you—?"

"You heard. Now, make this your last drink. We've got an early flight tomorrow and I'm exhausted. I'm going to the bathroom, and when I get back, I expect you will have ordered a taxi to take us to the airport hotel."

She picked her handbag up from the floor and strode off to the ladies. It wasn't until she'd gone that I noticed Lisa had been standing close by. She must have watched the scene unfold in front of her and heard the whole conversation.

Looking over her shoulder to ensure Amelia was out of sight, she stepped over to be by my side. She spoke as quietly as she could, leaning into my right ear. I could smell her perfume and felt her breath as she spoke. It may have been the drink, but I could quite easily have turned my head and kissed her. I'd noticed how pretty she had looked ever since she'd arrived at the registry office earlier that day.

"Can you remember your very first day in the office?"

"Hmm, some of it, why?"

"On my way out, I told you to be careful."

"Yeah, I sort of remember. What did you mean?"

"It's like I said in the café that day. There's something not right, but I'm not sure what."

She looked nervously over her shoulder again, before falling silent.

"And?" I asked. She looked exasperated and let out a groan.

"Oh, forget it. Maybe I'm just a little jealous."

Right on cue, Amelia returned. She looked Lisa up and down. Lisa's dress was low cut, showing off ample cleavage. Amelia couldn't resist.

"That took some squeezing into, Lisa."

"Hey, that's not fair," I defended my friend, who was blushing and attempting to cover herself with her forearm. Amelia turned to me.

"I see! Well, perhaps you married the wrong girl, did you?"

"Hey, come on. I just thought it was uncalled—"

"Have you booked that taxi yet, or have you spent the last five minutes chatting her up?" Amelia looked at Lisa like she was somebody who'd been dragged in off the streets until Lisa stormed off to the toilets.

"What's wrong with you? I've never seen you act like this before." I tried to stay level-headed. I knew the drink could easily lead to me saying something I'd regret later.

"Can we just go, please?"

She fixed on her best smile and made her way through the remaining guests, saying her goodbyes. I'd ordered an Uber, which would be outside within minutes.

With one eye on the bathroom, I reluctantly followed Amelia to the exit, wishing Lisa would appear before we left. Unfortunately, she didn't materialise. I hoped she was okay.

The taxi ride to Gatwick Airport was fraught with tension. We'd sat in the back seat together, but Amelia just stared out of her window all the way. After several failed attempts to start up a conversation with her, I finally chatted to the driver instead. We talked about football and the best pubs around Epsom. Amelia tutted at everything I said. The cab driver caught my eye in his mirror and winked. I couldn't help but smile – ironically, the only time that Amelia turned her head to face me on the entire journey. If looks could kill…

Once inside the hotel, I checked us in at reception. Amelia stood well back, avoiding the inevitable small talk. As soon as I had the keys, we wheeled our luggage to the lift and stepped inside. For the last time, I tried to lighten the mood.

"Fourth floor. Maybe it's a sign?"

"What are you talking about?"

"Fourth floor, just the same as Harrogate."

At last, she smiled. The lift arrived with a 'ping', and I allowed Amelia to walk out first.

"Yes," she said, "maybe it *is* a sign."

The room was standard airport hotel accommodation. Double bed, a small TV hanging from the wall, and a bathroom with a shower unit. We had to be up early for our flight, so it wasn't an issue.

"I'm going into the bathroom to change," Amelia announced, unpacking some nightwear from her case. It caught me totally off guard.

"Sorry?"

"I won't be long, then you can change."

I grabbed her arm, a little harder than I'd intended. She looked down at my hand as I spoke.

"Amelia, we're married now. I've seen you undress a hundred times before. Why do you need to change in the bathroom?"

Still she stared downwards, towards the floor now, purposefully avoiding eye contact.

"Will you please remove your hand from my arm?"

As soon as I let go, she made her way into the bathroom, closed the door and clicked the lock. I sat on the edge of the bed, vacantly glaring after her.

What the fuck is this all about?

Then I thought about Lisa, wondering if she was okay. She'd recently divorced, and Amelia's jibe really looked as though it had affected her. Grabbing my phone, I quickly sent her a text message.

Are you okay, Lisa? Sorry about what happened earlier xx.

Fuck knows why I put the kisses. Part anger at Amelia, and part something else; maybe the subconscious section of my brain trying to hold on to the past. Once a lad, always a lad.

I heard Amelia moving around in the bathroom and I immediately flicked my phone to silent. Hiding it in my suitcase, I fished out a pair of shorts to sleep in. I couldn't recall the last time I'd worn anything in bed with Amelia, but it felt right that I should make the effort tonight, given her mood and her strange request to change behind closed doors.

My phone vibrated in the suitcase. I listened for Amelia before retrieving it.

Am fine, Matt, thnx for asking. It's all forgotten. Have gr8 time. Lis xx.

"Who's that from?"

Fucking hell, how did I not hear the door unlock?

I quickly hid the phone in my hand, wrapping my fingers around it to create a fist. My thumb pressed the off button until I felt it vibrate one last time before switching off.

"It's the airline. Just a reminder that check-in opens at seven thirty."

She looked as though she didn't believe a word I'd said, and couldn't care less in equal measure.

"Oh, okay. Right, I'm shattered. Can you hurry in the bathroom please?"

I couldn't take my eyes off her – and not for the reasons I'd thought I would on our wedding night. Amelia was wearing pyjamas. Not sexy pyjamas, but fleece type PJs. She'd brushed her hair straight down, covering some of her face and looked as though she'd aged ten years since I'd seen her a few moments earlier.

She nodded towards the bathroom in a further attempt to get me to hurry along. I wandered towards it in a trance.

Brushing my teeth, I looked at myself long and hard in the mirror. All kinds of emotions cartwheeled around my mind, exaggerated by the alcohol still making its way around my system. Amelia had changed with a click of the fingers. As I stood there contemplating the day, I realised her whole demeanour had altered, bit by bit, hour by hour – all after arriving at the pub. She'd appeared so happy when she arrived at the registry office, her face lighting up the already glorious day. She'd looked me deep in the eyes as she said her vows, her hands gripping mine tight. It felt like true love, the kind I'd only ever seen at the movies. But then, at the reception, she'd begun to change. She only spoke to her family, avoiding everybody else. Maybe Melissa or Graham had said something, influenced her mood? She hadn't had an alcoholic drink at all, and she'd hinted frequently that she wished to leave – blaming everything on feeling tired.

And then the outburst at Lisa, before the whole silent treatment travelling to the hotel. And just to rub salt into the wounds, she'd changed in the bathroom, insisting on doing so behind a locked door.

My wedding day hadn't gone according to plan. I silently prayed that it wasn't a sign of things to come.

12

FORTUNATELY, my concerns were relatively short-lived. Once we'd stepped off the plane and into the intense heat of Corfu, Amelia's mood lightened. As I stood watching the wave-like fumes rippling the air, she voluntarily held my hand for the first time since we'd said our wedding vows and lifted her face to the sun, holding her straw hat to her head with her free hand.

"Hmm, feel that. It's gorgeous."

Although she was right – I'd always loved that initial sensation of being abroad, the sun somehow feeling different, more powerful, to how it felt at home – my mind was elsewhere, scrambling for explanations. Looking at Amelia right then, smiling, carefree and beautiful, in complete contrast to the person who had ended our wedding day with principles and morals beyond comprehension.

Amelia had stuck to her word in the hotel; when I returned from the bathroom, her bedside lamp was already switched off and she lay on her side, presumably asleep. In total contrast, I'd lain awake most of the night, staring at the ceiling whilst listening to my wife's steady breathing. We hadn't even had a solitary goodnight kiss to end our wedding day.

Next morning, her mood remained downbeat, but at least she'd made an effort with her appearance, wearing light blue knee-length shorts, new brown sandals and a bright white T-shirt. Her hair looked lovely again – shiny – and she carried a straw hat in readiness for the cloudless skies at the other end of the flight.

I'd showered, more in an attempt to wake myself up than any other form of excitement for the forthcoming honeymoon. I dreaded how Amelia would act; had it been wedding day nerves, or was there something else altogether; something much deeper?

The wedding day had brought back memories of my parents. We'd never been especially close, but I knew they would have loved to have seen their only son eventually marry and settle down. Until their car accident, the occasional phone call always ended with, 'Have you met anybody yet, Matthew?'. And, just over two years later, I had. I so wanted it to work out with Amelia; finally put those bachelor days behind me and plan out the rest of my life.

When my parents died, it had surprised me how little money they actually had. I'd thought they owned the house in Scotland, but it turned out they only rented it. There was around thirty thousand pounds in a joint savings account, and a tiny pension scheme my dad had set up and made sporadic contributions to. My mum had never worked, so I always knew there was only dad's solitary wage from the factory. They'd saved enough each year to take me on a family holiday, mostly to Norfolk, but we'd never travelled abroad together. They never did, unless you counted Scotland.

It wasn't until I was in my mid-twenties that I had sufficient money to travel. The bug soon hit me, and I would save enough to go on holiday at least twice a year. If I went a third or fourth time, my credit card took the hit. It gave me a purpose in life, a goal. Once I returned from holiday, I'd count down the months, weeks and days until the next trip. It had been something I'd wanted to do for the rest of my life. But now, I had to grow up, settle down. Who knows, maybe start a family.

Something struck me as I watched Amelia lift her head to the sun on the tarmac outside Corfu airport. Something I'd never addressed before.

"Have you been abroad before?" I felt her hand inadvertently tighten in my grip. She stopped looking at the sun and faced me instead. It was impossible to read her thoughts.

"Well no. I haven't. We're not all international jet setters, you know."

Although she smiled, it still felt like an underhanded dig.

The wind whipped up, leaving a feeling like a naked flame brushing my skin, and I followed Amelia's lead to make our way into the terminal building. As we walked, I looked back at the aeroplane, wondering what the week had in store before I boarded once again for the return journey.

The hotel was wonderful; even better than the online photographs which hadn't done it full justice. We had a suite on the top floor, with a huge wrap-around balcony, taking in views of both the sea to the front and the mountains to the side. There was a fridge – already stocked with both soft and alcoholic drinks – and the bathroom had the biggest walk-in shower I'd ever seen. The bed was enormous too.

When we first walked in, I wondered if we would consummate our marriage during the week. It was something I needn't have worried about.

Amelia immediately put her suitcase to one side and strode over to me. Inviting me to let go of my case too, she took both my hands and led me to the bed. At first, I felt apprehensive, a feeling akin to it being our first ever time together. But Amelia soon fell back into familiar territory; the way she had always been during those long weekends of bliss spent in my tiny flat in North London.

After a heavenly hour together, we both lay on our backs, mesmerised by the ceiling fan that slowly rotated above us. Amelia shifted herself onto her side and allowed her finger to trace the contours of my chest.

"I'm sorry about yesterday. I was nervous, scared even. It's all so new, for both of us..."

She looked as though she might cry. I slid my arm underneath her shoulders and pulled her tight into me. The sigh of relief came from the pit of my stomach.

"Hey, I know, I know. It's a big day, a massive change. We've committed to spending the rest of our days together."

My heart thumped in my chest, so much so, I thought Amelia would have to lift her head to relieve herself from the sensation. But she seemed to find comfort lying there, her breathing becoming shallow and regulated. I could listen to the sound of her inhale and exhale all day long.

She sprung up suddenly, making my heart skip a beat. I watched her, standing at the end of the bed in all her nakedness. I could have pinched myself, feeling the need to remind myself that I had just married this woman. She was far more beautiful than any other female I'd been with. It was at that moment, for the first time since I'd met her, I truly felt I had married above myself. Amelia was stunning in my eyes. I was just a lad who may have eventually grown up.

She grabbed my T-shirt off the floor and pulled it over her head. Moments later, I heard a small squeal from the balcony as soon as she stepped outside. The net curtain in the doorway blew inwards, the breeze rolling across my body. It was warm and felt wonderful as it caressed my skin. Amelia came running back inside the apartment.

"You've got to see the views. It's just…"

I watched her as she smiled, trying to find the right words.

"…it's just, paradise."

I laughed with her. This was exactly how I'd imagined married life to be.

I watched her excitedly explore the apartment. She screamed in glee when she saw the shower, grinning at me as she returned to the main room. Then she made her way to the fridge. She opened it with another gasp of excitement, leant inside and stood back to face me. She was holding two bottles of ice-cold beer.

"Shall we?" she asked.

What the fuck is going on here? Did I imagine last night?

I replayed the images of the room above the pub in Epsom.

Don't you dare ruin this for me, Matthew. I've not married a drunk, and my family doesn't want an alcoholic living in their house.

Amelia opened both bottles with the utensil she found in the small kitchenette area. She walked over to the bed and passed one to me. As I took it, still unsure if I was walking into a trap or not, she clinked my bottle with hers.

"Here's to us, the Walkers," she said, before taking a huge gulp of the beer. It was like she had saved up an entire day of not drinking just to devour that one.

As I took a long swig of mine, she took the bottle from my hand and placed both on the bedside table. Her fingers carried on from before and traced lines along my chest and down. She looked up at me, spoke softly, before following her fingers with her mouth.

"We need to make up for lost time."

The rest of the honeymoon went with no hint of a problem between us. We ate out every night, trying different restaurants dotted along the seafront. We drank beer, wine and cocktails, returning to the apartment every night slightly worse for wear. And Amelia hadn't been wrong; we made up for any lost time in the bedroom department.

During the day, we relaxed. Mainly by the enormous onsite pool and sometimes strolling down to the beach. We hired jet skis and took a boat trip to some nearby caves. It was idyllic. We both regretted not booking two weeks and vowed to return one day – to the exact same apartment.

The week flew by, and before we knew it, we were in a taxi on the return journey to the airport. We had a daytime return flight. Once inside, the airport felt muggy and the air conditioning gave only a brief respite from the heat pouring through the immense glass windows. It was the part of any holiday I hated. Hanging around in an airport, the initial excitement of the outward journey now dissipated.

After we had found two seats in the waiting area, I

stood and took out the few remaining euro coins I had in my pocket.

"What are you doing?" Amelia stopped reading her magazine and looked up at me.

"I'm going to grab a beer. It's so stuffy in here. Want one?"

"Er, no thanks. Can you get me a Diet Coke, please?"

"Yeah, okay, sure." I headed towards the bar.

"Oh, and, Matthew?" Amelia cried after me.

I turned, stepping backwards, smiling at my new wife.

"Make this your last one, eh?"

My smile disappeared as quickly as it had arrived. I stopped in my tracks and looked at Amelia for any sign that she might be joking. There was no such look. She spoke again, though.

"Don't forget we move in with Mother once we get home. We will need to abide by her rules."

13

AMELIA DIDN'T DRINK on the plane home either. She complained about the in-flight food and she'd had an argument with someone at the airport who she accused of pushing in front of us. By the time we landed, disembarked and made our way into the terminal, I needed a break. As soon as Amelia said she needed the bathroom, I made my way to the carousel to wait for our luggage. It would at least give me fifteen minutes of peace.

Her behaviour had become unpredictable. I'd asked frequently if I'd done something wrong, something to upset her. Each time, she brushed me aside and said she was getting nervous about us moving into her family home. I suggested we live at my flat until I sold it, but then she'd go straight back on the defensive and accuse me of hating her family. Feeling as though I just couldn't win, I decided not to mention it again. Besides, I was also beginning to feel slightly anxious about living with my in-laws.

Once we stepped out of the airport, I squeezed Amelia's hand and told her everything would be okay. She thanked me and stood on tiptoe to kiss me on the cheek. I smiled with relief and led us towards the taxi rank.

"Don't bother," Amelia cried after me. "I've arranged a lift."

Looking at her perplexed, I wheeled the suitcases back over to where she stood. Then Amelia put one foot into the road, smiled and waved frantically. I followed her gaze along the inner airport access road. A car was flashing its lights in response to Amelia's signalling. I couldn't believe my eyes. I ran to catch up with her before the vehicle reached us.

"That's my fucking car!"

She spun towards me, momentarily scowling her disapproval at my rant. She then fixed her smile back on and turned to face the car as it indicated and pulled in alongside us.

"Isn't it great? I arranged it just before we took off."

"But, but that's my fucking—"

She dismissed my complaints with a flick of her hand. As the car came to a halt, she inched herself closer to me and spoke through gritted teeth.

"Matthew, please keep your language down."

With that, the driver's door swung open and out stepped Graham.

"What the fuck—!"

"Matthew!" Amelia was no longer smiling. She stared directly into my face; a look of anger shot across her own. "Can't you *ever* be grateful? I really hope you change your ways, else you're in for a very uncomfortable time."

Then she turned again.

"Graham! We're so grateful." She nudged me. "Aren't we, Matt?"

Graham looked me in the eyes, then down at my car. He couldn't suppress his smile.

"She drives like a dream, mate. What's the top speed you've had out of her?"

I felt like throwing my fucking suitcase at him, but once he joined me on the pavement, I remembered just how big a guy he was. He held his hand above mine with the car keys jangling. I placed my open palm below, and he dropped them in.

"I'll let you drive home, mate." He paused for effect, letting my mood simmer. Leaning closer, he goaded me, now only inches from my ear. "But if I ever need to borrow it, you won't mind, will you? Especially now you're living in the family home."

Graham walked off and hugged Amelia before holding her at arm's length to take a good look at her. As I loaded the luggage into the boot a thought suddenly hit me.

"Er, Graham?"

They both looked up.

"Yeah?"

"What about insurance? This is a company car."

Amelia spoke for him.

"Oh, don't worry about that. I fixed it before we left. Mike said it was okay, you know, for emergencies."

"But this wasn't an emergency—"

Graham butted in.

"Behave, Matt. Mike will never know when I borrow it. If anything ever happens, that's when we'll say it was an emergency."

When I borrow it! Did he think it would be a regular thing?

They both giggled, and took their seats in the car, leaving me to finish loading the suitcases.

Before I got in myself, I heard the roar of an aeroplane taking off on the runway from behind the terminal building. I watched it take to the skies, silently wishing that I was on it; wherever it might be going.

We pulled up outside our new temporary home about an hour later. Graham and Amelia had chatted freely all the way back. It hadn't gone unnoticed by me that he asked her all the questions regarding the holiday, not once engaging me in the conversation. In all honesty, I found it a relief. I had no intention of making small talk with him anyway.

Again, they left me to deal with the luggage whilst they walked up the footpath to meet Amelia's beaming mother and sister, who were standing outside the front door. Melissa welcomed her daughter with open arms, and soon Graham and Tracy joined them in a group hug. It made me feel sick as I watched from behind the open car boot.

After I unloaded the suitcases and placed them on the ground, I looked up towards the happy family. Without a hint of acknowledgement towards me, they went inside and closed the front door behind them. The last thing I heard was the faint sound of laughter.

I turned back to the car, lifted the final two items of hand luggage out with one hand, and pulled down the hood with the other. As soon as I closed it, a figure standing only a few feet beyond startled me. I felt myself physically jump backwards; the breath momentarily gone from my lungs.

"What the—?"

"Hush, hush, Matthew. They do not allow swearing in your new house."

Katrina grinned, showing her yellowing teeth. Her

lips appeared chapped, with tiny cracks running their entire length. She licked them, as if reading my thoughts.

"Oh, hi, Katrina." I held my heart to stop it from thumping. "You made me jump."

Katrina giggled. Just like the first time I'd met her the day on the swing, her voice didn't match her teenage years. She looked like a child straight out of a horror movie. Pasty white skin, wild black hair and crooked yellow teeth. Her lips looked like they could split open and blood drip down her chin, just to complete the image.

Calming myself, I peered up at the house, ensuring nobody was watching.

"So, Katrina, tell me. What do you do all day?"

I knew I was speaking to her like I would somebody half her age. It was surreal, but the way she conducted herself made me feel that was the only means of communication.

"Oh, I play." She started sucking her thumb and swaying her body from left to right. Her eyes never left mine. She was scaring the shit out of me. Attempting not to show my discomfort, I asked her a further question.

"Okay. What do you like to play?"

From nowhere, her voice dropped several octaves. It was as though another person lived within her and it was their turn to talk. Removing her thumb, her mouth twisted into a snarl. Her teeth appeared sharper. But by now, my mind was all over the place. She replied in a slow, meaningful and terrifying manner.

"Whatever. I. Fucking. Want."

And then she turned and ran up the slope, her white dress flowing around her, ghostlike. I heard her giggling again as I watched her run all the way to the swing. Turning full circle, she hitched herself up, forcing the swing backwards with a firm push of her feet. The swing squeaked as it travelled back and forth. She gripped the metal chains, her knuckles white and bony. Not once did Katrina take her eyes off me, even when I begrudgingly made my way up to the house.

"Matthew!"

I put the cases and hand luggage down in the hallway. My heart still pumped so fast I thought it would be audible. Looking up, I saw Melissa's beaming smile. She held her arms aloft. Although my nerves were on the edge of exploding, I returned a smile.

"Welcome home," she said.

Before I knew it, she was hugging me. She had considerable strength, given her ageing years, and she held me tight in her grip. She whispered in my ear.

"Hold me back, Matthew. Like you would Amelia."

I looked over her shoulder, worried any of her siblings might be around. Reluctantly, I lifted my arms and placed them lightly around her back. This time she murmured.

"Tighter, Matthew. I want to feel you."

Holy fucking shit. What is going on?

For the second time in Melissa's private company, I did not understand how to react. I did as I was told.

She adjusted her head, her mouth now inches from mine. I could feel her breath exhaling warm air directly onto my face. What was she doing?

The door sprang open behind, and Melissa immediately stood back. It was too late for her to let go of me, so she held onto my arms. Glancing over her shoulder, she saw that Amelia had joined us. Amelia's expression showed no emotion.

"Isn't he well-tanned, Amelia?" Melissa's manner instantly changed. She looked me in the eyes, daring me.

"Yes, Mother. We had wonderful weather, didn't we, Matt?"

"Er," I coughed, clearing my throat, which by now had become parched. "Yes, it was lovely."

"That's great. I'm so pleased for you both."

Amelia asked me if I could carry the cases upstairs, and she left us in the hallway once more. I took it as my cue to pick up the cases, the perfect excuse to get away from the suffocating situation.

Melissa had to step sideways to let me pass. She still fixed her eyes on mine. As I shuffled past, she held out her hand and grabbed my arm.

"Matthew?"

"Yes?" My tone was much higher than I'd intended.

"I hope you're really happy here."

I let out a sigh of relief. I hadn't known what she was going to say, but I took it as a positive.

"Thank you. We won't be here long—"

She squeezed my arm tighter, stopping me from saying any more.

"Stay as long as you want. You're part of our family now."

I nodded and attempted to move on. I felt trapped, strangled by the palpable lack of air in the tight space. She grabbed me once more.

"And if there's anything..." She let it hang, knowing I'd have to face her to wait for her to finish.

"...if there's anything at all..." She let her hand slide down my arm until she reached mine, "...you only have to ask."

14

It wasn't until around midnight that I eventually fell into a deep, uninterrupted sleep. When I first went to bed, I had lain awake, motionless, listening to the summer rain ricocheting off the bedroom window. My thoughts danced from Graham using my car, to Melissa's salacious approach and then onto my weird, and scary, confrontation with Katrina. What a welcome to my new life.

It had surprised me they had allowed me in the same room as Amelia, half expecting a family announcement that it was against the rules to sleep together. We were to use Amelia's bedroom. It had a direct door into the bathroom that separated her room from the one I'd previously used. At least it acted as an en suite and we wouldn't have to go out onto the landing every time we needed to use the toilet.

Making my excuses that a full day's travelling had worn me out, I retired upstairs before anybody else. When Amelia came to bed about an hour after me, I'd pretended to be asleep. I had my back turned to her.

There was so much I'd wanted to say, but I thought it best to let things settle and allow myself time to adapt to our new arrangement. We'd only been married a week, and I loved Amelia. It would be stupid to fly off the handle so soon and start making demands.

Earlier, I had opened the calculator app on my phone and started crunching figures. I'd worked out that if we were scrupulous with money, we could be out sooner than the six months previously agreed. I planned on telling Amelia after a few days so it didn't look as though I wanted to leave as soon as I'd arrived, even if that was the truth.

Amelia made as little noise as possible as she got ready for bed. I thought it nice that she didn't want to wake me. She snuggled up next to me and kissed me on the cheek, before whispering 'good night, husband' in my ear. It made me smile and put my mind at ease. I did not roll over and kiss her back or let on that I was awake. I just wanted to feel her close to me, reassure me. Maybe my wife just belonged to a dysfunctional family and I was reading far too much into it.

Two days later, after beginning to settle into our new routine, I awoke at six o'clock to shower and get ready for work. I joined Melissa in the kitchen for breakfast – there had been no repeat of our encounter for the rest of the weekend, and I was already putting it to the back of my mind. We made small talk, whilst we waited for Amelia to join us.

Melissa saw Amelia walk in before I did. I'd been eating toast whilst reading the news on my phone, much to the bewilderment of Melissa, when I heard her greet her daughter.

"Morning, darling. You look smart today."

"Thank you, Mother," she replied, before walking over to me and kissing me on the cheek.

Amelia wore black trousers and a matching jacket. Underneath was a pale yellow blouse. Her mother had been right, she looked very smart.

"Hi, darling," I said, in between chewing my toast.

"Oh, Matthew. Please close your mouth when you're eating." Melissa looked over at me and tutted before returning to her daughter.

"Is there anything you need Graham to do today? He's coming over later."

"What a surprise," I said. I'd intended to speak under my breath, but it came out louder than expected.

They let it go, deciding to ignore me. Instead, I congratulated myself on my quick wit.

"Welcome back, Mr and Mrs Walker," Mike said as soon as we reached our desks. There had been a few hand-shakes from well-wishers as we'd made our way through the office. I nodded my head in a thank you gesture to Mike and likewise thanked the others in turn. Amelia took her seat, smiling from ear to ear. She looked pleased by the attention, whilst I just wanted to get back to work and earn some money.

Then I caught Lisa's eyes, the one person totally focused on me and not the new bride. I forced a smile, but her response was much more natural in return. It pleased me; it looked as though the incident at the wedding reception might be forgotten or at least swept under the carpet, and hopefully not mentioned again.

Throughout the day, I kept looking up at my new wife. She was beautiful. Her family was something I had to put up with, and it would be a small sacrifice now I had Amelia in my life. I contemplated the fact that her mother, Tracy and Graham were prudes, people who were stuck in the past. The way they conducted themselves was alien to me, but once away from their clutches, Amelia became a different person. Even as the day wore on, she flirted with me once more. When we were alone, making coffee, she promised me things in bed later that night – 'as long as we're quiet' – she winked. I needed to bide my time and then she would be all mine, forever.

That evening, Katrina joined us for the family meal. It was the first time she'd sat at the dining table with us. Graham had stayed for dinner too, which didn't surprise me – it appeared he'd *always* be there. There was a hushed silence around the room, as each member of the family took it in turns to watch Katrina. Tracy had observed her daughter's every move. Nobody dared to speak, as though in fear of igniting the touchpaper. I couldn't stand the tension any longer.

"So, Graham..." I began. I noticed Melissa jump at the broken silence, and Graham glared at me as if to dare me to say anything out of hand.

"Yes, Matthew?" All eyes were now on me. Katrina had stopped eating and looked directly towards me too. Her mouth was open and I could see chewed food inside. It made me feel momentarily sick. I focused my attention back on Graham.

"Is your wife due home soon? It would have been nice if she'd made the wedding."

Melissa dropped her fork, the sound reverberating around the room as it spun and dropped, slow motion-like, to the floor. Katrina laughed, her mouth now wider, showing all the contents, mixed with those crooked yellow teeth.

Amelia scraped her chair back.

Everything felt like an overreaction, but something obviously bothered them.

"I'll get you a clean one, Mother," said Amelia, and she walked towards the kitchen, glaring at me as she went. I shrugged my shoulders, almost enjoying the charade. Graham cleared his throat.

"Er, no. Not just yet."

I didn't want to let it go.

"And where do you live? I've never known where you walk from to get here." I put a mouthful of food into my mouth before looking up at him, chewing and smiling whilst waiting for a reply. I knew I had him trapped; he had to respond.

"Not far away. Down the hill, towards town." He was stuttering in his response.

"I know."

All eyes turned to Katrina as Amelia returned to her seat, handing fresh cutlery to Melissa. Graham stopped her in her tracks.

"Yes, yes. We know you know, Katrina—"

She wasn't interested in what her uncle was saying. Her eyes became fixed on me instead.

"I'll show you, Matthew."

It was Melissa's turn to speak. The authority of the house knew the conversation was drifting further than they'd expected.

"Do you want to go to your room, young girl?"

Young girl? Go to your room? What the fuck? She's a teenager.

Silence fell again. The sound of food being chewed

and cutlery scraping on plates irritating me in equal measure.

As soon as we finished eating, Tracy excused Katrina to leave the table. Shortly after, I heard the back door open and then close. It was a fine summer evening, and they seemed to have no issue with her wandering around the vast garden alone.

The rest of us retired to the living room. I'd enjoyed seeing Graham squirm earlier, so I pushed things a little further.

"I've been thinking." Again, silence. Amelia looked at me inquisitively. I shook my head at her, distinguishing any fear that I might say something untoward.

"If we are going to be residing here for a few months..."

The three of them exchanged a look which I couldn't read.

"...well, I will need broadband. The phone signal here is weak, too weak for me to connect my laptop."

Again, they traded stares. Amelia eventually spoke.

"He's right, Mother. Matt will need to work some evenings on his accounts and emails. It's part of the job."

Melissa looked at Graham for support. It was uncomfortable for them.

"What would you require?" Graham asked, as politely as he could manage.

"Well, there are some great deals at the moment. We'd need an external phone line—"

He interrupted me sharply.

"No. We don't need a phone."

"No, no, it's fine. We wouldn't have a phone, just the line connected to the house. Then you just hook a broadband router to it, and hey presto, we have internet. I'm guessing I'd be the only one using it."

Amelia supported me, convincing them it was nothing to fear. I showed them the one I wanted on my phone, and they reluctantly agreed for me to get the line installed. I thanked them and promised to put it all in my name so I could pay and then take it with me when we left to live in our own place.

Later that night, around ten thirty, we retired to our bedroom for the evening. About an hour before, I'd heard Tracy call Katrina back in once the light had faded outdoors. I'd deliberately held back in the hallway and watched them go up the stairs and make their way towards their respective bedrooms further along the corridor above.

As Amelia got ready for bed, I found myself wandering over to our bedroom window. The room faced the front of the house, and I watched Melissa walk with Graham down to the end of the footpath as he left for home. They were deep in conversation as they sauntered along. I took a step backwards as soon as they looked over their shoulders and up towards the house.

Amelia interrupted my monitoring of the two senior family members by calling me from behind. Turning round, I saw her lying on our bed with the blanket pulled tight to her chin.

"Are you coming to bed, Mr Walker?" She wore that sexy smile, the one that got me every time.

As I moved to join her, she pulled the blanket back, revealing there were no pyjamas that night.

Later, I lay awake watching the curtains wave in the breeze of the open window. I felt happy with the way the evening had panned out. Not only had I just spent a blissful hour with my wife, but I'd also persuaded the family to let me have broadband — a window to the outside world – and made Graham squirm around the subject of his wife.

It was Graham, and his inconspicuous wife, that preoccupied my thoughts before I drifted off to sleep. Something didn't fit where they were concerned, and I wanted to find out more.

15

AMELIA CONTINUED to fluctuate between the perfect wife and the over-dutiful daughter. Some nights she'd be thoughtful, affectionate, the Amelia I loved, whilst at others, she would clam up, and all but threaten to put our lives on hold if I pushed her into a corner whilst discussing our future.

Two weeks after agreeing to have broadband installed, we returned home from work one evening to find an installation guy working outside the house. Inevitably, Graham stood beside him, presumably overseeing his work. It wasn't until we left the car, and I walked over to join them, that I heard exactly what had been worrying Graham. Amelia carried on towards the house, obviously not interested in the new capability to connect to the world wide web.

"So, does this record what we're doing?" he asked. The installation guy looked at him incredulously.

"No, mate. It will just allow you to get onto the internet, that's all."

Thinking it a strange question to be asking, I ignored Graham completely.

"Good evening," I greeted the workman. "So, will this be up and running today? It's me who needs the internet." I couldn't resist adding, "as I doubt anybody else will know how to use it." Graham shuffled his feet and straightened his back. It read like a threatening stance.

"Yes, all being well. I'll have the phone line connected in half an hour or so, and then I'll hook your router up."

"That's great. Thanks so much. I'll leave you two to it." I turned to leave and offered a sly wink towards Graham. He narrowed his eyes and a deep frown spread across his forehead. He mouthed something towards me, but I couldn't make out what.

Katrina sat on the swing as I approached the house. She gave a friendly wave in my direction, to which I reciprocated. I couldn't help but wonder exactly what was wrong with her. She always looked wild, spaced-out, but she also seemed capable of holding some conversation, even if it was at a very basic level.

That evening, I tested the new Wi-Fi service. Although I'd known there would be some weak spots around the house, I'd specifically asked for the router to be stationed in the dining room, so the signal would be at its strongest in there and the lounge downstairs. I also knew I'd be able to connect in our bedroom immediately above. This would give me a ready-made excuse to spend time on my own in our room whenever I felt the urge.

Amelia tried her laptop too, but Graham was much more interested in mine. He watched every website I brought up – I purposefully stuck to Google, our company website and a few client sites – and read through a selection of my work emails.

"Is it good, Matthew?" Melissa asked as I finally closed the lid on my laptop.

"Yeah, great, thanks. Just what I need for work and stuff." I added the latter just to annoy Graham who, at last, stopped looking over my shoulder and took a seat next to Amelia. She too closed her laptop down, which appeared to agitate him further.

"What do you mean, 'stuff'?" Graham wanted to know more.

"Oh, you know, the internet allows you to find out all kinds of things."

The atmosphere shifted. Graham and Melissa exchanged a look. Despite their obvious concern, Graham kept his voice even.

"Yes, but you can't believe all you read on there. I've heard most of it is made up, anyway."

"True," I replied, "a lot of it is nonsense." I shifted my attention to Melissa. "But look at you."

"What about me?" She adjusted herself in her chair, suddenly looking worried. Graham inched forwards in his seat, perching himself on the edge, as if ready to pounce. Amelia looked at me wide-eyed, dreading what I could be about to say. Inwardly, I grinned.

"Your puzzles," I pointed at the pile of papers on the table next to her chair. "They're all from the internet, no doubt." There was an audible escape of collective breath.

"That's true, Mother," Tracy said, catching everybody out as she entered the room. "Without the internet, we wouldn't be able to gather all this…"

She stopped herself mid-sentence. Again the room fell silent. In a strange way, I found their discomfort entertaining.

"Gather all what?" I asked, searching from face to face, second-guessing which one would crack.

Suddenly, Graham stood, towering above everyone. It was more of a display of physical prowess than any attempt to defuse the situation with a logical answer.

"It's nothing, okay?" He chortled at his own words. "You ask a lot of questions, don't you?"

Ignoring him, I studied the pile of papers on the table next to Melissa. She caught my eye, and immediately picked them up and shuffled them into a neat stack before placing them on her knees, her hands pressed firmly on top.

"I'm going to make a move and get myself home," Graham announced before walking over to Melissa. "Do you want me to take those for you?" He took the papers without waiting for a reply and put them into an empty folder which sat on Melissa's side table.

After he'd kissed his in-laws goodbye, he asked if I could accompany him to the door. I noticed how flushed he had become, his face full of hostility. I was still more interested in the manilla folder tucked under his arm but reluctantly followed him.

Once outside, he turned so we were face to face on the doorstep.

"What's up?" I asked, somewhat cheekily given his expression.

He stepped even closer, our faces now only inches apart. He murmured, but the threat was obvious.

"Just be very careful. We have allowed you to have your stupid broadband, and we are letting you stay in our family home." He inched his face closer still. "Now, just be grateful and show us some respect. That way, nothing untoward will happen. Okay?"

He was barely audible by the time he finished, but the message left little doubt in my mind. Graham didn't like me or my snide little remarks. It was as though I might be a threat to their strange existence. My eyes followed him until he was out of sight. I couldn't move, dumbfounded by his ultimatum.

Just as I'd composed myself, I heard the familiar creepy sound of the squeaking swing. Meandering around the side of the house, I spotted Katrina, gently swaying backwards and forwards. The light was fading fast, and she appeared only a silhouette against the moisture-laden air. A storm didn't feel far away and the atmosphere was muggy in the late summer evening.

"Hi, Katrina," I managed.

"Grandmother likes her puzzles."

Again, Katrina went straight to the point, but it wasn't her choice of subject that concerned me. How did she know what I had said in the living room? As far as I could recall, she hadn't even been there.

"Yes, I'm sure she does, Katrina."

"Do you want to know why she likes them so much?"

Suddenly I became intrigued and walked towards her. Once I was within earshot without the need to raise our voices, I beckoned her to continue.

"Why does she like them, Katrina?"

The next voice made me jump.

"You coming back in, Matt?" It was Amelia, standing at the corner of the house behind me. I glanced back at Katrina, but she just smiled before pushing herself higher on the swing.

Once in bed that night, I waited for Amelia to join me. She had spent forever in the bathroom. She turned out the light on her bedside lamp and rolled away from me, thinking I was already asleep. I made her jump when I spoke.

"What's going on?"

"Holy shit. You scared me half to death."

"Why did Graham pick up those papers from your mother? What did Tracy mean when she came into the room, you know, 'the internet allows her to gather'? Gather what?"

Although she kept her voice low, it was crystal clear that my line of questioning annoyed her.

"It's absolutely nothing. Just let it go, will you?"

I had no intention of letting it go.

"She said something about, gather all this... All this what?"

She sat up with a jolt and felt for her bedside lamp. The light momentarily blinded me.

"What is wrong with you? My family has allowed us the internet—"

"Allowed? What the fuck is that supposed to mean? I need it to do my job. Big fucking deal that I'm so privileged to live with such an accommodating family."

For the first time, I thought she might swing for me. She was breathing deeply, undeniably trying to control her temper.

"Just let it go, okay? We all need to get along, and I think you need to make more of an effort. This is for our benefit, and it wouldn't go amiss if both of us remembered that. Mother is probably just embarrassed by the games she likes to play. Because it's not your high-tech gadget stuff, she must feel inadequate. And Graham, too. You don't help by questioning everything they do."

She lay back down and exaggerated the fluffing up of her pillow before flicking her lamp back off. I listened intently after she'd rolled over onto her side and, once she'd turned her back to me, I waited for the steady breathing. After it arrived, I had to get in a last word, and I made it as sarcastic as I could muster.

"Okay. Just for you, I promise to try harder."

16

AFTER THE ESCAPADE involving Graham picking us up from the airport – what had he said, *Mike will never know when I borrow it* – I always made an effort to hide the car keys. If we travelled to work on the train, I'd put them in my laptop bag. It gave me some reassurance that he wouldn't be using my vehicle without my permission.

When we caught the train, we could leave home around twenty minutes later. That allowed me to get into the habit of taking my coffee outside the front of the house on those particular days. I'd sit on the rusting bench, which was preciously perched underneath the turret. Although the atmosphere in the house was always positive in the mornings – Graham wasn't around for one – I still found ten or fifteen minutes in solitude deeply satisfying.

Invariably, each of my morning retreats coincided with the postman arriving. Bob was a cheerful man, and very close to, if not already past, retirement age. The amount of post had increased since I'd moved in, and Bob would always look out for me. If I was around, he'd hand the letters to me personally rather than post them through the letterbox. If truth be told, I think we both enjoyed a morning chat. We talked about mundane day-to-day stuff; the weather or the previous night's football results.

One day – I'd been living in the house for over a month – I sat outside on the bench during my early morning ritual. The sun lit up the sky, as summer held on to its very last strands. Bob walked up the footpath wearing his usual smile, exaggerating the creases on his weather-worn face.

"Morning, Matt. Lovely day." He handed over a pile of envelopes which were neatly held together with an elastic band.

"Morning, Bob. Yeah, too nice to go in to work."

He soon changed tack, looking cautiously towards the house before speaking again.

"How you settling in? Is everything, you know, okay in there?"

"Er, yeah." I thought the question a little strange but played along anyway. I too looked over my shoulder before continuing. "Apart from the in-laws that is." I laughed, tapping my temple with my finger to point out they were a little crazy. Bob laughed too.

"Yeah, I can imagine. Down at the depot, we call them the Adams family." Although he laughed, he gave the impression he was only half joking. I hunched forward, purposefully lowering my voice.

"Do you know much about them?"

"No, not a lot. See little of them, to be honest. However, there's a bloke with ginger hair who sometimes—"

"Graham, my brother-in-law."

"Well, he's odd. He was nasty to a postwoman on

more than one occasion. Her name is Carol. He told her she used to bend the letters when she put them through the letterbox and stuff. One day, he accused her of opening mail and reading it before posting them. She soon asked to change to an alternative route. Couldn't stand the guy."

"Yeah, that sounds about right. He's here every night —" Bob interrupted me.

"I've noticed he isn't around in the mornings anymore. Ever since you moved in, mate. Why does he come round so often?"

I hadn't known Graham used to be around in the morning too.

"To tell you the truth, I haven't got a clue. He says he lives local…" then an idea crossed my mind, "…you don't know where, do you?"

"Well, that's the strange thing. Ever since Carol complained about him, nobody's really seen him. There's nobody around here with the first name Graham on any letters, so unless he goes under a different name, I've no idea. Do you know his surname?"

It made no sense. Graham had said he was a self-employed accountant. He must receive post if he ran his own business. It also dawned on me I didn't know Graham's surname.

After Bob left – I'd asked him if he could keep his eyes and ears open to see if he could find out any more about Graham's mystery home – I undid the elastic band on the pile of letters and looked at who they were for, one by one. It wasn't something I'd thought about before; I'd normally just fish out the mail for me and Amelia.

Four were addressed to me; letters forwarded from my flat, two for Amelia and one for Melissa. The one for Melissa was large, A4 size, and white. It had a hand-written address on it. I stared at it for several moments;

somehow the writing looked familiar, but I couldn't quite place it. However, it was the contents that grabbed my attention. The envelope was stuffed, threatening to break the seal on the back. Somebody had reinforced it with clear tape. I held it up to the sunlight, trying to peer inside. Twisting it, pulling each end tight, but to no avail. I couldn't make out anything hidden inside.

"Is that one for Mother, Matthew?" Amelia startled me. I'd been so intrigued by the letter I hadn't heard her step outside.

"Actually, yes. I thought it was coming undone, that's all."

She snatched the letter from my hand, took the two addressed to her, and marched off back inside. She halted at the front door.

"We need to leave in five minutes. Get yourself ready."

On the train, I asked Amelia if Graham had a company name, or even operated under a different personal name. Amelia wasn't forthcoming, declaring she knew nothing about her brother-in-law's business. Not for the first time, I asked further questions, determined to find out more. I wanted to know where he lived, when his wife was due home, and anything else that might give me a clue to his elusive place of residence and why he always turned up at the family home. I also asked if Amelia missed her sister, all of a sudden realising she hardly ever got a mention in the house. Each time, Amelia dismissed my questions. She eventually said it was none of my business. And why did it matter about Graham and his wife so much? She explained her sister had chosen her own way of living and we wouldn't be visiting their house anytime soon.

Taking on board that I'd exhausted my line of questioning, I changed the subject onto something else entirely.

"Oh, I forgot to tell you. I've transferred all my savings into our joint account. There's quite a bit in there now. I think we should start looking at some places. It will take weeks for any sale to go through, so we'd better get started."

Amelia turned to face me from her window seat on the train. She'd been staring out of the window for the entire journey. She smiled for the first time in what felt like an age.

"That's splendid news. It really is."

"So, why have you been acting so glum lately?"

"Oh, I've just been preoccupied thinking about Mother. Ignore me." Finally, a bigger and much more natural smile spread across her face. She leaned over and kissed me. "Yes, it's great news. Shall we look at some properties online tonight?"

"Yes, that would be great. Oh, and, Amelia?"

She snuggled in against me, both her hands wrapped around my arm.

"Yes?"

"Can we spend next weekend away somewhere? You know, just the two of us, for a break and—"

"Yes, darling, we can. That would be wonderful."

That evening, we never had time to look at properties online. Graham was there when we got home from work and Katrina joined us for the evening meal. Just as on the previous occasion when Katrina had joined us, the atmosphere was fraught. Katrina kept screeching her knife across her plate, something everybody else appeared to ignore. Each time, it went straight through me, making my teeth tingle.

After we'd eaten, I made my excuses and explained that I needed to work on some business proposals. Graham suggested I did it with the rest of the family in the living room, but I'd annoyed him when I said I needed to concentrate and I'd be best on my own.

For the best part of an hour, after I'd tried to get on with some work, I looked for properties by myself. I thought I could show Amelia later if I found anything that might be suitable.

Without realising, I had left the bedroom door slightly ajar. As I searched through the property website, I heard the distinct sound of the four adults talking downstairs. Suddenly interested, I crept out onto the landing and leaned over the bannister to see if I could eavesdrop on their conversation. But it was muffled, and they were keeping their voices low.

Suddenly, the living room door sprang open, and I stepped back into the shadows. I could make out the fuzzy hair of Katrina leaving the room.

"Just be careful, darling." It was Tracy talking. "I'll be up to your room to help you in a little while."

Help you? Help her with what?

Having been certain that Katrina hadn't seen me peering over the bannister, I waited until she disappeared before resuming my position. But, just as she opened the kitchen door, she looked up, flashed her yellow teeth, and gave me a brief wave.

Has she got some kind of fucking sixth sense?

I sarcastically smiled back. But she hadn't finished with me yet. She craned her neck at an awkward angle so she could get a better view up the stairs.

"I like Bob the postman too," she said, before grinning and skipping off into the kitchen and out of sight. As I tried to take in what she'd just said, the sound of the three voices drifted back up from the now open doorway. They were still keeping their voices low, but I could make out the occasional words. I tried to form sentences from what they were saying.

"Too soon", "how much", "not ready" and "all in good time" were little snippets I could pick out. Nowhere near enough to understand the gist of the conversation.

Then, after it had gone quiet for several moments and I was about to retreat into the bedroom, Graham spoke again. This time, he raised his voice to a level none of them had previously used and, as a result, he was much clearer.

"Do you think there's any chance that he saw what's in the letter?"

17

WE SPENT the following weekend away, and it turned out to be the best weekend we'd had since we'd become a married couple. Amelia booked us three nights in a hotel on Brighton seafront. It meant we didn't have to travel far, and it gave us room to breathe and to be alone; it had been perfect in every way.

Amelia had returned to her endearing self; full of fun and sexy traits. She'd packed some of her clothes I recognised from our pre-marriage days and we ate out, got drunk and had breakfast in bed every morning. She had been perfect company; reminding me exactly why I'd fallen for her all those months ago.

What was it about that house – that family – that made her so different? I pushed all negative thoughts to one side as I didn't want to ruin a lovely weekend by talking or thinking about that. Three days in each other's company acted as the perfect reminder that we needed to get away and start afresh; I for one couldn't wait.

During the weekend, we'd spent some time looking at properties online. We found one that we both fell in love with, and I called the agent to arrange a viewing as soon as we returned home. It was modest, but was full of charm and quintessentially the perfect British cottage. The only downside that I could see was that it was less than twenty miles from her family, but even I could put up with seeing them once a month, maybe less. I figured that Amelia could easily see them rather than the other way round. Besides, deep down, I knew there had to be a compromise along the way and, whatever I thought, they were a very close family.

On Monday morning, we drove directly to work from our weekend by the seaside, Mike and Lisa were already sat at their desks when we arrived at the office. Lisa winked in my direction as I took my seat; I'm not sure why, but somehow her action unnerved me, especially in the presence of Amelia.

Just as we were settling down, Mike asked Amelia if she would join him in a meeting room. He needed her to go over some figures for a client she had a very good understanding of. Amelia looked up at me, and then across to Lisa, before agreeing to join Mike.

"We'll be an hour at most if anybody wants us," said Mike, picking up his laptop and following Amelia to the meeting room. As soon as I heard the door click shut, I stood and sneaked over to Lisa. I don't know why I thought I needed to creep silently over to her. Maybe paranoia was taking its hold on me, frightened I might say or do the wrong thing.

"Morning, Lisa. Don't fancy a coffee across the road, do you?"

She collected the papers in front of her, shuffled them into a neat pile and placed them in her in-tray as soon as I suggested getting out of the office.

"Didn't think you'd ever ask," she giggled.

We both walked as silently as we could as we passed the meeting room.

This time, I bought the coffees and Lisa found us the same table at the back of the café.

"Something on your mind?" she asked before I'd even sat down.

Looking around, I pulled my chair out, sat down and hunched in as close to the table as it would allow. Even though Amelia and I had had a fantastic time, and things were looking up on the property front, something still niggled away deep inside me.

"As a matter of fact, yes." I looked around again. "Can I ask you something in complete confidence?"

She looked intrigued and scraped her seat as far forward as it would go too. Our faces were only inches apart across the table. Again, I noticed how pretty she looked.

"Do you know anything about Amelia's brother-in-law? The guy at the wedding. Graham."

She sat back in her seat, her eyes now wandering around the café. I couldn't work out if she was angry or just disappointed at my question.

"What about him?" she asked, almost dismissively. It must have been disappointment that I hadn't asked something more scandalous. I would not give up that easily, though. There was something about the guy that didn't add up, and Lisa could be my only friend to help me find out what. Even when Amelia and I moved out, I knew he'd still play a huge part in our lives.

"Well, to begin with, where does he live?" I wanted to tell her about the envelope, and me overhearing

Graham's comment asking if I'd seen inside it. However, I didn't feel I had Lisa's full attention.

"Won't he tell you that?"

It struck me as a stupid question. If he'd told me, I wouldn't be asking her. My reply was rather abrupt.

"Of course, not. I've asked Amelia too. Everybody tells me to mind my own business."

Lisa gave my comment some thought. Her interest appeared to be ever so slightly invigorated.

"I'm guessing he must live local, you know, if he's around as often as you say he is."

What?

"I haven't told you how often he's around. Have I?"

Lisa reddened, something I hadn't noticed her do before. She'd always struck me as a confident person.

"Oh, no. It wasn't you. Amelia told me last week. Said she couldn't wait for you guys to get your own place—"

"Amelia said that?" I couldn't stop the smile spreading across my face. To know she had confided in someone else that she wanted us to move in together meant the world to me. The thing that surprised me, though, was that she'd spoken to Lisa about it.

"Yeah. Me, Tracy and Amelia were chatting. You know, girls gossip."

I moved the conversation on to ask Lisa about Graham's wife too, but again she couldn't help me at all. Said she'd never met her and didn't even know what her name was. That's what struck me too; I didn't even know her name.

Giving it up as a dead end, we spent the next ten minutes chatting about work instead, before making our way back to the office. Just as we turned the final corner, Lisa grabbed my arm.

"Matt, is everything alright? You know, everything okay between you and Amelia?"

The question surprised me.

"Yeah, sure. Why do you ask?"

"Well, maybe I didn't come across as very helpful, you know, just then in the café."

"It's fine, don't worry about—"

"No. I need you to know that I'm here for you. I'd like to think we are more than just good friends."

I did not understand where the conversation was heading, but I remained silent, something stopping me from interrupting her.

"Amelia told me, well, us, about you losing your parents. It can't be easy having no family at all to speak to. That's why I want you to know you can always speak to me."

She walked away, glancing over her shoulder towards me. I quickly caught her up.

"That's very kind, Lisa. It's nice to know there's someone I can rely on. I appreciate it, I really do." I reached out and squeezed her arm. She didn't push me away.

That evening, as we drove back towards Epsom, Amelia broke the amicable silence.

"Did you have a nice coffee with Lisa?" She didn't take her eyes off the road in front of us. I glimpsed her face – which was non-committal – before replying.

"Yeah, sure. We just walked round to get a decent cup of coffee. You know, that stuff in the office is awful." Although I had been caught out by Amelia's question, I thought I'd made a reasonable attempt at covering myself. Again, Amelia's eyes didn't leave the road ahead.

"Just be careful. Don't confide everything in her, will you?" Finally, she turned to look at me. She looked concerned. Her comment left me feeling uneasy.

"You can talk. She said you'd told her my parents were dead." It was her turn to go on the defensive.

"I was talking to Tracy about that actually," she exaggerated the last word. "Lisa was within earshot, eavesdropping no doubt. Tracy is a wonderful sister. Women sometimes chat, that's all. It's not as though I've given away any secrets."

She was babbling, her words tripping over themselves as she backtracked. I held her hand to calm her down.

"Hey, it's okay. I know you all gossip. As long as you don't share too many secrets." I squeezed her thigh, and she reddened.

"As if," she replied, letting out a snigger at the same time.

There would be no more sniggering, or holding hands, or squeezing of thighs once we got back inside the Reid house that night. Back to the formal way of conducting ourselves. No swearing, no drinking, no fun. I reminded myself that we'd only been living there for two months, but at least there were now two months extra savings in the bank. After our lovely weekend together, just sitting around the fire that night in silence made me realise more than ever how much I needed to get away.

As we sat in the lounge – I thought it was best that I try and stay with them for a couple of hours – it surprised me to see Katrina join us. She seemed relaxed; more so than I'd seen her before.

After a while, she sat on the floor in between Graham's legs, both facing the roaring fire. At first I ignored them, thinking it was just uncle and niece being close, affectionate. Besides, it wasn't something I'd ever had first-hand experience of. Maybe my lack of family life could be a reason I struggled so much in their presence.

However, after a while, their initial affection developed into something else. I became transfixed with them. Especially when Graham played with her hair. He pulled it up in strands, allowing his fingers to gently tease out the knots. Katrina's hair was wiry, but he made it look effortless as he glided his hands through it. She leaned her head back against him, pushing herself deep into his lap. It made me feel sick, the way he touched her. His hands moved to massage her shoulders; she moaned and smiled in return. I looked at Amelia and then at Tracy. It amazed me that nobody paid any regard to what was going on in the corner of the room. Even Melissa appeared oblivious.

I cleared my throat, but I couldn't garner anybody's attention. Graham continued to massage his niece. She bent her head forward, between her knees, and Graham moved his hands across her back. His fingertips kneaded every muscle and joint. Katrina continued to moan. It sounded repulsive now, the touching getting more and more sensitive. Both appeared to be lost in their thoughts, their actions.

Then Katrina shifted her position again, this time leaning right back into Graham's lap. Her head pushed against his groin; it was his time to sigh. His hands slid down from her shoulders. I'd become mesmerised, not only by what I was watching but also by the total lack of concern from anybody else. I couldn't take my eyes off them.

It was when Graham's hands reached his niece's breasts that Katrina finally appeared to snap out of her trance. Her head turned, almost in slow motion, until her eyes became fixed on mine. A smile spread across her face; not a normal, pleasant smile, but one of evil, accentuated by her yellowing teeth.

I stood to leave the room; the silence finally broken by Amelia asking where I was going. I noticed my breathing had become irregular, and I felt faint. I could feel sweat had formed under my arms and around the back of my neck. Katrina stood too, pushing her hair back off her face. She looked at me once more before saying goodnight and leaving the room. Not once did Graham look up.

As I helped myself to a glass of water in the kitchen, I jumped when someone tapped me on the shoulder. Spinning round, Melissa stood directly in front of me. She was smiling.

"Did you enjoy that, Matthew?"

I felt myself blush and took a swig of the cold water to buy myself a few seconds. Melissa placed her hand on my hip. I couldn't move. She then positioned her head next to mine. I could feel her lips brush my ear as she spoke.

"I think you did, Matthew."

"I... I..." It was pointless trying to speak as I couldn't form a coherent sentence. The whole situation had rendered me speechless. Melissa must have known. She held her finger against my lips.

"Shh, Matthew. You're one of us now." Her hand slid from my hip, further to the front. It felt like someone had drugged me, unable to move, however much I tried.

18

AMELIA DENIED anything had happened and accused my imagination of working overtime. I'd confronted her as soon as she came to bed; asking what Graham was doing, touching his niece like that. Once she'd refused to believe me about her brother-in-law, I knew it was futile trying to discuss her mother's actions too.

After I'd turned out my bedside lamp, it surprised me to feel Amelia snuggle up close to me. We lay together for several moments, not speaking, not moving, just holding each other. It felt comforting. Eventually, Amelia spoke, breaking the perfect silence.

"I'm worried." I didn't reply, just altered my position so I could hear her clearly. She continued once I'd settled.

"I really need you to like my family. We're very close and I thought you'd fit in much better than you seem to be doing." The concern in her voice was almost tangible. I held her tighter, desperately wanting to comfort her.

"It's not that I don't like them. It's more I'm just not used to such a close-knit group of people. We were never a close family; more conventional I'd say. We ate meals together; we went on annual holidays and the occasional weekend away. But we didn't sit down together, night after night. We would never touch each other—"

Amelia shifted, momentarily easing herself away from me.

"We don't *touch* each other," but she didn't appear angry with me and soon snuggled up close again. "Not like that, anyway. As I explained, we're just very close." Both of us were trying our best to keep things as amicable as possible. We'd become exhausted with falling out over the same things.

"Okay, I don't want to argue. I guess what I'm trying to say is that it's alien to me. I just want us to be together, alone."

"I understand that but this has to work."

"What do you mean? *Has* to work?"

She lifted herself up onto her elbow, her face just above mine. It was dark, but my eyes were adjusting to the light. In the shadows, I could make out her facial features.

"I love you, but I love my family too. I can't love one more than the other. Will you please accept us, the way we are?" She kissed me passionately. It felt so good. Once she pulled away, she moved to her side of the bed, now reaching out and holding my hand.

"I'll try, I really will," was the last thing I said before we both closed our eyes in an attempt to drift off peacefully to sleep. At that moment, I couldn't have meant it any more than I did. I loved Amelia, and I was determined to hold onto what I had.

The following evening, I worked on my laptop in the bedroom. This time it was genuine. I had a client in South London who wanted to invest in several commercial properties. It would be a good deal if I could pull it off.

The knock on the door caught me by surprise. I couldn't recall anybody knocking before. The door opened before I had time to react. Katrina stood watching me, motionless. She unnerved me, as she always did, standing there, staring. Had they sent her to see me or was she there of her own volition? Deciding to play her at her own game, I glared back, waiting for her to crack. I had no time for her games. Eventually, she spoke.

"They're talking about you, downstairs."

I strained to hear, listening for voices beyond her. I could make out faint mutterings, supposedly coming from the direction of the living room.

"Are they, Katrina?" I asked, non-committal. I tried not to show it, but Katrina scared me. Her mannerisms, her ghostlike appearance, her sixth sense. Wild and unpredictable.

"Mother said she doesn't think you like us." Katrina took one step into the bedroom. Now she had my full attention, and I sat upright on the bed, my back stiff against the headboard. In fear of saying the wrong thing, I remained silent. Katrina glanced over her shoulder and took another step into the bedroom.

"But I like you living here," she ultimately added.

"Thank you, Katrina." It hadn't surprised me that the family talked about me. Amelia had made it no secret that she was desperate for it to work out.

Now that I had Katrina in the room, out of earshot, I thought it an ideal opportunity to question her.

"Can I ask you something now?" She remained a step or two inside the doorway, but her face took on a less confident appearance.

"Have you always lived in this house with your mother?"

For the first time, she looked a little afraid of me. She glanced over her shoulder, downstairs towards the living room.

"Don't worry, Katrina. They can't hear us." She turned back to face me, looking slightly more relaxed. I waited for her to reply, knowing by now that if I left a question hanging, she would eventually crack.

"Yes. I live here."

Had she heard me correctly?

"Yes, I know you live here, Katrina, but have you always?"

"We like it here."

"We? Who else likes it here?"

"Me, Mother, Grandmother, Auntie Amelia." She looked over her shoulder again, before lowering her voice fractionally above a whisper. "But not everybody liked it here."

What does that even mean? Liked? Past sense.

Inching myself forward on the bed, I knew any sudden movement might make her turn and run. Although she looked nervous, she also gave the impression she could be on the cusp of saying something; something that maybe she shouldn't say. Again, I sat and waited, not wanting to interrupt her train of thought. But she didn't speak, she just backed out of the bedroom, not taking her eyes off me.

"Who didn't like it here, Katrina?" I asked, knowing I was losing her.

With that, she turned, and she ran. I leapt off the bed and took two giant steps to the doorway. I made it just in time to see her disappear along the landing and out of sight; around the corner and towards the other end of the house. I realised I didn't know where her bedroom was, along with Tracy's, or Melissa's. I wanted to find out, see what her room was like; but when? The house was never empty. I also needed to find out exactly who Katrina had been talking about. 'Not everybody liked it here.'.

Three weeks later, on a chilly November morning, Amelia and I walked into the office together. Two weeks earlier, we had viewed the house we'd found online. It had been small, but a lovely quaint little cottage. It came complete with a long, narrow garden where we'd planned to grow some vegetables. We talked and talked about how we'd decorate the place, what furniture would fit where, and what we'd need to buy. Our imaginations ran wild. I loved every second when we discussed it.

Once inside the office, I immediately felt a tension in the air. I looked towards Amelia for any sign she knew what might be happening. She looked non-committal, but I knew she was aware of something. She knew everything that was going on. All the team were there, even Don, who I rarely saw or even spoke to. Once I reached my desk, I noticed Chris sitting and staring at his computer. His face looked ashen. Lisa watched me take my seat as my eyes flicked between her and Chris. She gave me a weak smile and a look of pity towards Chris.

Mike called me and Don into a meeting. Once we'd sat down, he told us they had decided to let Chris go. He was to clear up any loose ends that morning and leave by lunchtime. Once he'd gone, Don and I had to go through any of his remaining accounts and split them up between us. I felt awful, knowing that I'd already taken most of Chris's clients, especially the good ones. Had that ultimately led to Chris's demise? When I returned to my desk, Chris offered me a watery smile. He didn't look angry with me, just worried. And very sad.

As lunchtime approached, Chris said his goodbyes to various people around the office. It didn't go unnoticed that he shook both Mike's and Amelia's hands without saying a word. Had they been the catalyst for this? Chris gave that impression.

Leaving it a couple of minutes until after Chris left, I made an excuse that I needed the bathroom. I noticed Amelia glance up at Tracy and they exchanged a look that I couldn't read. I didn't have time to deliberate anyway.

Running straight out of the front door and into the chilly air, I saw Chris take a right turn out of the car park. He would have been making his way to the nearby tube station. I ran after him, and once I'd turned the corner and was on the same street, I started calling his name. He turned, gave me a half-smile, and waited for me to catch him up. The first thing I noticed was how out of breath I was. I needed to get myself fit again.

"Hey, Chris, I'm sorry about—"

He held up his hand to stop me.

"Don't worry. It isn't your fault."

"But I feel so guilty, with taking some of your clients and stuff."

For the first time since I'd met him, Chris showed some emotion. He put his hand on my shoulder and composed himself before speaking. He looked close to tears but equally determined not to show himself up.

"It's not you." He looked back up towards the office block as if he could see through the walls and direct his accusation at the person, or people responsible. "I know who wanted me out, and I know why." I couldn't get my words out fast enough.

"Who, why? What are you talking about?"

But Chris clammed up, crawling back into his shell.

"I'm not saying any more. But put it this way, I don't belong. I have nothing to offer them anymore."

What the fuck are you talking about?

"They do their homework. They know."

"I don't know what you're talking about. What do they know?"

He let go of my shoulder, shaking his head, forlornly. He turned to leave, back towards the tube station. I stood, watching. He stopped again after a few steps. Chris had one last thing to say to me.

"Just be careful. They loved me too when I started."

19

As I SAT in the café, deep in thought, it startled me when somebody tapped me on the shoulder. Looking up from my coffee, there was Lisa, standing over me. She rested her hand on my arm and wore a sympathetic look on her face.

After I'd watched Chris trudge out of sight, I'd needed to spend some time alone. My mind was doing somersaults. Ever since I'd joined Opacy, there'd seemed to be some kind of vendetta against Chris. I'd only been with the company a couple of months when I had been offered one of his clients, Jayavant Packaging, totally out of the blue. They had spent a considerable amount of money on a few properties; surely Chris, and others, had known they were on the brink of doing business with us? I recalled asking Amelia about taking some of his clients the day we drove to Harrogate. She'd dismissed it, telling me to concentrate on making a name for myself. The day after our initial meeting with Mr Jayavant, Mike had asked if I'd wanted any more of Chris's customers; why, when I'd only been there five minutes?

Then there had been the occasion when I first met Graham. I tried to picture the scene. After dinner, we'd been sat in the lounge, sitting in the uncomfortable sagging armchairs. It had been just us two. What had he said? I racked my brain, searching for his words. *You'll have Chris out on his ear before you know it.* He had caught me off guard; I recalled feeling uncomfortable. *From what I hear, he's useless anyway. The dead wood has to go.* I remembered asking myself what could Amelia have possibly told him. Now, I knew. But why? What had Chris done so badly that the company wanted him out? And why had Amelia thought it necessary to tell her brother-in-law about him? If he had done nothing wrong, then why did they want him to leave?

I forced myself to smile up at Lisa and indicated towards the empty seat opposite me. At first, she seemed reluctant to let go of me, but she relented and sat down.

"I guessed I had better come and find you. It didn't take much to work out where you'd be." Lisa was smiling, but she looked worried, not comfortable being there. It had surprised me that Amelia hadn't come to find me herself. Lisa read my mind.

"Amelia has gone straight into another meeting with Mike. I sneaked out."

"I just needed five minutes. I'm a bit shook up about Chris, and I can't help but feel I'm responsible." Lisa sat in silence and listened to my concerns as I recalled the day we'd visited Jayavant Packaging; Mike asking if I wanted any more of Chris's clients. Then the lack of contacts we'd given him after Don and I had received far too many from the Harrogate conference to cope with ourselves. I left out the part about what Graham had said.

"Listen, it's not your fault that Chris is no longer with the company. Once we'd read your CV—"

"Whoa, Lisa. What do you mean, 'once *we'd* read your CV'? Who's 'we'?"

Lisa blushed slightly before regaining her composure.

"Mike asks all of us to look through the applicants. It's no big deal."

She went onto explain that Chris's days had been numbered before I'd even started, and it had only needed the right applicant to come on board and rejuvenate his side of the business. It made more sense once Lisa had explained it. She described how poorly he acted in front of clients; something that I found impossible to argue with. Perhaps I had been taking it too personally. Maybe Graham had been correct when he said the dead wood has to go. But it was Chris's last words to me I couldn't get out of my mind. 'They do their homework. They know.' and 'Just be careful. They loved me when I started.'. I asked Lisa what he could have meant.

"Sounds like sour grapes to me. Everybody can say they were loved when they first start with a company."

True enough, but what about doing their homework?

"I honestly do not understand what he meant by that. But you saw how he acted. He had no passion for the job." She rested her hand on mine. "Please, don't take it personally."

It felt good to get things out in the open, and Lisa had made perfect sense. She was also a good listener, and I knew she had my best interests at heart. I was pleased she'd rescued me in the café and not Amelia. I loved Amelia, but Lisa offered something different; a genuine friendship. Walking back to the office, she informed me that the company was looking to replace Chris, so her job would be safe. She also told me she had booked us on a conference that was held in Cheshire, northwest England,

and although it's not as big as the Harrogate show, it purposefully coincides with the same dates as the key event, again biennially. As before, it would be three nights away. Just as we were to step out of the lift and back onto our floor at work, Lisa grabbed my arm and did her best impression of Amelia.

"Oh, and I've booked us into a lovely hotel."

That made me laugh a little too loud.

Graham appeared to be making more of an effort with me in the evenings. He tried to make jokes and even persuaded Melissa to let me have a couple more beers; after all, I'd been working very hard, he'd said. It hadn't gone unnoticed with me that Graham's change of attitude had coincided with the evening Katrina had visited my bedroom. She'd said the others were talking about me downstairs and were worried I didn't like them. It had only been two weeks previously, but there had been a fresh attitude towards me since then.

The weather had turned bitterly cold during November and I'd noticed Katrina had taken to sitting in an upstairs window in the turret, rather than rocking back and forth on the swing. At first, I'd been pleased not to hear the incessant squeaking, but it now unnerved me whenever we returned home from work and saw the ghostlike figure staring at us upon our arrival. Amelia didn't seem to notice, but I was spellbound by her appearance. She always wore a long white dress; the same as the girl I'd seen on the edge of the woods on my first visit to the family home. By then, despite Amelia's denial, I knew it had been Katrina, standing amongst the trees. It sent shivers down my spine.

During that fortnight, Melissa had received two more thick envelopes, stuffed with papers. I'd taken them from Bob as I'd continued my morning ritual of drinking my coffee outside, even if it was freezing cold. On both occasions, first Tracy and then Melissa had apprehended me and taken the post out of my hands. They would give me my letters before strolling off inside with theirs. There was obvious interest in the mail for their mother. They were pleasant towards me though, and there had been no further accompanying sarcasm or ill feeling. It finally felt as though the family were attempting to like me, or more likely, to get me to like them.

Bob hadn't been able to find out where Graham lived, although it had been very difficult to find time to talk to him alone. As soon as Bob turned the corner and began the approach up towards the Reid house, somebody would appear at my side. Once or twice I'd heard Katrina shout something out when he came into sight. Did she watch from her bedroom window and then let the others know that the postman was arriving?

Each evening, we'd sit around the fire. It became cosy as the weather made its turn for the worse. The heat in the living room made for a pleasant change when compared to the rest of the house. Although our bedroom had a small electric heater, Amelia told me we had to be careful how much we used it because of the heating bill. The bathroom, which doubled as our en suite, was especially cold. Each morning I could see the breath escape my mouth as I walked in to take a shower.

Katrina complained of the cold more than anybody else. Graham constantly told her to be grateful she had a roof over her head, adding that many people around the world weren't so lucky. Even though they argued around the dinner table, they would always make up by Graham playing with her hair afterwards in the lounge. There had been no repeat of his excessive touching – not in my company at least – but it still made me cringe to sit and watch them being so uncomfortably close. Tracy and Melissa always appeared oblivious; something that I found just as cringeworthy as the act itself.

The weekends were still the highlight, for me especially. Our relationship felt so different when we had the opportunity to be alone. We both relaxed, spent time together being a normal couple, doing normal things. We went for long walks, drove around looking at other potential properties and stopped off at village pubs for lunch; plus a beer or two, of course.

It was late on a Sunday night as we sat on the two-seater sofa, that I had an idea. The rest of the family had retired upstairs for the evening, giving us some rare time in the house alone. I knew it would please Amelia if I took the initiative.

"I'd like to buy some portable heaters for your mum. You know, with winter approaching."

Amelia snuggled even closer to me and kissed me.

"That's so sweet, but it won't be necessary."

It is fucking necessary; they'll all die of pneumonia if they don't heat the place up.

"But the house is freezing."

She put her head back on my shoulder and continued to stare at the dancing flames in the open fireplace.

"Oh, I don't mean that they don't need heating. I mean it's unnecessary to give them money."

I left her words deliberately hanging and waited for her to clarify what she meant. Eventually she spoke.

"Graham told me he's got a feeling that everything

will be okay soon." I shuffled uncomfortably, not knowing what she could have meant. She squeezed my arm, an attempt to stop me fidgeting, or worrying. I settled again, but Amelia hadn't finished.

"You know something else? Graham's rarely wrong."

20

HOWEVER HARD I tried to get along with that family, something would always kick me back to where I started. I decided not to press Amelia on Graham's premonition. Maybe he earned more money than I'd been privy to, or maybe she just wanted to deflect from us spending cash unnecessarily. Besides, I was tired of trying to fathom out what any of them meant when they only spoke in riddles. Secretly, I'd been pleased; we needed every penny for the deposit.

Later that week, we returned to the Reid house after work, and for the third night running, Graham hadn't been there. It had been the only time since we'd moved in that he hadn't been around in the evenings. Apparently, he had some business to attend to; further cementing my thoughts that he could be busy and coming into some money.

The weather had taken another turn for the worse. Although the skies were clear and bright blue by day, an extremely sharp frost overnight subsequently followed. As soon as the sun set, the temperature would plummet; as low as minus ten degrees in the countryside. After we'd eaten, the five of us would retire to the lounge. Katrina had volunteered to join us more and more during the past couple of weeks. She must have craved the warmth of the open fire as much as everybody else. She mostly sat in silence, but now and then, she would make me jump by inadvertently laughing or squealing out at nothing in particular. Occasionally she would start humming an indecipherable tune. The three women would ignore it, but each time I couldn't peel my eyes off Katrina; always wondering if she had been born that way or something had happened to her to make her act so unpredictably. I still needed to get her on her own and try to get her to talk; especially since the night she had knocked on my bedroom door.

The fire was almost out, and I noticed there weren't any spare logs on the hearth. I exchanged a look with Amelia, and she instantly read my mind. With her pleading eyes, she silently asked me to brave the cold and fetch more from outside.

As I put on my boots at the back door, Melissa made a coughing noise behind me. I hadn't even heard her follow me. With my boots tied up, I stood upright to face her. We hadn't been alone for a long time; ever since the night in the kitchen, in fact. She had that same look in her eyes; a look that both scared me and intrigued me in equal measure.

"It's so kind of you to do this, Matthew."

She spoke slowly, every syllable articulated. Her hand reached up and clasped the side of my head. She stroked my cheek with her thumb. With all my inner strength, I willed myself to get away, but I was under her spell; I couldn't move.

"It's fine. I like to help." For some unknown reason, I

matched her voice, and spoke slowly, quietly. It felt so wrong, yet somehow…

Melissa moved even closer to me, our mouths only inches apart. Attempting to pull my head back, her hand clasped harder and held me in a vicelike grip. She had strength, both mentally and physically.

"We want you to be so happy, Matthew." Our lips were almost touching and her voice had dropped to a whisper.

"I am. I am happy."

"Good boy," she said, before letting go. Just as before, she'd pushed it as far as she'd wanted to, all on her terms. I knew I wouldn't have let anything happen, but somehow Melissa held the power.

She moved over to one side, removed a coat that was hanging up and lifted an axe from the hook underneath.

"You'll need this, Matthew. Chop some fresh logs, will you? Just enough for tonight. Graham can do the rest tomorrow."

She stroked my arm as she passed me the axe, before turning and walking back to the lounge. She acted as though we'd just been chatting about something nondescript. Opening the back door, hitching my coat collar further round my neck, I walked out into the welcoming frosty November air. I chuckled to myself as I made my way around the back of the house, towards the coal bunker and the pile of logs.

You've still got it, even if she is old enough to be your grandmother.

I chopped nine or ten logs, more than adequate to keep the fire going for a couple of nights, before loading them into a wheelbarrow and finally taking them back inside.

After I'd placed two large logs on the fire, and stoked it to create a flame, I made my excuses and went to work upstairs.

As I sat on the bed, working my way through some emails, I heard footsteps on the landing. I instinctively knew it was Katrina. Glancing at the clock, I realised it was the same time that Katrina always went upstairs – just before ten o'clock – the set routine. Waiting for her to disappear along the landing, I quietly placed my laptop on the bedside table and crept over to the door.

To my annoyance, as I pulled the handle, it opened with a squeak. Taking my time, I stuck my head outside, peering up and down the landing. I noticed the living room door was closed, with just a sliver of light escaping from the crack at the bottom. I could make out Amelia's, Tracy's and Melissa's voices. Although very faint, they sounded deep in conversation.

Taking a step out onto the landing, my eyes followed the corridor towards the corner at the far end. It occurred to me that I'd been living there for over three months, and I had never visited half of the property at all; upstairs or down. The principal part of the house stood forward, more pronounced, whereas, when approaching from the front, the structure to the side was hidden before expanding upwards into a single turret. Beyond that, the corridor continued into further bedrooms. I guessed they didn't use the corresponding downstairs area, concentrating on keeping the primary rooms as warm as possible.

Following a further glance over the bannister, I convinced myself the coast was clear, and it was time I discovered what lay around the corner on the upstairs landing.

Once I reached the bend, the first thing I noticed was

how dark and forbidding it appeared ahead. The little light escaping from my bedroom door didn't stretch that far, and it became difficult to distinguish the layout in front of me. Placing my hand on the cold bare wall, I slowly stepped forward, one gentle pace at a time. Soon, I passed an open door to my left. I could just make out a dressing gown hanging from a hook. I'd occasionally seen Melissa wearing it in the mornings, so that must be her bedroom.

After a few more uneasy paces, I noticed a glimmer of light ahead. It appeared to be coming from beneath a door further along. As I got closer, my hand accidentally moved from the smooth, icy wall and onto another door. It wasn't closed tight, and I inadvertently pushed it open under my weight. Just like our bedroom, the door squeaked on its hinges. I stood motionless, expecting the sound of footsteps from below or further along, but all remained silent.

Inching forward, past the now half-open door, my eyes became more adjusted to the gloom, further aided by the light escaping from underneath the next door along. The one I'd accidentally opened must have been Tracy's room, and Katrina's was adjacent; the last room. That would make sense, Katrina kept furthest away. Tracy would know if she ever left during the night.

I crept ever further forward until I stood next to the room with the light on. At first, I thought the door was closed, but once outside, I could see that the latch hadn't quite caught. There was a tiny gap along the length.

Should I knock or should I push it open?

Whichever choice I made, I knew Katrina's reaction was unpredictable. Would she scream, would she run? There had to be a reason the family had never given me a guided tour of the house, and why Katrina only joined everybody else on rare occasions. Were they embarrassed by her or worried about repercussions of her erratic behaviour? Or was it for her own safety?

As I contemplated my next move, I heard a key turn in the front door. I froze to the spot. My mind raced. Should I stay put or should I run? Too late; as the front door swung open, the pressure of the onrushing vacuum of air filtered through the house, up the stairs, along the landing, past my rigid body, and pushed the bedroom door wide open in front of me.

Katrina opened her mouth wide. I was convinced she was going to scream. On impulse, I held my finger to my lips. Unbelievably, in that split second, she obliged.

I heard the faint voice of Graham saying hello to his family downstairs, but I didn't take my eyes off Katrina. She stared back at me; her back pushed hard against her headboard. But it wasn't Katrina's back or headboard that held my attention; it was the pile of pills laid out before her on the bed.

Her eyes followed mine. There must have been four or five different jars, each with one or two tablets lying next to them. She held one tablet between her fingers and a glass of water in her other hand. Quickly she swallowed it, before gathering the rest from the bed. She stuffed them all into her mouth and took a huge gulp of water to wash them down. Swallowing hard, with an exaggerated bending of her neck, they were gone. She smiled at me before gathering the little brown bottles in front of her.

Katrina stood and placed the pills onto a dressing table next to her bed. I looked around her room. It wasn't a typical bedroom for somebody of that age. Apart from the small dressing table, there was no other furniture. No wardrobe or chest of drawers for clothes. There were no books, no make-up. Where were her clothes? A teenager's room should be full of make-up, music, magazines. I couldn't even see a mirror. It had to be the barest room I'd ever been in.

She made her way back to her bed and sat in the same position she'd been in when the door had flown open. Just as I was going to ask what the pills were for, I heard Graham mention my name from the living room. It had been the clearest I'd heard any of the adults speak downstairs.

Shit.

Katrina caught my attention. I must have looked like a rabbit trapped in headlights. 'Run', she mouthed, 'he's coming'.

How the hell does she know?

Turning on my heels, I heard Graham from downstairs. He said, "I'll say hello to him then."

Fuck, fuck, fuck. He's coming upstairs.

I crept along the corridor, my hand feeling my way and keeping me as close to the furthest wall from the staircase. I heard Graham's foot creak on the first step.

Picking up my pace, I walked as fast as I dare without becoming so heavy-footed it would be obvious I was above him.

Once I turned the corner, I could see over the bannister. Fortunately, Graham was taking his time, with his head bowed downwards. Pushing my shoulder against the wall, I increased my pace even more. I didn't take my eyes off Graham, who was now halfway up the staircase. My luck was holding out, and he kept his focus on the steps beneath him.

Reaching my bedroom door, I took one step inside as he called my name.

"Matthew!"

I spun around, aware of my heavy breathing. I had

one foot in the room and one foot out. I turned my body at such an angle it looked as though I had been leaving the room rather than going in.

"Oh, I thought I heard your voice. You okay?"

He looked at me, inquisitively. Instinctively, I peered back along the corridor. His eyes followed mine into the darkness.

"Yeah. I'm good, thanks." He looked up and down the corridor again. "Everything alright up here?"

"Yep, all good. Just catching up on some emails." My breathing gradually returned to something like normal. "Have you been away?"

He retreated down the stairs, his hand gripping the rail as he went. About halfway down, just as I thought he was going to ignore my question, he stopped and looked back up at me. He spoke slowly.

"Yes, Matthew, I have. I've been taking care of a bit of business." A smile spread across his face. "I hope you've been behaving yourself too." He continued walking away and reached the living room door before craning his neck to look back. I observed him from the bannister.

"Goodnight now, Matthew. Sleep well," he added before disappearing to rejoin the others.

I didn't move until the living room door clicked shut behind him. Heaving an enormous sigh of relief, I turned to go back into the bedroom. Then something caught my eye.

Taking a step sideways along the landing, I peered into the darkness. At the beginning of the bend, half hidden in the shadows, stood Katrina. She watched me, standing motionless, with her arms by her side.

How long had she been there?

I had no time to deliberate or attempt to fathom out

how she moved around so quietly – ghostlike. No, I knew I may not get another chance to get Katrina on her own.

If I wanted to find out more about this family, I had to make the most of the opportunity that lay directly in front of me.

21

GLANCING OVER THE BANNISTER, I reassured myself that Graham had definitely closed the living room door behind him. The low murmuring beyond bolstered my confidence; I knew they were engrossed in conversation.

I turned back to face Katrina along the corridor. But she had gone. Disappeared as quick as she'd materialised. I heard the faint click of her bedroom door, so I made my way along the landing for the second time that night.

Knocking as gently as I could, I opened her door, trying my utmost not to startle her. Katrina had resumed her position on the bed, sitting upright with her spine square against the headboard. She smiled as I took a solitary step inside.

"Hello, Katrina. Do you mind if we talk?"

Although she shook her head slowly from side to side, it didn't fill me with any confidence that she would reciprocate. I had to try at least, and I kept my voice low.

"What are the pills for, Katrina?"

"Mother says they keep me happy."

At least she spoke, even though her eyes kept darting

to the door behind me. Aware that she noticed things before me, I realised I had to keep my wits about me. I also knew time would not be on my side.

"Why would it make you unhappy, Katrina, you know, if you stopped taking them?"

This time she clammed up; instead of responding, she began to gently sway back and forth.

"Is it anything to do with when you told me that not everybody has been happy in this house?"

Katrina let out an inaudible murmur and continued to rock.

Shit.

"You can tell me, I'm your friend."

At last, she spoke, but completely avoided my questions. However, what she said startled me more than any reply I'd been expecting.

"You should leave."

"Leave where? Your bedroom?"

"No!" She snapped. I convinced myself they must have heard downstairs, and I listened for any movement. Katrina hadn't finished though. "You should leave our house. They know you don't like us."

"Why would they think that, Katrina?" I eased myself out of her room. She was becoming agitated.

"Because you don't. Everybody knows you don't."

I smiled, trying my best to keep her calm. Still, I edged backwards and reached for the outer door handle, ready to pull it closed it behind me.

"I shall leave you now, Katrina. But one last thing." I glanced behind me, convinced I'd heard a door open downstairs. "Who did you mean when you said they didn't enjoy living here?"

She clammed up again, just staring after me. As I was pulling the door shut behind me, I noticed her open her mouth. Was she going to say something? I waited for long as I dare, but she offered no more words. Smiling and giving up, I stepped back. But just before I clicked the door to, I heard Katrina say one last word.

"Father."

My heart pumped hard in my chest as I sat down on my bed. I placed my laptop on my knees, so I could justify myself if anybody came upstairs to check on me.

What on earth did she mean? I recalled Graham telling me that Tracy had lost her husband a few years ago. He'd said it was tragic, but nobody had elaborated on the subject. From memory, no sooner had they had mentioned it than it had been dismissed.

And then there were the pills. 'Mother says they keep me happy.'. I knew nothing about uppers or downers or any kind of prescription tablets. A childhood memory sparked from somewhere deep in my mind, and I recalled how I used to avoid taking tablets as a boy. I'd lost one of my teeth at the back whilst playing rugby at school. Whenever my parents gave me painkillers, I'd always push them into the space at the back of my mouth, swallow some water, and then retrieve the tablets when mum or dad had turned away. It became more of a game than any kind of refusal to take the drug.

My mind snapped back to the present. Was Katrina depressed? I didn't need a doctor to tell me she was mentally unstable.

The bedroom door opening made me jump.

"Hey, darling. You okay?" It was Amelia. Although her voice appeared pleasant, she had the look of somebody with important issues on her mind.

"Yeah, yeah, fine. Everything alright, you know…?"

I couldn't control myself, and I knew I was mumbling. Amelia stood at the end of the bed, watching me.

"Alright with what, Matthew?"

I hated when she called me Matthew. It always coincided with when she knew something was wrong, or she wasn't happy with me.

"You know, downstairs. Did Graham have a pleasant break?" I felt myself redden. My words were tumbling over themselves. Amelia knew something was amiss.

"What's wrong? You seem confused." She sat on the bed, goading me. "Graham came downstairs and thought he'd seen you walking along the landing. Where had you been?"

Shit. Get out of this.

"No, not at all. I haven't left the room. I only went to the door to see Graham. I'd heard him coming upstairs."

Amelia's smile dripped with self-congratulation. She knew she'd got one up on me. However, I realised she hadn't addressed my question.

"You didn't answer me." The look of one-upmanship disappeared from her face.

"Answer what exactly?" She stood and busied herself at the dressing table, purposefully turning her back to me. She slowly removed her earrings.

"I asked if Graham had a pleasant break. I've not known him to go anywhere before."

Amelia swung back round to face me. Her friendly outward appearance had completely vanished.

"Why are you so preoccupied with Graham? He helps Mother out whilst his wife is away all the time. Do you think it's easy for him with her being abroad?"

"Because something isn't right." It was my turn to go on the attack. "Where does he live, for example? Why did everybody want Katrina to shut up when she said she knew where he lived? Where on earth *is* his wife?"

The words came blurting out, but I didn't care. I didn't like the guy, and I didn't like the secrecy surrounding him.

Amelia glanced at the bedroom door as if expecting it to open. I looked over too. Was somebody listening on the other side? Shifting myself to move, Amelia quickly joined me on the bed, halting me from going any further. She took my hand in hers, composing herself before she spoke. Her voice became more placid, no doubt taken aback by my sudden outburst.

"Listen. I've told you before, we just need you to get along with us. There's no big deal. Graham's not a drug smuggler or anything. He just likes to be around us, look after us." She kissed me. After, I noticed her look around at the closed door again, before continuing. "His wife is away. Think about it, it can't be easy for him."

She had a point, and I hadn't previously given too much thought to his personal circumstances.

"That's fair enough, but I still can't understand the secrecy—"

"Maybe he just wants to keep himself to himself," she interrupted me. "Does it matter? What's the big deal?"

"If it's not such a big deal, why won't anybody tell me?"

Amelia instructed me to move over so she could sit next to me, before leaning in close to me. Her whole demeanour had changed, like the flick of a switch.

"Okay, I'll let you into a little secret, but only if you promise not to ask me, or anybody else, about it again. Deal?"

"Deal," I replied.

"Graham feels embarrassed by where he lives. It's a

tiny, one-bedroom house near town. He sees what you earn, even what I earn, and he feels inadequate. His wife does charity work, which only covers her costs. It's why he spends so much time here. Does that explain it more?"

Although she sounded convincing, something still niggled away inside my mind.

"Okay, but…"

That was Amelia's cue to jump off the bed. Her face contorted again, and she flushed from her neck up.

"But what?" she shouted. "Forever questioning me, questioning us." She marched to the door and gripped the handle. I noticed her bare knuckles protruding.

"Okay, I'm sorry…" I tried to reconcile with her, but she wasn't in the mood. As she turned the handle, I'm sure I heard a scuffle of feet from outside. Amelia must have heard it too, as she paused a few seconds before leaving.

Slamming my head back down on the pillow, I sighed with exasperation. I lay there for ages, thinking things over repeatedly. Maybe I had been too hard on Graham and the family. It couldn't be easy with his wife being away, Tracy losing her husband, the upbringing of Katrina and the house falling into disrepair. But why be so defensive, so secretive? And why did Amelia's attitude change at the slightest enquiry? I'd offer to help if they just opened up a bit. One thing had been cleared up though, Amelia's explanation also dispelled my theory that Graham earned decent money.

I went downstairs to be sociable, to make an effort, for Amelia at least.

Once I was out on the landing, I heard the voices from the living room again. Although the door was closed, the conversation sounded more animated. I crept downstairs rather than make a pronounced appearance.

After convincing myself that Katrina wasn't along the corridor, I cautiously made my way, one steady step at a time, down to the hallway. Standing as still as I could, I turned my head sideways and positioned my ear as close to the door as possible without touching it.

They didn't all speak loudly enough for me to fully understand the gist of the conversation. Some parts I couldn't hear at all; maybe when Tracy or Amelia spoke, but Melissa, and especially Graham, were more discernible.

At one point, Graham said, "...but how long until he accepts us?" But again, I couldn't hear the reply. Then, Melissa asked, "... and how long until he'll want to move into a new house?" Again, the replies became muted.

I looked around me, dumbfounded that I should be the sole topic of conversation. Why were they so bothered about me? Graham's voice drew my attention back to the room.

"...well, at least my trip was worthwhile. We just need to hang on for a little while—"

But he stopped himself mid-sentence. Everything went eerily quiet. The next voice I heard was Katrina's, also from inside the living room.

How on earth had she crept by my room and made her way downstairs? The scuffle of feet from outside?

"He's outside the door," she said in a raised tone.

Quickly, I bolted to the kitchen. Amelia was the first to appear. I spun around and put on my best surprised face.

"Er, hi, Matt. What are you doing?" She looked sheepish, her eyes darting between mine and the occupants of the room behind her.

"Just grabbing a glass of water. Didn't want to disturb you all."

Melissa appeared next.

"We were just talking. You don't have to sneak around here. You know that."

They sounded apologetic, and maybe a little apprehensive of what I may have heard. I tried to appease them.

"I've just this second come down. I'm not sneaking around, honest." I glanced towards the room. "Chatting about anything interesting?"

Melissa shot a look at Amelia, who looked lost for words. Fortunately for both of them, Graham appeared.

"Hey, Matt. Didn't hear you come downstairs." He looked at Melissa before continuing. "If you're thirsty, I'm sure we can arrange something stronger than water, eh?" He laughed, before strolling past me and returning with a cold bottle of beer. "Here, have this one on me."

He returned to the others before I could reply. I heard him say his goodbyes to everyone, before reappearing in the hallway.

"Right, I'm off now. Enjoy that beer, Matt."

"Yeah, I will, thanks," I said as I watched Graham leave.

I sipped the beer whilst standing awkwardly in the hallway, unsure if I should go into the lounge and join the others. Amelia reappeared from the living room, removing any choice I had.

"Ready for bed?" she asked, before beginning the walk up the stairs. As I turned to follow her, I stopped at the open doorway.

Melissa and Tracy each offered me a weak smile and wished me goodnight. Katrina stood behind them, grinning.

Nobody moved or said another word, their intention obvious that I should follow my wife. Dumbfounded, I made my way slowly upstairs, beer in hand. As I began to close the bedroom door, I noticed Katrina standing in the hallway below.

Her eyes never left mine and she looked full of consternation. My hand shook as I clicked the latch and locked the image away.

22

DURING THE FOLLOWING FEW WEEKS, I found myself caught in two minds. That night in November, when the entire family had been talking about me, had left me feeling vulnerable, precarious even. There was something about Graham saying 'we just need to hang on a little while' that played on my conscience; what could he have meant? Ever since I'd first met them, the Reid family had made it clear that they wanted me to accept them. Now, it felt more like I *had* to accept them. I couldn't decide whether to forget about the situation and hang on until Amelia and I moved into our own house, or to take things into my own hands and find out if there was an ulterior motive.

Amelia begged me to hold out, especially the following weekend when we'd viewed the small house for sale, for a second time. As a result, we'd put in an offer – which was refused – followed by a counter-offer, one that the vendors had finally accepted.

By the time December arrived, we were only another

two salaries away from saving the full deposit. Our mortgage was in place, in principle, and the vendors had agreed to wait until the end of January for us to complete the move.

But Amelia didn't appear as excited as I thought she would be. She kept stalling, forwarding documents late to the solicitor or delaying in sending her payslips through to the bank for the mortgage. Everything felt as if it was taking far too long, and my frustration made me irritable. This inevitably led to more arguments with Amelia – and therefore the family. Something didn't fit. It hadn't been right since Amelia had stormed out of the bedroom and my subsequent eavesdropping outside the living room door.

'We just need to hang on for a little while…'

Amelia woke early on Christmas morning. She'd told me to stay in bed whilst she went downstairs to finish wrapping presents. It came as no surprise when Graham informed us all that his wife wouldn't be returning in time for the festivities, but he had confirmed that she would be back early in the new year. He'd told us she could be back for good, giving up on the charity work once and for all. Maybe that's what had been meant when Amelia said Graham had a good feeling that everything would be okay? Perhaps I had been reading too much into the whole thing. It would be nice to meet his wife, at last.

I'd dozed back off to sleep when the commotion downstairs woke me. There were lots of excited voices. Suddenly, the bedroom door flung open and Amelia beamed towards me from the end of the bed.

"Happy Christmas," she exclaimed, before coming to kiss me.

"Happy Christmas, darling," I replied, trying to sound as enthusiastic as I could.

"Come on, we're opening presents in a few minutes. We're all waiting for you."

With that, Amelia skipped off and shortly afterwards I heard her telling everybody that I was on my way. I resisted having a shower until later.

Once downstairs, the Reid family gathered around the Christmas tree. Presents were stacked neatly into individual piles; maybe three or four for each person. There was lots of kissing and hugging as everybody wished each other season's greetings.

We all opened our gifts; they were modest, although Katrina had done the best in monetary terms. A few weeks before, I'd suggested to Amelia that we kept our spending to a minimum. She hadn't exactly been enthused by my lack of Christmas spirit and had sulked off mumbling under her breath. I'd let it go, knowing that getting our own place would be the best present ever, even if she didn't see it at the time.

After I thought we'd all finished, I made a move to grab my shower.

"Where are you going?" asked Amelia. All eyes were on me.

"I kind of thought I'd freshen up. Take a quick shower. I won't be—"

"We haven't given our presents to mother and Graham yet," said Amelia, stopping me in my tracks.

What on earth does she mean?

"Oh, right, okay? Where are they then?"

I offered Amelia a confused look. Her mouth straightened and her eyes narrowed. It was a *don't you dare ruin this* look.

Her smile returned to her face as quickly as it had left.

"Right, Graham. You first."

Melissa let out a little squeal of excitement. Katrina starting clapping her hands, following her grandmother's lead.

"Well, what is it?" asked Graham, trying to appear nonchalant but obviously as excited as the rest of them.

My mouth had gone dry. What on earth had Amelia got them?

"It's outside," said Amelia. She brushed past me without looking at my face. She would have known exactly what I was thinking.

I let the others file out, one by one, before following them into the pleasant December sunshine. It was cold, but the weather was almost as opposite as you could get from the idyllic snowy Christmas scene; bright sunshine without a cloud in the sky.

At the end of the makeshift driveway was my car. I squinted into the low sun to see where they were all going. That's when I saw it. There was another car parked, tucked neatly away behind mine. I couldn't believe what I was seeing, but somehow, my legs reluctantly led me to accompany the Reid family down the drive.

It wasn't a new car, and I noticed the number plate, which dated it at four years old. It was a small hatchback; bright red. The paintwork gleamed under its newly polished wax. Melissa had tied a yellow bow from the side windows down to the front grill.

Graham was speechless as Amelia passed him the keys. He hugged her over and over whilst the rest of the family walked around the vehicle, grinning in admiration. Melissa was the first to look back and thank me. But I just stood there, staring in disbelief. I couldn't form any words or even raise a smile.

The next thing I knew, the entire family was running back up the driveway. Amelia screamed that it was Mother's turn next, and everybody followed her back inside.

Again, I trudged after them, feeling as though I needed to pinch myself. What was my wife doing?

Once in the kitchen, the family had gathered around a brand new cooker and next to it, a brand new freezer. They looked state-of-the art. As with the car, she had tied a yellow bow around them. Melissa began to cry, before hugging her daughter so tightly I thought Amelia would have to ask her to stop for air.

Finally, it went quiet, apart from the occasional sob of joy from Melissa. Everybody turned to me as I stood propped up against the door frame. Were they expecting me to say something? Fortunately, Amelia spoke on our behalf – just as well, as I found myself in total shock.

"It's just our gift to say thank you to Mother for putting us up for so long, and to Graham for being such a great help around the house." She turned to me. "Isn't it, Matthew?"

"Well, yeah." I was still speechless, even though Amelia's expression dared me not to join in. As before, she took over and spoke for me.

"And the car means Graham won't have to borrow yours again."

They all laughed in unison. It felt as though she aimed it as a jibe towards me rather than for the benefit of keeping the conversation light.

"Well, thank you both again," said Graham, before focusing his attention on me. "It means the world to us all that you've accepted us."

Accepted you? What the fuck do you mean, 'accepted you'?

"I'm going to grab that shower now," was all I could

say. I knew I had to get away. I was on the brink of exploding with anger.

I'm sure I heard a suppressed giggle as I marched up the stairs, purposefully stamping as I took two steps at a time. Once inside the bedroom, a hideous thought entered my mind. Grabbing my phone, I immediately tapped my online banking app. My hands were shaking as I waited impatiently for it to load up the details.

Tapping on our joint savings account, I gasped for air and had to sit on the edge of the bed. It was several thousand pounds short from when I'd last looked; about three weeks previously. There were two new transactions; one to a local car dealer for just over seven thousand pounds, and one to an electrical store for twelve hundred pounds.

She's spent our fucking joint savings on presents for her family!

Pacing the room, I frantically considered what the hell I should do. I couldn't ruin Christmas Day for everyone, but I had to do something. We were now at least another two months from saving the deposit, and we had already stalled the deal by demanding a moving date at the end of January. What on earth do we tell the estate agents, the solicitors and the vendors?

The bedroom door sprang open, and amazingly, Amelia stood there, grinning from ear to ear.

"Thank you. They're so hap—"

"Thank you? How fucking dare you spend our joint money without asking?" I held my mobile phone in the air, displaying the banking app towards her. The thing that surprised me more than my wife spending money behind my back, was that she looked shocked that I'd be pissed off about it.

"Matt, calm down." She glanced behind her, before closing the bedroom door. "We had to say thank you to Mother, and you said you didn't want Graham using your car again."

"But the house. We need the deposit in five weeks!"

"No, no. I've spoken to the estate agent and solicitor. We have put it back until the end of March. Everybody's fine about—"

"Everybody's fine?" I interrupted her again, my voice still raised, hoping this time that the other occupants in the house *could* hear me. "I'm not fine!"

The thought of three more months in that house whirled round and round my head. I had to sit down, suddenly feeling light-headed. Amelia sat on the bed next to me and tried to put her arm around me. I brushed her away and hunched myself further along. It was her turn to take on a more aggressive approach.

"Matt, you need to stop being so selfish. We're stopping here for free and it's allowed us to save up much sooner than we would have elsewhere. Everybody's happy, apart from you. Maybe…"

She let her words trail off.

"Maybe what?" I asked.

She stood to leave, shaking her head at me. There was a look in her eyes. At that moment, she looked angry, or more likely, ashamed of me.

"Maybe you're not the person I had been expecting."

"And what the hell is that supposed to mean?"

Amelia left the room, slamming the door behind her. I listened as she raced back downstairs. Everybody must have been waiting at the bottom for her, and I immediately heard voices.

"Is it bad news?" I heard Melissa ask. Amelia either

replied extremely quietly or had made a gesture in silence. However, the next voice sounded purposefully loud.

"That's it," said Graham. "He's had more than enough chances."

PART III

23

WHAT HAVE I DONE? And what do I do?

For the rest of the Christmas break, I tried to immerse myself in my work. But my enthusiasm for that was waning too. This time, it wasn't the usual three or so months into a new job that caused my passion to decrease, but the worry and apprehension that I'd never get away from the Reid household. Two more months could quickly extend to another two, then another...

At least my work, or pretending to, kept me away from the rest of the family. Although the office was closed over the holiday season, I spent hour after hour in the bedroom alone. One day, I ventured out to the library in town. Graham and Melissa hadn't been keen on that idea when I announced it over breakfast.

"Why can't you work here? It's just as quiet in your room."

"It's a change of scenery, and allows my brain to function." My reply had intended to sound sarcastic, but Graham had read my mind and just grinned at me. His attitude immediately put me ill at ease. It surprised me when Tracy spoke up; by then, I'd realised just how quiet Tracy could be around the house.

"Matt can do the same work upstairs that he can in the library, Graham." Her words seemed more of a way to placate him rather than any form of explanation.

My productivity was no more inspired in the library than it had been at home; in fact, the holiday period turned out to be one of the longest weeks of my life. By the time the year ended, I was staying in bed longer and longer, rather than claiming to be doing any work. Sleeping – and therefore hiding – felt like the best course of action.

It wasn't until New Year's Day that Amelia and I sat down to talk. It had taken all week for me to be civil towards her, and I sat and reluctantly listened as she explained that we would have enough money by the end of March for the house. I've no idea how she'd persuaded all parties to hang on for two more months, but she assured me that everything was in hand. I'd even lost the will to check with the agent that she'd been telling me the truth.

Amelia still couldn't understand why I'd reacted so negatively about the Christmas presents. So, she prompted me to get dressed and suggested we had a ride out to see the new house. She said it might cheer me up. I tried to argue my point of view again, but it fell on deaf ears. Amelia said that family would always come first, and I knew that when I'd agreed to marry her.

As we drove out to the countryside, I changed tack and asked Amelia about her father.

"Didn't you say he left home when you were four years old?"

She momentarily hesitated, my question catching her off guard. She bought herself some time by looking out of the passenger window. I let my question hang, knowing she couldn't rely on the rest of her family to reply on her behalf, not when we were alone. I noticed her take a deep breath before answering. She looked straight ahead.

"Yes, that's right." Then she turned to face me. "Why have you asked about that again?"

I looked directly at her.

"What?" I asked incredulously. "I've never asked about that."

"Well, I already told you all you need to know."

But I wanted to know more.

"There must be a reason he left. Nobody just gets up and walks away." I felt like adding, 'even though I wouldn't have blamed him' but thought it best to avoid another massive confrontation.

"I was only four. I don't know." She said it in such a manner that it was clear that would be the end of the conversation.

We sat in silence for the next mile or two. I purposefully listened until her breathing had returned to normal. She thought the subject was closed.

"Perhaps I'll ask your mother then."

That truly lit the touchpaper. Amelia made me jump when she slammed her hand onto the dashboard. She leant forward, straining her seatbelt until I heard it click into the final locked position. She spoke in a low growl.

"You'll do no such thing. It's none of your damn business."

I remained calm, knowing that would wind her up more than anything else.

"Oh, but it is my business. You see, I need to know what kind of family I've married into."

Before she could reply, I pulled the car to a halt; we were outside our new house.

"Doesn't it look nice with the sun shining on it, darling?" I said. Amelia was seething. She glared at the house through her side window, but I knew her mind was on anything but the property in front of her.

"I want to go home now. Can you turn around, please?"

The next day – Tuesday, January the second and a whole new year ahead – we were due to go back to work. Although my enthusiasm for the job had waned over the holiday, I still felt relieved to wake up and know that I could get away from the house for several hours.

I woke early and made my way downstairs to make breakfast. The weather had turned much duller, but at least the temperature had risen a few degrees. Once I'd eaten my toast, I took my coffee outside and sat on the bench to get some fresh air, trying desperately to motivate myself.

My mind wandered through all that had happened. It was a new year, but I struggled to muster up the energy to face a new day, let alone for another twelve months.

A familiar voice broke me from my trancelike state.

"Penny for your thoughts."

It was Bob. I hadn't even noticed him walking up the driveway. I fixed on a smile, but even Bob's presence annoyed me. I had been enjoying my moment of solitude.

"Ah, hello, Bob. Happy New Year to you." I wanted him to give me the pile of letters and leave me alone.

"Same to you."

Presumably reading my thoughts, he turned to leave. It wasn't until he was halfway back down the drive that he spun around to face me.

"Oh, Matt." I looked up. Bob lowered his voice. "I've

found something out." He slowly walked back towards me. I stood, now interested in what he had to say. I checked that I'd closed the front door behind me.

"What is it?"

Bob nodded towards the house.

"Your brother-in-law friend."

"Oh, him," I added, my tone dropping as if to convince Bob that I didn't have any time for Graham.

"Yes, *him*." He inched himself a little closer and lowered his voice even more. I had to turn my head so I could hear him properly. "Well, I've found out where he lives."

"You're fucking kidding——"

"Shh," Bob said. "Keep your voice down."

My enthusiasm had got the better of me. At last, I might have some information on the family.

"Well?" I asked, trying to curb my eagerness in case it turned out to be a red herring.

Bob fished around in his jacket pocket. He retrieved several elastic bands and paper clips.

"Shit," he said, before trying another pocket. I impatiently turned to look at the house. It had surprised me that nobody had come out to collect the letters.

"Come on, Bob, hurry up," I pleaded with him.

"Aha," he exclaimed, and salvaged a piece of paper from deep inside the third pocket he'd tried. He had crumpled it up into a ball. Putting my cup of coffee down onto the bench behind me, I took the paper from him and unfurled it. Just as I saw the writing, Bob cleared his throat. I followed his eyes and noticed Melissa standing on the doorstep. She glared at me before fixing a smile for Bob.

"Morning, Bob. Happy New Year to you."

I scrunched the paper back up and held it tight in my

fist. Taking a step towards Melissa, I forced a smile onto my face and picked up the letters from the bench before handing them to her.

"Morning, Melissa. I haven't checked who they're addressed to yet. Maybe you can—"

"Yes," she replied, taking the mail from me. "I'm sure I can manage that." She glanced at my other hand, still forming a fist. I could feel my palms beginning to sweat. "Is that everything?" she asked.

"Er, yeah. That's everything, Melissa." I looked at Bob, who I noticed had gone white. He was clearly out of his comfort zone. I turned back to Melissa, willing her to walk away.

"Hmm, let's hope so, shall we, Matthew?" She went back indoors. I turned to face Bob.

"Shit, do you think she saw?" I asked him.

"I don't think so. She didn't seem to look at you until after you'd scrunched it back up."

Although I prayed he was right, I wasn't convinced.

"I hope so. But one thing I've noticed about that lot. They don't miss a fucking thing."

24

THE PIECE of scrunched up paper remained in my trouser pocket until we reached the office. I'd checked it was still there several times throughout the train journey. Fortunately, Tracy had travelled in with us that day, and she and Amelia had kept each other in conversation. I'd put on my headphones, more to block out the incessant buzz all around me rather than to listen to anything in particular.

It was nice to see familiar faces once we arrived at work. Everybody was in, and judging by the noise level, they were pleased to be back and exchanging stories of how their respective holiday breaks had gone. It came as some relief that nobody asked me any specific details about mine.

Lisa caught my eye as I set up my laptop. She gave me a slight nod of her head before glancing toward Amelia. It was an 'is everything alright?' type of nod. Had she noticed the tension in the air between me and my wife? What do they call it? Women's intuition? I reciprocated with a slight shake of my head. That's when I noticed Tracy watching us. She immediately busied herself by rearranging some items on her desk. Lisa must have noticed too, and she thought on her feet much faster than I could react.

"Don't forget the conference, will you?"

Shit.

With all that had been going on, I'd completely forgotten about the conference. I noticed Tracy and Amelia exchange a look across the office. Lisa's reminder sent a small wave of excitement through my body, and when I faced her, I recognised she was wearing the same satisfied smile as me.

"Yeah, next week. What day do we head up to Cheshire?"

"I booked the hotel from Tuesday night. The conference is Wednesday and Thursday."

"Yes, that's right," I replied. I hadn't given it any thought. Only a few weeks earlier I would have been planning for it, but my lack of enthusiasm for work worried me now. "I'm looking forward to it."

"Yeah, me too," Amelia added from behind me. I shifted to face her and the first thing I noticed was the satisfied grin written across her face. Lisa tried to keep her temper under control.

"But it's not a huge conference. Matt and I can handle this one on our own."

"It's okay. I've passed it with Mike. After the success of Harrogate, we both thought it best that we could cover any amount of prospective clients." She shuffled some papers on her desk, before looking back up. "It'll be fun."

Before either of us could reply, Mike called me and Don into a meeting. I trudged off disconsolately to join them. As my mind kept flicking back to the conversation in the office, Mike informed us that the company had received several CVs in response to the position to replace Chris. I took it as a cue and asked who looked at the CVs and what the process of elimination was. I recalled Lisa telling me that Mike always asked the three secretaries to go through them, one by one. It still felt strange that all of them would be so involved.

Apparently, the aforementioned secretaries had whittled down the list to just three applicants, but Tracy and Amelia had both indicated that one particular candidate stood out from the rest. Mike told us he and Amelia would interview them all before making a final decision.

When we returned to our desks from the meeting, Amelia gave me an inquisitive look. I shook my head, signalling that it was nothing to worry about. Again, I noticed her and Tracy exchange glances.

The day dragged on and on. Although I had plenty of work to do, I just couldn't concentrate or drum up any enthusiasm. I didn't even give the shock news of Amelia coming to the conference much thought. It was as though I'd gone past caring. My mind kept wandering to what Amelia and I had to sort out for the house move, and every time I thought about it, my anxiety levels crept back up. Would we move at the end of March, or would they put another hurdle in the way? I couldn't get excited about it. The entire experience of living in that house, with that family, was having such a negative and detrimental effect on me.

Then I remembered the piece of paper in my pocket. The one Bob had passed to me earlier that day. I felt my trousers, and once I'd satisfied myself it was still there, I decided to go somewhere alone. I stood, a little too abruptly, and my chair fell backwards before crashing to the floor. I felt several eyes look up at me.

"Everything alright?" Amelia asked.

"Yeah, sure. Just need the gents, that's all." I bent down to retrieve the fallen chair.

Her expression showed that she wasn't convinced that I'd require the toilet in such a hurry, but she left my words hanging without response.

Once in the bathroom, I went into a cubicle and locked the door behind me. I fished the crumpled piece of paper from my pocket. Bob's writing wasn't the clearest, and the ink had faded in places – not helped from where I'd gripped it earlier with sweating palms. However, I could make out the address, and I made a point of memorising it, repeating it over and over in my head. I didn't know the area around Epsom at all, so didn't recognise the street name. But there it was; at last, I had some information on Graham. It might not prove or lead me to anything in particular, but it felt good to have something that he'd gone out of the way to stop me from knowing. Just then, the main door to the toilet opened.

"Everything alright in here?"

It was Don. I quickly folded the piece of paper and placed it back in my pocket.

"Yeah, fine."

"Okay. Amelia thought you might be sick or something and asked me to check on you."

I shuffled around a little before flushing the toilet, trying to make out it had been a genuine call of nature. I unlocked the door and headed over to the basin to wash my hands. Don watched me until I'd finished. After I'd dried my hands, I made for the exit.

"Back to it then, I guess," I said. I'd never been able to hold a conversation with Don, and this occasion felt especially awkward.

Once I got back to my desk, Amelia asked again if I was okay. I reassured her before Don reappeared from the bathroom. He walked directly to my desk.

"This fell out of your pocket, Matt. It was on the bathroom floor."

Don placed the folded piece of paper on my desk.

Fuck.

Amelia stood up to get a better look. I felt myself redden as everybody seemed to show an interest in what I'd left on the bathroom floor.

"Ah, thanks, Don," I said, returning the paper to my trouser pocket, this time ensuring I'd stuffed it right to the bottom. Amelia sat back down but continued to glare at me. Not for the first time, Lisa came to my rescue.

"Is that the name of that client I wanted you to call?"

"Yeah, yes, that's right. I'll put it into my laptop soon. Thanks."

The quiet that ensued added to the atmosphere, which now crackled with tension. I knew Amelia didn't believe a word that Lisa had said, and I knew she'd want to know exactly what was on the piece of paper. I needed to get rid of it before we left the office.

About an hour later, I collected two sheets of paper from my desk and walked over to the shredding machine. Once more, I felt Amelia's eyes bore into my back. I didn't need to turn around. The sound of her chair scraping backwards told me she was following me across the office.

I quickly retrieved the folded note from my pocket and placed it between the two pieces of paper in my hand. Gripping it tightly, so the small piece didn't drop to the floor again, I lifted the sheets directly above the shredding machine.

"Hold on, Matt."

Shit, Amelia was approaching fast across the office. I turned to look at her, my hands poised over the shredder. Amelia held out a few more sheets of paper in front of her. "I've got some more here. I'll shred it all for us."

I knew there was no way I could let her see I had Graham's address in my hand, and so I dropped the pieces of paper into the machine. It immediately sprang into life, and I watched the razor-sharp teeth whirl backwards and forwards as it tore the paper into tiny pieces. It automatically stopped itself just as Amelia arrived by my side.

"Why did you ignore me?" Her volume increased with each word. Yet again, the eyes of the office fell onto me.

"Sorry, didn't hear you, darling." I looked at the papers in her hand. "Want me to do yours too?"

Amelia pushed me to one side before placing her sheets into the machine. As soon as it whirred into action, she spoke into my ear, ensuring only I could hear.

"What are you up to?" she asked through gritted teeth. I shrugged my shoulders whilst smiling at her. We returned to our desks without another word.

Although I took pleasure in my victory over Amelia, there were more pressing issues on my mind. I unrelentingly repeated the address over and over in my mind until it became etched on my brain.

Tracy had returned home early, so Amelia and I took the train soon after five o'clock. She brought up the subject of our new house during the journey and appeared upbeat, despite our exchange in the office. Amelia gave me the impression that she definitely still wanted us to move in together; it just felt it all had to be on her terms.

We drove home from the station, and as we turned the last bend before reaching the Reid household, I noticed Graham. He was at the bottom of the driveway, right next to the public road. It was as far from the house as he could legally be, but still be on their property.

As we pulled up alongside him, I noticed he held a large mallet in his hand. There was a wooden post secured in the ground. I stopped right next to him and pushed the button to open my side window.

"What are you up to?"

On the floor, next to his feet, was a red, oblong tube of metal. I immediately knew what it was, even before he'd lifted it up to show me. It had the word 'MAIL' printed along both sides.

"It's a new mailbox. Saves poor old Bob having to walk all the way up our driveway every morning. He's not getting any younger." Graham smirked as he spoke. He winked towards Amelia before bending down to retrieve the rest of the contents. I shot her a look. She smiled, although she appeared more embarrassed than satisfied. I noticed she couldn't look me directly in the eye. I turned back to Graham.

"But I enjoy chatting with Bob. And he enjoys walking up the garden for a chat with me. It's why I sit on the…"

I looked up. The old, rusting bench wasn't outside the house anymore. Graham followed my eyes.

"Got rid of that too, mate. It was dangerous. We wouldn't want Katrina sitting on it and cutting herself, would we?"

Pushing the button to bring my window back up, I put the car back into gear and left Graham to his task.

As I climbed out of the car, I allowed myself one last look towards him. The smile never left his face.

25

THAT EVENING, after dinner, Melissa announced that she had instructed the post office to drop the mail off in our new post box. She'd added that Bob wouldn't be doing our postal round anymore either. When I asked why not, she said she thought he had tampered with some of our letters and she wasn't satisfied that Bob wasn't behind it. It all felt so familiar and I thought of the postwoman Bob had told me about – Carol – and the family asking for her not to deliver the mail anymore. Melissa had looked at me throughout her announcement, daring me to object. I let it go. I had all I needed from Bob anyway, and I guessed it would please him to move onto another postal round anyway.

The following Monday morning, Mike again asked me to go into a meeting room with him. As I stood to follow him, I looked towards Amelia. She shrugged her shoulders as if she didn't understand what it could be about either.

Once inside, Mike closed the door behind me before taking a seat on the opposite side of the desk. It all felt very formal; so unlike any other meeting I'd had with him before. I pre-empted the talk, trying to keep it light-hearted.

"What's wrong, Mike? Bad round of golf yesterday?" Mike didn't laugh. Instead, he nervously shuffled some papers in front of him.

"No. Nothing like that." He cleared his throat before continuing. He looked as though he was finding the situation as difficult as I was. "The thing is, somebody has brought it to my attention that you've missed a couple of, shall we call it, opportunities with clients recently."

What the hell did he mean? I realised over the Christmas break that my interest in the job had waned, but I couldn't think of any business that I'd missed out on. I glanced outside the glass meeting room, but couldn't see Amelia from where I sat. Did she know anything about this?

"Which clients are those? I can't recall anything off the top of my head."

Mike pulled out two separate sheets of paper, which he passed to me. Each one had the name of a company as the header, with a paragraph written underneath containing an email chain which had supposedly taken place between me and the clients. They detailed a few offices that the prospective customer had requested to see, and follow-up emails, allegedly from myself, promising I would arrange subsequent viewings. The clients' emails were the last in both chains.

"So, why didn't you follow these up? It's so unlike you."

At first I couldn't answer. I read the pieces of paper

for a second time, shaking my head throughout. Eventually, I looked Mike in the eye.

"Mike. I have absolutely no idea where these have come from. I've—"

"Matt, they've got your email address on them. They're definitely from you. That's not even open to debate."

I looked at the printed sheets again. My mind raced, trying to recollect sending or receiving the messages. I couldn't even place the names of the customers. What was happening to me? Had I agreed to sort out these viewings? If so, Mike was right, it would be so unlike me not to follow them up. If there was one thing they could trust me upon, it was my reliability to follow things through until they either ended in a sale or a dead deal. No way would I forget to do it.

"Mike," I pleaded, "I need to look on my laptop. Even if I can't recall sending the emails, I would definitely have made notes in my calendar to follow these up."

Mike allowed me to fetch my laptop. I could feel my palms perspire. The number of properties these clients were supposedly interested in could have resulted in thousands of lost revenue to the company. Once I reached my desk, Amelia cleared her throat to grab my attention. Picking up my laptop, I shrugged my shoulders, unsure how to communicate to her that I could be in deep shit. Turning to go back to the meeting room, I noticed Tracy looking sheepishly towards Amelia. Meanwhile, Lisa looked full of concern.

I trawled through my laptop. Sure enough, the string of emails that matched the copies Mike had printed off were on my computer. It made little sense. Next, I went through my notes, scrolling up and down. Mike shuffled in his seat, his impatience becoming apparent. Finally, I admitted defeat.

"I'm so sorry. I don't recall this at all…"

I grabbed the printed sheets again.

"…hold on. Who gave these to you? Has somebody been accessing my emails?"

"Matt, calm down. Somebody made me aware of these clients, so I got the techies to look at your emails. They forwarded them to my inbox. This isn't about who told me, or how I got your emails; it's about your work. We can't let this kind of business go. This is exactly the same as the slippery slope Chris found himself on."

His last words were obviously a threat. If I carried on missing opportunities for new business, then I'd be following Chris out of the door. What had Chris said to me? 'They loved me when I started'.

Our meeting went round and round in my head for the rest of the day. I couldn't shake it from my mind, even long after we'd returned home that night. I kept thinking of the dates – late November – when the emails had been exchanged. That would be around the same time that Chris had been sacked. So much had been happening in my private life around then, but surely not enough for me to take my eye off the ball and let two excellent business opportunities slip through my fingers?

Amelia probed me on the train journey home. She wanted to know all about my meeting with Mike. I told her everything, even showed her the emails in question on my laptop later that night. She appeared sympathetic, but it still annoyed me when she took Mike's side. As soon as I offered my defence, she said I couldn't argue with black and white; the emails incriminated me.

She had been right, though. Both communications were there in front of me. However, it wasn't the fact that

Amelia had backed up Mike that annoyed me the most that evening. Soon after we'd arrived home, Graham appeared to know all about what had happened.

"What's this I hear about you at work today, Matt?" he asked as we sat at the table for dinner. I immediately glared at Amelia who was taking her seat on the far side of the table. I couldn't contain my anger.

"It's nothing, Graham. But what the fu—". I stopped myself mid-sentence. Katrina giggled.

"Matthew!" Melissa looked suitably embarrassed on my behalf. "Please don't swear. And Graham's just interested, that's all. We all are. We've just been discussing it in the kitchen."

I knew that arguing was pointless. The Reid family would defend each other to the death. It was that evening when I realised that Amelia discussed *everything* with them, and in return, the family knew everybody else's business. I'd even guessed that they knew how much money we had in our account, what our salaries were, and how much we intended to borrow for the house. It would be futile to even discuss it. Still, the gratification on Graham's face riled me. Why on earth would he be so pleased that I'd screwed up at work?

After dinner, I reluctantly agreed to join them in the lounge for an hour. Amelia had asked me to show some solidarity after my outburst at the dinner table, but the primary reason I'd agreed had been the roaring fire. The weather had turned much colder, and I knew our bedroom would be freezing; at least until some heat from the fire had radiated upstairs.

Tracy and Melissa sat at the small table at the back of the room. I noticed them going through a pile of papers again, strewn across the table in front of them.

"Is that more puzzles?" I asked, more out of politeness than any interrogation. Graham shuffled uncomfortably in his seat.

"It's, well, it's just some question papers for Katrina. Maths, English, and others. We're putting them in order," said Tracy, picking up a few of the sheets and stacking them neatly into a pile furthest away from where I sat.

"Must be interesting," I said, standing. "Can I look?"

Graham stood up, blocking my view of the table.

"Maybe not, Matt, yeah?" He tried to keep the conversation light. "It's best to leave them to do that. Tracy knows best when it comes to Katrina."

I sat back down. "Yes, okay. Best leave them to it," I mimicked, smiling to myself.

Shortly afterwards, despite the clear chill in the air, I made my excuses and went to bed.

That night, I tossed and turned and sleep evaded me. I couldn't let go of those emails; something didn't add up. There would be no way I would miss two prospective clients. One at an absolute push, but two would be impossible.

And, in the middle of the night, as I lay wide awake, staring at the ceiling, the entire day's events clicked into place. That's when I knew that somebody had planted the email chains.

26

THE SOUND of a faint tapping on our bedroom door made me sit bolt upright. After convincing myself about the emails, I'd eventually dropped off, falling into a deep, disturbed sleep. I tapped Amelia on the shoulder to wake her, without taking my eyes off the door.

A second knock followed. I checked my phone. Four thirty in the morning.

"Who's there?" asked Amelia, easing herself slowly upright to join me.

The door opened gradually. Still adjusting my eyes to the dark, I could just make out the faint outline of Tracy standing in the doorway. After what felt like an eternity, she eventually whispered.

"It's Mother. She's not well. Can you come, Amelia?"

I sighed with relief.

"Stay there," Amelia instructed me.

As if I wanted to go, anyway.

"Okay," I replied, before lying back down and pulling the blankets back up to my chin. The house was freezing at the best of times, but at its worse in the middle of the night. I took comfort under the covers.

When I went down for breakfast the next morning, it came as no surprise that Graham had arrived early and sat in the kitchen with the others. Of the grown-ups, only Melissa was missing. Graham spoke first, his voice full of sarcasm.

"I'm glad somebody got a good night's sleep."

Ignoring him, I filled the kettle and busied myself making my first coffee of the day. I turned to Amelia.

"How's your mum?"

"Mother," she corrected me, "is not too good. We think it's flu, or something similar. She's got a sky-high temperature."

"Oh, that's not great," I replied, non-committal. I heard Graham tut, but again I ignored him. "Are you still coming to Cheshire today then?"

Amelia, Tracy and Graham went white in unison.

"Oh bugger," swore Amelia, in her own house of all places. "I'd forgotten all about that. You must cancel it."

I stared at her, incredulous.

"No way. It's a big conference. We've booked everything; the hotel, the stand in the hall. We can't pull out the day before."

Secretly I was loving watching the family squirm but tried to maintain a businesslike look on my face. Graham set about pacing the room as if contemplating the next move in some cosmic game of political chess. *Why the huge concern?*

"What about you, Tracy? Could you take Amelia's place?"

"With all due respect, Graham," I butted in, "it's got nothing to do with you. This is business and it's my job."

Fortunately, Tracy interrupted, momentarily defusing the situation.

"I can't, Graham. I need to be here for Katrina. By the looks of Mother, it will take up all of Amelia's time looking after her. There's no way she can care for both of them. I'll phone in sick for us both, Amelia."

"Thanks, Tracy," said Amelia. She could see the worry etched over Graham's face and moved to placate him.

"It'll be fine, Graham. Besides, I'm sure Matthew and Lisa will be professional." She turned to me, "Won't you, Matt?"

"Sure," I couldn't help a little dig toward Graham. "We'll make a great team."

As soon as I reached the office, the news had already circulated that Amelia and Tracy wouldn't be in, and Amelia wouldn't be able to make the trip to Cheshire. The sheer look of relief on Lisa's face was a picture. She smirked when I arrived at my desk. Her travel bag lay next to her feet, and she spoke excitedly about the excursion for the rest of the morning.

Mike had a few words with me in private. He said that Amelia had phoned in and had shown concern that Lisa would treat the trip as a holiday rather than a serious business conference. She'd even suggested that Mike came with me instead, but fortunately, he had prior arrangements which couldn't be altered at such short notice. Don was out of the country, supposedly on a work-related trip.

It baffled me why there had been such concern that Lisa and I shouldn't go together. Only the week before,

Amelia had surprised us both when she announced she was accompanying us. After my initial shock, I hadn't given it much thought, but now it felt as though she hadn't trusted me and Lisa to go alone. It also made me realise that Amelia and Tracy were always around in the office. The only time I'd been away from either of them was when I'd been for a coffee with Lisa, or in a private meeting. I suddenly felt claustrophobic, trapped by their persistent hold over me. I looked at Lisa and smiled. More than ever before, I needed to get away for a few days.

Amelia phoned me three times as we drove to Cheshire during the afternoon. The weather had turned even colder, and the forecast was for snow in northwest England. Amelia wanted to know our progress, where we were and if we had been talking about business. I had to keep pressing the mute button so she couldn't hear me and Lisa laughing. After the third call, Amelia asked if I was ever going to enquire about the health of her mother. I'd completely forgotten about Melissa, who apparently felt slightly better, even though she still had a high temperature.

"Send her my love," I said, attempting to end the call. Amelia promised she would and asked me to phone her as soon as I'd checked into my room.

As predicted, the snow began falling just before we arrived at the hotel. We were staying outside town, roughly two miles along a narrow country lane. The scene was picture postcard as we pulled into the car park; white powder beginning to settle all around. I heard the snow crunch underfoot as we huddled under our coats and scurried to reception. Thoughts of turning up at Harrogate with Amelia entered my mind. It had been a year earlier, almost to the day. I tried to recall how I'd felt about Amelia back then. The adjoining rooms, the gala dinner, spending our first night together. It had felt like a fairy tale, but it also felt like a lifetime ago. What had gone wrong between us?

Once we'd checked in for the next three nights – no adjoining accommodation on this trip – we made our way to our respective rooms. On arrival in Harrogate, I had been so enthused at the prospect of meeting new clients and building my portfolio, but this time, as I unpacked, it felt as though I was just going through the motions. Work was becoming a chore and the whole job situation turning into the same feeling of boredom I'd experienced before. I lay on the bed, my thoughts drifting around in circles.

The phone ringing on my bedside table woke me from my intermittent sleep. It was Lisa, asking when I wanted dinner. She had booked us an evening meal in the hotel each night but at no set time. We agreed to meet downstairs in thirty minutes. In reality, I just wanted to sleep. I phoned Amelia to check on the patient before getting changed and making my way downstairs.

Lisa had made an effort, and she looked quite stunning when I joined her. She was waiting in the hotel bar where a log fire roared in the corner. I could have happily bought us both a drink and spent the evening relaxing in one of the several comfortable-looking armchairs. My spirits were momentarily lifted.

"You look nice," I said, approaching her at the bar.

"Are you saying I don't normally?" Fortunately, she smiled as she spoke, as I realised what I'd just said could easily have been construed the wrong way.

"You know I don't think that."

The conversation flowed freely throughout dinner. Lisa sounded more upbeat about her ongoing divorce, explaining that she and her ex-husband had come to an amicable agreement. I felt awkward asking too many questions, but I didn't want to appear uninterested and rude. I hadn't noticed before, but since the turn of the year, Lisa's glow had returned. She had regained her flirty side and was once again full of laughter. For the first time in months, I was enjoying my evening – and the company.

The time flew by, even though we'd taken our time eating. I hadn't realised that we'd made our way through two bottles of wine. We'd only talked about work once, and that was because of me. I'd asked Lisa about the CV situation and how much influence the three secretaries had over recruitment. I recalled how Mike had told me that Amelia and Tracy had a favourite to replace Chris; something I still found strange that they could be so authoritative about. Lisa told me it had gone on since before she'd joined. She said she hadn't given it much thought, but since I'd asked her about it, she had discreetly asked Don. He'd confirmed that it had only started when Amelia joined; before that, he and Mike went through all applications with no other input. Don had told Lisa that Amelia had been insistent that she'd be involved, and once she started, she drafted in Tracy, and later, to a lesser degree, Lisa. It appeared that Don found it strange too.

After dinner, I asked Lisa if she wanted to join me for a nightcap in the hotel bar. I recalled the log fire and the comfortable-looking chairs surrounding it. I was enjoying Lisa's company, and my thoughts of Amelia and her family hadn't entered my head for hours. Fortunately, Lisa agreed, even though she admitted to feeling tipsy already.

We had two nightcaps, both opting for brandy. We had the bar to ourselves and pulled two of the chairs directly in front of the fire. The curtains were still open and we could see snow settling in the corners of the windowpanes. It felt so cosy inside.

Lisa made me laugh all evening. She was just the company I'd needed. I thought of telling her all my worries and woes, but I didn't want to spoil the relaxed ambience which had settled between us. Instead, we talked about ex-boyfriends and girlfriends, all of whom were unsuccessful relationships. We laughed out loud at each other's stories, each one becoming more and more outrageous.

Eventually, we knew we had to get some sleep. It was almost midnight, and we had to be at the conference hall by nine in the morning. After a last visit to the hotel bathroom, I escorted Lisa back to her room.

As we arrived, Lisa turned to me.

"Thank you for a lovely evening. It was just what I needed."

"The pleasure was all mine. You've been great comp—"

Before I could finish, Lisa leaned forward and kissed me. At first, it was a small peck on the lips, but within seconds of looking each other in the eyes, we embraced and kissed passionately. I was oblivious that we were in a hotel corridor. Anybody could have walked past at any second.

Lisa fumbled for her key card, before sliding it down the locking mechanism and clicking the door open. We stumbled awkwardly into her room, still kissing and laughing as we attempted to walk at the same time.

Once inside, we continued to kiss, whilst drunkenly undressing each other. I quickly became lost in the moment, alcohol-fuelled, and weeks and weeks of pent up tension spilling out. Lisa looked lovely to me, and she knew exactly how to turn me on. We fell onto her bed, still kissing. For the next hour, we kissed, made love, laughed and talked, before making love again. We were very compatible, and in no way did it feel like our first time together. There was no awkwardness, just pure passion. It felt so right being with her; even though I knew it was so wrong.

My alarm woke me with a jolt. Scrambling for my phone, I switched it off at six thirty. At first I couldn't adjust to my surroundings, the room looking so unfamiliar. Rolling over, I saw Lisa staring directly into my eyes. She was smiling and looked just as pretty as the night before. She threw the sheets back, and I realised we were both naked. She kissed me, this time much more gently than the crazy passion of the early hours. Again I became lost, and again we made love.

Half an hour later, I got dressed. I put my jeans and shoes on, leaving my shirt undone. My room was just along the corridor and I needed to get back to quickly shower and change. We agreed to meet downstairs for breakfast in half an hour. I said goodbye to Lisa before scurrying to my room.

Thirty minutes later, my hangover began to materialise, and I felt my head throbbing as I made my way downstairs. I groggily walked past the bar and on towards the restaurant for breakfast. The thought of food made my stomach churn, but I knew I had to force something down to get me through the morning. We had to talk about what happened, and I prayed that Lisa would agree to it being our secret. Suddenly I realised just what I'd done.

Shit..

I queued at the self-service to help myself to a buffet-style breakfast, before piling my plate high, full of non-healthy, greasy food. Next, I walked to the drinks machine and poured myself a strong black coffee. As I turned to find myself a table, the shock of what I saw almost made me drop my tray to the floor. My hands shook, and I felt my mouth drop open. The hairs stood up on the back of my neck and the entire room spun before me.

He smiled in my direction. I found I couldn't move my legs, and I watched, motionless, staring directly back at him. I must have had sheer disbelief etched across my face.

On the far side of the dining room, all alone at a table, sat Graham.

27

"MORNING, MATT," said Graham cheerfully, after I'd slowly dragged my way across the dining room and sat down opposite him. "Hope you don't mind me saying so, mate, but you look awful."

Having no time for his small talk, I went straight to the point. I tried my level best to keep my voice low and even.

"What on earth are you doing here?"

"Hey, don't be like that. We thought it would be a good idea if I—"

"We?" I interrupted. "Who's 'we'?"

My anger appeared to take Graham aback. He must have known I wouldn't be happy with him just turning up, but I was on the brink of losing it.

"Well, me, Amelia, Tracy. We just thought I should come up, you know, make sure business is okay."

I leaned across the table, my face snarled and creased. I spoke through gritted teeth. I couldn't recall ever feeling that way.

"Well, you can just get back in your car and drive

back home and tell everybody that everything is perfect. Do you under…"

A huge smile spread across his face. He sat back in his chair and lifted his mug of coffee to his mouth. After taking a long gulp, he placed it back on the table between us. This time it was Graham's turn to lean in close to me. The smile never left his mouth, but the tone of his voice sank to a new level of contempt towards me.

"If I drive home now, Matthew, I'll go straight to Amelia and explain to her that I arrived at the hotel at midnight last night." He leaned in closer still. I could see white spittle forming in the corners of his mouth. "And then I'll tell her I went to your room to check that you were okay. But you weren't in your room, were you? Where should I tell her you were?"

I felt like picking up the knife in front of me and stabbing him directly in the neck. I clenched my fists tight and I could feel my entire body shaking. I had to think on my feet; there could be no way he knew for certain where I was, even if he knocked on my door at midnight. I sat back in my chair, trying to give the impression of somebody totally in control of the situation.

"And did you check the hotel bar, Graham?"

The look of arrogance slid from his face. If he'd said 'yes' I would have been screwed, but he fumbled and that gave me the upper hand; for the time being, at least. He remained speechless.

"Well, if you had, you would have found me in one of the large comfortable chairs, directly in front of the fire. Yes, I admit I had too much to drink, but I needed to unwind."

He had no choice but to believe me. Even if he asked the hotel manager, I knew he would back me up, and that

I'd been there until gone eleven. I would argue that he'd got mixed up, and I was still there at midnight.

"Ahem." Lisa's voice from behind completely threw me. I'd forgotten all about her coming down for breakfast. Spinning around, I could see the look of horror on her face as she stared at Graham sitting opposite me. I pre-empted the conversation, knowing I had to get her on my side to back me up.

"Hey, Lisa." I stood up, somehow making me feel more in control if I towered above Graham for a change. "Graham arrived last night, around midnight." The colour drained from Lisa's face. I had to talk quick and leave no space for Graham to interrupt.

"Oh, okay," she said.

"Yes. He came and knocked on my bedroom door to check on me…" Lisa held onto the back of my chair. She looked as though she might faint. "…and I told him I was still in the hotel bar."

Lisa caught on quickly and played along with the game.

"Did you stay down and have another drink?" She turned to Graham. "What's he like, eh?"

Lisa managed a stifled laugh. Graham's eyes flicked from Lisa to me, looking for signs that our story may not be valid. I sat back down. Eventually he spoke.

"Were you in the bar last night as well, Lisa?"

"Well, she was," I answered for her, "but you went to your room earlier, didn't you? When was it? About ten?"

Lisa's eyes darted between mine and Graham's. She was struggling to concentrate. All the words bombarding her at once.

"Erm, yeah. Ten o'clock, maybe a little later. I was so tired." She pretended to yawn. I could have kicked her. There was no need to act out the scene too. I looked at Graham, who had remained seated through-out. I knew he had nothing on us; nothing definite anyway.

"Okay," he announced, "that's got that cleared up." He smiled, before standing. He then made me jump when he clasped his huge hand on my shoulder. "Matt?"

"Yes, Graham?" I suddenly felt powerless once he towered above me.

"I'd like you to get me into the conference today, you know, get me a pass. I'd love to know how you operate at these kinds of shows."

I glanced over at Lisa, hoping she could ad lib this time. But she offered nothing but an empty gaze.

"Well, I'll try. But I can't promise—"

He squeezed my shoulder even tighter. I didn't want to show it, but his tight grip hurt. I felt his fingernails digging in.

"I'm sure you'll do your very best. After all, Amelia won't be pleased if I return home and tell her I couldn't find you last night. It would be even worse if I couldn't get to see you during the day either."

With that, he released his hand from me and placed his plate and coffee mug onto his tray.

"I'll leave you two to have breakfast together then. Nice meeting you again, Lisa." He sauntered off, before turning and walking backwards as he spoke.

"What time, Matt. About ten, shall we say? Make sure there's a pass on reception for me."

With that, he left, whistling some damn awful tune. We remained silent until he'd completely disappeared from view.

"Fucking hell," I exhaled, before turning to Lisa. "What the fuck is he doing here?"

Lisa sat down; I guessed before she fell down. The

way she inhaled made me think she'd been holding her breath for the past ten minutes.

"Does he know?" I thought she might be sick.

"Listen, it's okay." I wanted to hold her, comfort her. "He can't prove anything. I don't even know if he's telling the truth about knocking on my bedroom door. Who the hell would do that at midnight?"

"I don't trust him at all. I don't trust any of them. Something isn't right with that family."

I sat down beside her, careful not to get too close. The last thing I wanted was for Graham to reappear like a magician and take a photograph of us in an uncompromising position. Nothing would surprise me anymore.

"Do you know something? Something you're not telling me?"

Lisa had told me on my very first day with the company that I needed to be careful. When I'd asked her about it on my wedding day, she'd clammed up, explaining that she couldn't put her finger on it.

There's something not quite right, but I'm not sure what.

"Whenever I've tried to talk to Tracy about her husband, she's changed the subject straight away. Then there's how Amelia changed her appearance, as if just for you."

"But that's nothing. Tracy never talks about her husband in the house, and Amelia obviously couldn't resist me." I laughed, trying my best to get Lisa to at least smile. She didn't though.

"And what about that lunatic then?" She nodded towards the restaurant exit, making it abundantly clear who she was talking about.

"Okay, fair enough, but I'm stuck in the middle here. I love Amelia…" Lisa looked hurt, although sympathetic.

"…and I really want our marriage to work out. She's nice when I have her to myself."

"I know. And don't worry, what happened last night will stay there. We were both drunk, and we needed something happy in our lives—"

"Lisa, please don't think I used you." Suddenly I felt awful. It was true, I loved Amelia, and the thought of getting a house together still felt the right thing to do. But I also knew that the family would always be around, with their strange behaviour and making my life miserable. I had some serious thinking to do.

"We probably used each other, Matt—"

"No, don't say that," I pleaded. "There's something between us, a connection. It's just, how should I put it? It's come at an inconvenient time. I feel like I'm trying to save my marriage before it's even begun. But, Lisa," I looked her in the eye, "I want you to be here for me, and I want to be there for you. We can help each other. Does that make sense?"

If I tell the truth, I didn't really know what I was saying. I wanted Lisa's friendship, but did I want more? Was I doomed to be the guy who couldn't stop moving from girl to girl, or had I met two at once and fallen for both? That must be a plausible scenario, and life can all come down to circumstance. Lisa appeared to understand anyway.

"I think that would be great." She hesitated before finishing, "I also think you need to find out more about that family and what you've let yourself in for." She paused, then added ominously. "Before it's too late."

28

I MANAGED to get Graham a pass for the conference. I'd told security he was a client who had turned up without registering. Because of the bad weather, the attendance numbers were down, so I think the organisers were pleased with anybody else turning up.

He spent an hour on our stand, listening in to mine and Lisa's chats with new and existing clients. He soon moved away, however, once it became busier and prospective customers began talking to him instead. I couldn't help but smile when he said he was going to walk around and see how other companies interacted. I knew he had nothing on me when it came to this business, so I let him wander off, to stroke his ego.

It finally gave me and Lisa time to talk; albeit in between bloody customers turning up. I opened up more and told her about the emails, and the company losing out on business. Then there was Mike's threat that this was how Chris's demise had begun. She couldn't believe that I would miss such a thing either, and she found me an email address of one of the technical guys to get to the bottom of it. I also told her all about the postman, Bob, and the subsequent removal of the post box and it being repositioned at the end of the garden path. Lisa asked me if I'd checked on Graham's address yet. I had to admit; it had completely slipped my mind. I'd originally hoped I could have asked Katrina – after she'd blurted out over dinner that she knew where he lived – but I'd never had the opportunity. But now I had no excuse since Bob had provided me with all I needed.

Lisa suggested that I sorted out the mystery of the emails first and then find out where Graham lived. She said, 'one step at a time' and take things from there. She also recommended that she and I get a burner phone each; just for us two to communicate. It all felt so underhanded and disloyal to my wife. However, I knew I couldn't trust the family any longer. I agreed for Lisa to get them, but warned her that any hint of collaboration between us would end in an almighty argument between myself and Amelia; maybe even the end of my marriage, such was the family's unity. She said we just needed to be discreet.

In the evening, Graham asked to join us for dinner at the hotel. He was sat at the bar when I went downstairs, waiting patiently. He then stayed with me and Lisa throughout the meal and for after-dinner coffee. I couldn't wait to get away, feeling suffocated in his presence. As soon as possible, we made our excuses and retired to our respective rooms.

The next day, Graham announced over breakfast that he had some 'other business' to attend to, and he'd be checking out of the hotel first thing. Lisa and I exchanged looks across the table. Yet again, something felt strange about his actions and the way he spelt it out. It sounded top secret and immoral.

On our last night at the hotel, Lisa and I had another meal together followed by a couple of drinks. We both decided it would be best not to repeat what had happened on the first night, and we retired to our own rooms. I think we both secretly wanted to spend more time together, knowing this could be our last chance, but we also feared that Graham could turn up at any moment, playing his ridiculous games.

However, I was dealt a pleasant surprise when a knock on my door awoke me from my intermittent sleep just after midnight. Instead of finding an inquisitive Graham standing outside, there stood Lisa, complete in her dressing gown. I checked the corridor up and down several times before letting her into my room.

The conference hadn't been as successful as Harrogate. To begin with, it wasn't as big, but the weather had also affected the numbers. We drove home mid-afternoon after the organisers had stopped the show early to give everybody a chance to get on the roads before the fore-casted snow returned.

After dropping Lisa off at her home – with a peck on the cheek – my mood deteriorated rapidly. A feeling of gloom and fear descended as I made my way ever closer to Epsom.

Amelia waited in the doorway as I pulled my car behind Graham's. I've no idea when he'd returned from Cheshire, or where he'd been on the way back. The only thing that concerned me was whether he'd relayed his version of events in the hotel before I'd had the opportunity to talk. The smile on Amelia's face suggested that at least she wasn't angry.

She walked down the drive to greet me, offering me a

hug and a peck on the cheek. It felt civilised, but not how I'd imagined I would be welcomed home by my wife after three nights apart. She asked how the conference had gone but showed far more interest in how Lisa and I had interacted. If she knew anything or Graham had spoken to her, she gave nothing explicit away, just seeming over-inquisitive. As soon as I was convinced my secret was safe, I told Amelia how angry I'd been that Graham showed up as he did. She insisted it had been his idea, but although she realised it would annoy me, she still couldn't see why I found it such a big deal.

"He only stayed on the stand for two hours, and you had one evening meal with him. What's the problem?"

"You know that's not the issue. It's him turning up for something that's got nothing to do with him."

Amelia tried her best to defuse the situation.

"I think deep down, he's always been interested in what we all do. It was more of an excuse to tag along and watch you at work, to see what's involved."

Amelia knew I couldn't argue with that. She put it in such a way that I'd come across as heartless to suggest otherwise. She also wanted to have the last word; leaving me with no option but to drop the subject.

"Anyway, if you've nothing to hide, I honestly can't see why Graham turning up would bother you at all."

The following day, a Friday, Melissa still hadn't fully recovered so Amelia agreed to stay home with her again. Tracy also showed some symptoms that she might come down with the same thing, so she stayed off work too. Amelia asked me to work from home, but I made the excuse that I needed to go through the list of prospective customers we'd met in Cheshire. Although they were short in numbers, they still needed dealing with.

Nothing could have been further from the truth, though. I couldn't care less about the clients, but I knew it gave me my first opportunity to be in the office with Lisa without either Amelia or Tracy being around.

As soon as I arrived, Lisa told me she'd booked a meeting room for us both to debrief after the show. Mike appeared impressed and hoped some of my enthusiasm had rejuvenated itself. Not a fucking chance, Mike.

First, we went to the café for coffee. We took our usual table at the back. The snow that had fallen up north now fell as rain in the capital, and the sky was leaden grey. We watched people scurry by, their umbrellas futile against the frequent gusts of wind. It felt cosy, and safe, at the rear of the café. Lisa took a plastic bag from inside her larger shoulder bag and put it on the table. She removed two new mobile phones. They were cheap looking, and not state-of-the-art technology. But it didn't matter. We could message or call each other from them, and that's all we required. It still felt wrong, immoral, but I took mine anyway, thinking we'd probably never use them. Lisa said she'd put some credit on both, but I needed to check on the balance so we could always keep in touch. I got the impression Lisa intended to use them more for flirting rather than anything either of us found out about the family.

Once back at the office, I went into the meeting room alone. I'd already explained to Lisa why and asked her to join me a few minutes later. After I'd set up my laptop, I emailed the tech guy who Lisa had given me the address of; somebody called Paul Prosser. I gave him the dates of the emails of the two prospective clients I'd apparently missed out on, and I explained that I couldn't recall ever seeing them, even though both chains of conversation were on the screen in front of me. I clicked 'send' and sat back in my chair, not knowing if I'd hear any more about it. As I sat waiting, I realised I was putting a lot of trust in Lisa. First, not knowing if this technical guy would say anything to Mike, and second, accepting the burner phone from her. The fact that we'd slept together two nights earlier that week didn't seem so daunting; that could always fall into the category of her word against mine.

Just as the door opened and Lisa walked in, all smiles, my laptop 'pinged' as a new email arrived. Lisa hurried over to join me. Even though the meeting room had glass walls, facing out onto the open-plan office, she still squeezed herself as close to me as she could. She put her arm around me, furthest from any prying eyes, and placed her hand on my waist. She pushed her chest hard against me. Although I was aware of what she was doing, I did not manoeuvre myself away. It felt good, and I enjoyed the closeness.

As I opened the email from 'Paul Prosser', I noticed my hand shaking. I could feel Lisa's breath on my neck. Turning to face her, our lips were almost touching. She smiled, and it took every ounce of willpower not to wrap my arms around her and kiss her as passionately as on our first night together. I knew the situation could so easily get out of hand.

Get a grip.

Paul explained in the email that it had only taken him five minutes to understand the issue. For some bizarre reason, once the first email had been sent, I had deleted the chain within seconds. When a new reply had been received, I then answered it, a new email sent, before immediately deleting the chain again. He could see the full history of the chain swapping between the two fold-ers. Eventually, the full correspondence had been recov-ered from deleted items and put into the inbox; all exceptionally easy, but something I would never have noticed. I looked up towards Lisa, whose face was still within inches of mine.

"I never look in my deleted items. And I would *never* keep swapping an email chain between two folders. No wonder I had no recollection of these."

Finally, Lisa stood up, allowing her hand to slide the length of my arm, finally resting it on my shoulder.

"Then somebody else has been using your laptop."

29

As soon as I walked out of the train station in Epsom, I saw Amelia standing by our car. A wave of panic rode over me; I hadn't been expecting her to be in the car park. I thought I'd have time to find a suitable hiding place for my new phone once I got back to the house. Approaching her, I secretly felt for the device which I'd hidden in my inside coat pocket. I tried to remain calm, on the exterior at least.

"Hi," I said, once I'd reached her. I kissed her on the cheek. "Have you walked here?"

"Hi. Yes. Thought I'd get some fresh air. How was your day?" She sounded cheerful enough, but I still felt as though something troubled her and I was under some kind of surveillance.

As we drove home, I made up some story about going through leads from the conference and making the odd phone call to catch up with correspondence. I couldn't have sounded less enthusiastic if I'd tried, but Amelia appeared satisfied with my story; maybe she didn't care either. We made more small talk, but the conversation became strained, unnatural. Neither of us had mentioned our new house for weeks; well, since the Christmas debacle. We both knew it was something we couldn't put off forever, yet the mood never felt right and my lack of enthusiasm for everything weighed me down.

I needed to find out about the emails, but where did I even begin? Proving who had done it would be nigh on impossible. It would be my word against theirs. Amelia had access to my laptop most of the time, but then Tracy knew I left it around the house too. Could Graham or Melissa have the knowhow after all? They both came across as computer illiterate, but by now I knew either could be capable of anything. And then there was Katrina; could she be computer savvy?

Outside of the family, there was Mike and Don. Whilst in the office, I was forever leaving my laptop on, and unattended, which would give anybody ample opportunity to set me up. Without proof, I had nothing to go on.

When we arrived home, I made my excuses: I needed to shower before dinner. As I climbed the stairs, Amelia shouted after me.

"Matt, don't you want to hang your coat up first?"

Shit.

I stopped mid-flight, one foot perched on a step higher than the other, my hand gripping the bannister.

"It's okay, I'll bring it down after."

Without turning to see her reaction, I galloped up the remaining steps and closed the bedroom door behind me.

Think, Matt, think.

There were two individual wardrobes in our bedroom, which we'd always used for our own clothes, shoes and other personal keepsakes. I had a plastic bag at the bottom of mine. It contained several family photographs, which I'd taken from my parents' house soon after the accident. Most of their belongings, furniture and clothes, had gone to local charity shops. I'd kept a few special items. Suddenly I felt ashamed that I'd not looked at any of them since.

Taking the new phone out of my coat pocket, it vibrated in my hand. It almost squirmed loose, such had been the shock of it going off unexpectedly.

Fucking hell.

The phone lit up, and I looked at the small screen. There was a message welcoming me to my new network. Without bothering to read the text, I quickly fished out the bag of photographs and scrabbled around for the bottom, before placing the phone underneath. I positioned the keypad outwards so nothing could press on the buttons and start phoning people randomly. Why the hell had I even agreed to have the stupid thing? I had to find a better place to hide it once I had more time to myself.

To keep my excuse genuine, I took a shower. I let the water run as hot as I could bear it, feeling as though I needed to burn all my guilt away. If anybody found out what had happened between me and Lisa, then I knew my marriage would be over. However, that wasn't what bothered me the most. The thought of what Graham might do to me filled me with more dread. He was a massive guy. A wave of panic washed over me as I luxuriated in the shower as I recalled the time when he spoke to me about Amelia's ex-boyfriend. He had been spinning an axe around in his hand as he spoke. '...once he messed her around, I had to make sure he never did it again...' What on earth did he do to him?

Even though I'd been running the water as hot as I could stand, I still felt an icy shiver run over me. It prompted me to turn off the shower and step outside to dry myself. I needed to pull myself together. One little crack and this family would be down on me like a ton of bricks.

After I'd dried, I wrapped the towel around my waist and stepped back into the bedroom. I'm not sure who had been most shocked to see the other; me or Amelia. She had her hand in my coat pocket. I'd discarded it onto the bed along with my other clothes. I played it cool, knowing I had the upper hand.

"Looking for something in particular?"

She looked suitably embarrassed and dropped my coat back onto the bed.

"Yes, I wanted the car keys. I think I've left my phone on the seat."

Her pathetic lie made me smile, but I didn't want to push my luck.

"They're downstairs, on the hook."

She left me standing there, pleased to have an excuse to get away. As soon as she'd gone, I closed the door behind her. I went back to the bed and noticed she had turned my trouser pockets inside out. My overnight case lay open on the bed too. She must have gone through everything. What did she know? What was she looking for?

I crept over to the wardrobe, and as quietly as I could, removed the new phone from the bottom of the bag. After a couple of minutes, I'd worked out how to send a message, and as there was only one number to send it to, I quickly typed out a message.

. . .

```
Need you to find out about Tracy's ex. Can
you discreetly ask around? x
```

Lisa replied almost immediately. I still had the phone in my hand.

```
Sure - I'll try. And thanks for the last
few days. Loved every minute. xxx
```

Shit, shit.

My hands began to sweat. I couldn't allow things to escalate; not yet at least. I found an old zip-up sweatshirt hanging in my wardrobe. I hadn't worn it for years, but I knew it had an interior pocket. I placed the phone inside without replying to Lisa.

The bedroom door swung open, followed by a giggle. I spun around, suddenly aware that I still only had a towel wrapped around me. Katrina stood in the doorway. I gripped the top of the towel.

"Hi, Katrina. You okay?"

She just watched me; I'm not sure what she wanted, but I didn't have time for her games.

"Was there something, Katrina?"

"Amelia says dinner is ready." And without another word, she skipped off. I listened as she went down the stairs, humming an indecipherable tune to herself.

Staring at the open doorway, something suddenly struck me. I recollected my conversation with Katrina. She had told me her father didn't enjoy living in the house. If only I could get her on her own, talk to her without fear of Graham, or anybody else, appearing from nowhere. Katrina was traumatised. It must be why she took all the pills.

As I formulated a plan in my head, I heard footsteps along the corridor. This time, Melissa appeared in the doorway. She looked a lot better than the last time I'd seen her the day before I'd left for the conference – so much had happened in such a brief space of time. For the second time in as many minutes, I became self-conscious at my lack of attire. Again, I gripped the towel. Melissa's eyes scanned my body from head to toe.

"Hmm, I can see why you attract all the ladies."

Feeling myself blush, and reaching for a shirt in the wardrobe with my spare hand, I realised what she'd just said. Before I could reply, Melissa walked away, and I heard her taking the stairs, just as Katrina had moments before.

I quickly got dressed, fearful of who might walk in next. As I scooped up my dirty clothes off the bed, I remembered Amelia going through my pockets. That's when I realised.

Quickly, I went back to the bed and looked through my overnight case. My hands shook as a fumbled through the clothes. I recollected buying the condoms from the hotel bathroom, just before I'd walked Lisa back to her room. It had been spontaneous; in anticipation of what may happen. I'd bought a packet of five and knew I'd used three during the week away. Had I put the packet back in my overnight bag, or had I left them in the hotel bedroom?

I felt inside all the hidden pockets, but they were all empty. Rushing back into the bathroom, I took my toiletry bag off the shelf and tipped the contents into the sink. Toothbrush, toothpaste, razor, miniature shampoo and deodorant, but nothing else. Scooping everything back into the bag, I returned to the bedroom, my mind doing somersaults. Surely I'd left them behind then?

Amelia stood in the bedroom door. I didn't know how long she'd been there, but she wore a smile of self-gratification across her face.

"Lost something?" she asked.

30

"Just my shaving foam. Have you seen it?"

My quick thinking surprised me. Amelia dismissed my question and told me dinner had been served over five minutes ago, and the family were waiting for me downstairs. I couldn't read her face; had she found the packet of condoms and removed them, or had she just watched me frantically searching for something without understanding what I'd been looking for? I'd be foolish to own up to missing two contraceptives. I had no choice but to keep quiet.

Amelia returned downstairs, and I followed her a couple of minutes later. I stopped outside the dining room door; Graham was talking inside, quietly. Pushing my ear to the crack in the opening, I tried to listen in. But it was pointless; he spoke so softly that deciphering any words at all was impossible. Instead, I entered, trying to catch him out mid-sentence.

The room hushed immediately. Graham had the grace to blush slightly, and the sheepish looks all around proved that I'd been the subject of conversation. Taking my seat, I addressed Katrina instead.

"Hello, Katrina. I haven't seen you for a while. Are you alright?" Everybody stopped what they were doing. I knew the very thought of me talking to Katrina filled the rest of the family with fear. If only I could get her alone.

"Katrina's fine, Matthew." Tracy spoke on her daughter's behalf, before helping herself to food. She didn't look too well, her face ashen, but still redirected the discussion onto more neutral ground. "Did you enjoy the conference?"

The chat soon became mundane, before dropping into predictable silence; just the squeaking of cutlery on plates and Katrina humming whilst chewing on mouthfuls of food. The entire scene made me cringe, and I shovelled my food down as quickly as I could. It wasn't until we'd retired to the lounge, and Graham made an announcement, that the idea came into my head;

"I'm going away for a few days," he declared, as I lifted two fresh logs onto the fire. "It will be impossible to contact me. Will you be able to help around the house this weekend?"

Pacifying Graham – and the others – that he would leave the house in safe hands, I took my seat and waited patiently for him to leave. It was bitterly cold outside, and I knew he'd want to get home soon. Sure enough, he made his excuses and asked me to accompany him to the door. I stood silently waiting for him to speak. Eventually, after putting on his coat, scarf and gloves, he turned to face me.

"I can't prove anything, but I'm not impressed with the way you are treating Amelia. What happened in—"

"I've no idea what you're talking about, Graham." He looked angry that I'd had the audacity to cut across him, but I continued anyway. "As far as I'm concerned, me and Amelia will move into our house soon, and…"

A wry smile spread across his face. Did he know something I didn't? What had they been talking about whilst I finished up in the shower? Come to think of it, what did they talk about whenever I wasn't in the room? I suddenly felt the centre of very unwanted attention.

"Well," he continued for me, "we'll see. But in the meantime, look after her, won't you?"

"As always, Graham. By the way, are you going somewhere nice?"

He tapped his nose and grinned, before stepping out into the frosty night. I slammed the door shut behind him. As soon as I re-joined the others, I fixed a smile on my face.

"It's so cold out there tonight," I said, before sitting next to Amelia and giving her hand a little squeeze. She gave her mother an awkward glance, surprised at my newfound attention.

"Yes," she said, eventually acknowledging me. "You're in a good mood."

"Yeah, I'm feeling positive, darling." I turned to Melissa, my forced expression now beginning to make my face ache.

"You're looking much better, Melissa. How are you feeling?"

She appeared just as flummoxed by my approach as Amelia had moments before. I remained silent, knowing it would leave her no option but to open up.

"Yes, thank you, Matthew. I'm much better now." I turned to face her other daughter.

"And you, Tracy. I couldn't help but notice you looked a little poorly over dinner. Do you think you're catching it too?"

They all looked surreptitiously at each other, nobody having a clue what my game was, but having no choice but to play along. Katrina giggled in the corner.

"You know what?" I continued, all of them visibly frightened by what I might say next. "I've had a great idea."

I let my last sentence hang. The fire crackled in the background as the new pieces of wood took hold.

"Well, what is it?" Amelia eventually asked.

"Oh yes, where was I? Well, tomorrow night, I'm going to take you three to the pub. The one where we held our wedding reception."

They stared at me, unable to comprehend what they were hearing.

"I'll drop you off, come back and stay around for Katrina, and return to collect you once you've finished."

"That's very nice of you, but—"

"No, Melissa. I'm not taking no as an answer. I absolutely insist. It's my way of saying thank you, and I'm giving you girls a lovely night out to spend together." I turned to Amelia, who looked shell-shocked. "Come on, when was the last time you three had a girls' night out?"

The following evening, I waited patiently for the three of them to get ready. I needed to be around when Tracy spoke to Katrina. I knew she'd give her the usual instructions, but I also needed to know where she kept things. As soon as they went into the kitchen together, I followed, pretending to be looking for something in the fridge. The window against the pitch-black sky outside made for the perfect reflection, and I watched Tracy point out where everything was.

I'd found it hard to keep up my cheerful demeanour

all day, and Melissa had twice tried to get out of the evening, making lame excuses on the spot. If only they'd had Graham around to think on their behalf.

After I dropped them off at the pub, I quickly drove back, knowing my entire plan depended upon Katrina's somewhat erratic mood swings. I stopped off at a twenty-four-hour garage and picked up an enormous bar of chocolate. This would be my bargaining tool. I couldn't think of another opportunity I'd have to get her on her own.

As soon as I walked in the door, I went directly to the kitchen. I knew Katrina would be in her room; it was Tracy's last instruction before we'd left. "Only come down when you need your stuff and a glass of water. Okay?" Katrina had nodded. Tracy watched her go upstairs and waited for her bedroom door to close.

Once in the kitchen, I removed the cereal cartons and immediately saw the plastic tray containing Katrina's pills. Quickly, I put them into my pocket before replacing the boxes. I went into the living room, stoked up the fire, and waited patiently until I heard Katrina make her way down. It would be tight. Bedtime was ten o'clock, and I had to pick the women up at eleven – including a fifteen-minute drive.

Time dragged on and on. At one point I went to my room and took out the burner phone from inside my sweatshirt. There were no messages from Lisa. I contemplated calling her, somebody to chat to, but thought better of it before returning to the lounge.

At last, and to the minute, I heard Katrina making her way down the stairs. It was nine fifty-five. I stood, waiting for her to walk past the lounge, before slowly opening the door and following her into the kitchen. After she removed the cereal packets, she fumbled on top of the shelf, frantically searching for the pills. I knew I had to time this perfectly and not freak her out. I cleared my throat and Katrina spun around sharply.

"Looking for these?" I asked, holding the plastic tray in front of me. She sprang forward, desperately trying to grab them from my hand. I pulled my arm back just in time. I could see the fear etched across her face and I needed to act quickly. I brought my other hand from behind my back and held out the chocolate bar. Fortunately, the panic immediately disappeared from her face and was replaced with a gigantic smile.

"Give it to me," she said, panting like a dog. She was so excited.

"In a minute, Katrina. First, I have to ask you some questions."

She followed me into the lounge where I instructed her to take a seat. She did as she was told, without taking her eyes off the chocolate.

"Now listen carefully. I want to know what happened to your father."

Katrina immediately recoiled, sitting as far back into her chair as she could and lifting her knees up to her chest. She wrapped her arms around her legs and began to gently rock back and forth. I'd been expecting a similar response. Snapping a piece of chocolate from the end of the bar, I offered her the treat. She sprang forward again; her reaction speed unbelievable.

She sat back in her seat, quickly devouring the chocolate. I noticed it spread around her lips and mouth, such was her greed to eat it.

"More," she said, now sitting forward as if ready to pounce. I held the bar behind my back.

"No more, Katrina. Not until you tell me about your father."

She had the taste, and I knew she wanted more. I'd never seen her with chocolate or sweets before; obviously not permitted. She rocked again; her eyes focused on what was behind my back. I tried to remain patient.

After a few minutes of stalemate, I stood up.

"I'll take this to my room and eat it myself then." I took a couple of steps towards the door.

"No!" Katrina rocked more furiously. I waited for her to say more, but she just stared at my hand. I took another step forward. The squeal from her mouth made me step backwards.

"In the woods," she said.

"What's in the woods, Katrina?"

She breathed harder. Short, shallow breaths. I realised the pills were in my pocket. Time was against me. My voice became more forceful.

"Tell me, Katrina, and then you can have some more."

"More now," she screamed. Her behaviour scared me. No wonder she needed so much medication.

"Tell me, Katrina." I dangled the chocolate bar in front of her, before walking away again.

"Father's in the woods!"

Fucking hell.

Snapping another segment off the bar, I held it in my hand. She fixed her eyes on it. I knelt in front of her so our eyes were level. I didn't want to scare her. I smiled as I spoke.

"Listen to me, Katrina," I passed her a chunk which she shoved in her mouth and chewed on frantically. "If you show me tomorrow, I'll give you this entire bar of chocolate." I passed her another piece. It felt like feeding time at the zoo.

Katrina nodded.

"But it has to be our secret. Do you think you can keep a secret?"

She nodded again. I broke off another piece, knowing I had to keep her on my side.

"Tomorrow, after lunch, when you go for your walk, wait for me in the trees. Just like you did when I first saw you all those months ago." I paused, ensuring she had taken in what I just said. "Can you do that for me, Katrina?"

She nodded.

"Good," I stood up and broke off about a third of the bar. I also passed her the plastic tray containing her pills. "Now, go up to your room, eat the chocolate quick, and then take your tablets. I'll follow you up with a glass of water."

Katrina sprinted up the stairs, devouring the confectionery as she went.

After watching her take the four tablets, I waited a few minutes for her to calm down. The excitement dissipated, and the medication kicked in. She lay her head on the pillow and her eyes drifted. I leant over her, taking the glass of water from her hand.

"Remember, Katrina, this is our secret."

For a last time, she gave me a brief nod of her head.

31

I'D HARDLY SLEPT. My imagination had gone into overdrive, and every single noise I heard made my eyes pop open. I visualised Katrina walking into her mum's bedroom, or worse still, Melissa's, and telling them everything. How I'd bribed her or hidden her tablets.

My plan with the three women had been a success. After we'd returned home from the pub, Tracy had gone to look in on Katrina. Once she'd checked that the pills were gone from the hiding place, she reported back that her daughter was fast asleep and thanked me for looking after her. I said I hadn't even seen her, just heard her come down and get a glass of water or something from the kitchen. Amelia and Melissa smiled in unison that nothing had gone awry, and they too thanked me for their evening out.

The morning dragged on and I wished I'd arranged to meet Katrina earlier in the day. But I knew she rarely went out until after lunch. I had to keep everything as normal as possible.

I helped make the lunch, much to everybody's

surprise. As soon as I volunteered, I could have kicked myself. I knew I was trying too hard, and Amelia gave me a suspicious look as I made my way into the kitchen.

"Just making myself useful," I said, thinking on my feet. "You heard Graham. He asked if I could help around the house whilst he's away. I'm just sticking to my promise."

Melissa helped me in the kitchen and I put the radio on to avoid meaningless conversation. Fortunately, she turned it up when a song came on she recognised, and we spent the majority of the time preparing food rather than making any idle chat.

By the time we sat down to eat, I'd completely lost my appetite. I pushed my food around the plate whilst watching Katrina devour her own. I prayed she didn't eat so much that she no longer wanted the chocolate.

After we'd eaten, Amelia and Tracy cleared away whilst Melissa and I retired to the lounge. Katrina went to her room and I tried to get her attention as she left us alone. She didn't look back once.

Having stoked up the fire, I told Melissa that I fancied some fresh air. I implied I had a headache – which is why I hadn't eaten my lunch – and that a stroll should clear it.

"Don't you want to wait for Amelia?" she asked.

"No, I doubt she'll want to go out there today. It's freezing."

She looked towards the window. It was grey outside and the wind rattled the old wooden frames.

"Perhaps you're right. Walk through the village. It's a pleasant enough stroll that way."

"I will. See you soon."

I purposefully closed the door with a bang, hoping Katrina would hear and she'd keep her part of the bargain. I'd put the rest of the chocolate bar in my coat pocket earlier that day, but I still tapped it to double-check.

Aware that any of the females might watch me from the window, I made my way towards the village. Once I was out of sight, I doubled back and approached the side of the house; the area you can't see from the living room. I'd gambled that nobody had gone upstairs to the turret and looked out, but there was no other way into the woods.

Hurrying across the overgrown garden, past the squeaking swing and skimming beyond the coal bunker, I broke into a gentle jog to get to the trees. Stepping a few metres inside, I couldn't believe how quickly the daylight was replaced by the dark and forbidding woodland. Although it felt eerie, it doubled up as the perfect shelter from the wind and any prying eyes; a different world to what lay outside in the open air.

I made my way to my right, hoping to find the area where I'd seen Katrina on that first night. I shivered when I thought of the girl in the white dress.

The branches hung low and the ground beneath was unforgiving. There was no footpath that I could see; just dense bracken and years of rotting foliage. Carrying on as best as I could manage, I eventually found a spot where I could see the small opening in the trees. It had to be the place where Katrina entered the woods.

Fearing she might not turn up; I checked my phone for the time. I cursed myself for not bringing along the burner phone too. I doubted that I'd need Lisa's help, but I could have at least texted her to see if she had any news. It would have been nice to hear her friendly voice too.

Out of the blue, and as I thought she would never come, I heard humming in the distance. The same tuneless noise that seemed to accompany Katrina whenever she ventured outdoors. I saw her crossing the field, walking directly towards the opening in the trees. She was carrying something in her hand; something colourful that I couldn't make out. It wasn't until she reached the edge that I noticed she was carrying a posy of flowers, complete with a small yellow ribbon.

Waiting for her to walk inside a few metres, I coughed to get her attention. She didn't look scared at all. She just smiled instead.

"I knew where you were. I watched you."

She really freaked me out when she acted like that. I stepped out from my pathetic hiding place.

"You haven't told anybody you're meeting me, have you, Katrina?"

She smiled again. Her feet were placed together, and she rocked gently. Eventually she shook her head.

Nodding at the flowers, I knew I needed to keep her sweet.

"They're pretty. Why have you brought them?"

Ignoring my question completely, she glanced at the flowers before fixing her eyes back on me.

"Do you have the chocolate?"

Taking the bar out of my pocket, I snapped a segment off and gave it to her. An overwhelming feeling of déja vu swept across me. The game bored me now, but I had to keep up the pretence.

"You need to show me, Katrina."

Without asking for more, she walked into the woods. I could see there was a faint footpath. I guessed she must have created it herself, as I'd seen nobody else venture this way. I made a note to myself to ask Amelia if the land belonged to them, surprised I'd never asked before.

Even though I wouldn't have thought it could be possible, the light faded more as we hiked deeper into the trees. Although it wasn't a bright day, I had presumed more natural light would find its way through. Katrina carried on as though she'd trodden the trail a thousand times before. She effortlessly glided along the makeshift pathway, whilst I tripped and stumbled my way behind.

Knowing that without Katrina I could become lost quickly, I was pleased when she slowed to a halt. She spun around to face me. It took me several moments to catch her up.

"All of it."

I took out the packet and gave it to her without question. She gobbled down a section before telling me to stand still. Doing as I was told, I watched Katrina walk off to the left. The footpath had completely disappeared and she had to tread on brambles and step over fallen branches to make her way forward. She still made light work of it, and it amazed me when she soon faded out of sight. I stood waiting, expecting her to call me forward. But she didn't.

After a few minutes, I panicked, my eyes darting around the woods. I could hear faint birdsong and the odd gust of wind rustle the very tops of the trees. Leaning backwards, it astounded me at how tall they were; stretching forever upwards towards the dark grey sky.

"Katrina," I called as loud as I dare. Silence.

Taking a step in the direction in which she'd disappeared, I called her name again.

My heart beat faster and, despite the cold air, I could feel sweat form under my arms. I walked deeper into the terrain, having to lift my feet higher and higher with each step to trample down the debris underfoot. My progress had become ridiculously slow.

"Katrina!" This time I shouted her name. Something

scurrying off nearby made me jump. I spun round, only to see a rabbit or hare shooting off into the distance.

Where the fuck is she?

The sky was darkening ever more and the visibility becoming more and more precarious. I kept walking, hoping to see Katrina. I suddenly realised she could be my only chance of finding my way out of there.

The flash of colour caught my eye. The posy of flowers stood out against the muddy brown of the soil that surrounded them. I ambled over towards the slight mound, oblivious to whether Katrina was watching me or not. Kneeling down to take a closer look, I saw a makeshift cross protruding from the soil. It had been crudely made; two twigs tied together with what looked like some old green wool. The flowers lay next to it, now looking as sad and crestfallen as the cross itself. The entire scene depressed me, sorrowful and extremely unsettling. Did Katrina really believe someone buried her father here?

A snap of a branch made me jump to my feet.

"Katrina?" This time it was a plea rather than a question. I felt scared, alone and very lost.

She was nowhere in sight. I backtracked and was pleased when I found myself back on the makeshift path. Although the light was fading fast, I knew if I stuck to the track, then eventually I would find my way back. I cursed myself again for not having the burner phone. My mind raced as I walked, ever gradually, back towards civilisation. Could that truly be Katrina's father in an unmarked grave? How the hell had he got there? Why hadn't he had a proper burial place, a normal funeral, an ordinary resting ground? No, it had to be Katrina's imagination. There would have been a full investigation, a complete search of the area if he had just disappeared.

Fucking hell. What the fuck have you got yourself into?

The further I walked, the more I recognised my surroundings. A fallen tree at an acute angle, a pile of logs, an old iron gate laying on the ground covered in moss. Not much further now.

At last I reached the clearing. I felt dizzy with relief, exaggerated by the thoughts of what the hell I was going to do next.

After a last glance around for Katrina, I doubled back around the house and ran down the side to get back to the road coming from the village. Catching my breath, I trudged back up the driveway to the house. Just as I reached for the handle, the door swung open. Graham towered above me. I spun around and saw his car there. How had I missed it? I must have been miles away with my thoughts.

"Not expecting me back?" he asked, as I turned back to face him.

"Well, no. Thought you'd still be away."

I stepped by him and walked into the lounge. Amelia, Melissa, and Tracy were sitting around the fireplace. It was deathly silent, and the atmosphere crackled louder than the flames.

"Matthew?" I spun around; Graham took up almost the whole of the door frame.

"Yes?" I looked back towards Amelia, but she just glared at me in return. Graham spoke again.

"Katrina got home a little while ago."

Oh fuck.

"Oh, okay, did she?"

"Yes, she did. And she said you've been in the woods."

32

___

Looking back, I think that must have been the point when I knew my marriage to Amelia was over. We would never move into our dream house together. In their eyes, I hadn't played along and I hadn't accepted the family way. They questioned everything I did and constantly talked about me behind my back.

However, something stopped me from running away right there and then. Even if I'd gone upstairs and packed my bags, I knew my departure would not have been tolerated, or even allowed. No, I'd become so deeply entrenched with the Reid family that upping and leaving wasn't even on the agenda. But there was something more. Even if they had agreed, something deep in my subconsciousness wanted to know exactly who this family was.

After admitting I'd been into the woods – I said I'd started in the village, walked back towards the house and decided I wanted to walk further – I gambled that Katrina had told them she'd seen me in there, not that she'd led the way. The three of them looked at each other, mentally gauging the credibility of my story. They appeared pacified, or more likely, unable to refute my claims.

That evening, we ate in silence. Katrina was absent from the dinner table. Nobody volunteered to explain her whereabouts and I thought it best not to bring the subject up. I also resisted asking Graham about where he'd been the past two days; again, I didn't want to risk further friction.

Amelia and I were drifting. We spoke about work; well, she talked, I listened, albeit without interest. Neither of us had mentioned the new house or the fact that we needed to chase our solicitor and estate agent to get things moving again. It was like an amicable silence. If we didn't discuss it, it might just go away.

We also hadn't been intimate for weeks. Even a good-night kiss became strained. We would both switch off our respective bedside lamps and offer a quick peck on the cheek, before rolling onto our sides with our backs to each other. There were so many questions I wanted to ask her; did she know where Graham kept disappearing to? Did she know anything about the emails at work? And was Katrina's father buried in the woods? But it became impossible to talk. If we couldn't hold a civil conversation about clients at work, we didn't stand a chance of discussing potential murder scenes on our doorstep. By then, I'd decided my only option was Lisa.

The new week in the office dragged by. I'd suggested phoning in sick on the Monday morning, again feigning a headache, but Amelia said I had some important meetings to organise.

During the next three days, it transpired that Amelia

set up the consultations anyway, and either accompanied me to the face-to-face discussions or joined me in a meeting room for a video conference. She also led most of the talks whilst I found my mind drifting aimlessly during the repetitive exchange of words.

It wasn't until the end of those three days of mundane conversations, that I saw Katrina for the first time since our venture into the woods. She hadn't been at any of the family meals, and I hadn't seen her sat in the window; something that had happened every night on our arrival back home following a day's work. I'd politely asked Tracy if her daughter was okay, to which she'd replied she had been feeling a little unwell and was eating and staying in her room. The strange thing was, I'd never seen Tracy take anything upstairs. Surely she would put some food aside and carry it up on a tray?

On the Wednesday evening, however, Katrina was sat in her window when we arrived home. As usual, her eyes followed me from leaving the car until I was out of sight near the front door. My initial anger at her telling the others I'd been in the woods had soon dissipated, and I had replaced my annoyance with worry.

When she came down for the evening meal, she looked awful. Her skin had taken on an even paler complexion, and her eyes had sunk further into her skull. Large dark rings extended from her sockets and cracked red veins spread across her eyeballs. Her lips were chapped and looked as though they would split open if she attempted to smile. I couldn't help but stare at her.

She pushed her food around her plate – which I noticed had all been mashed up – pureed, like baby food. Tracy told her she needed to eat up, to get her strength back. Katrina attempted a few mouthfuls before giving up altogether. She just stared into open space, looking completely out of it.

What the fuck had they done to her?

After dinner, I said I needed to work in my room. Amelia pacified the others by explaining we had quite a lot going on in the office, so they had excused me like an obedient child. The atmosphere was overwhelming, but the family somehow held an imaginary grip over me.

I purposefully left my door ajar, knowing Katrina would be along any minute. Sure enough, moments later, I heard her heavy feet slowly ascend the stairs. It sounded as though every step was an individual struggle.

Inevitably, she stopped at my bedroom door. She looked even worse than she had at the dinner table; ghost-like, haunting. She didn't smile, just stared at me. I murmured.

"Hi, Katrina. I've been worried about you."

She continued to look at me, but her eyes bored straight through me rather than focus on who I was. As I sat more upright on the bed, Katrina flinched, taking a step backwards. I'd never seen her act this way before.

"It's okay, I won't hurt you." I smiled, willing her to trust me. "Where have you been?"

Eventually she spoke. Her voice was so soft, whisper-like. I strained to hear what she said.

"Asleep."

"Asleep? For three days?"

"Mother gave me my special pills. She said I'd been very naughty."

What the fuck?

"Why have you been naughty, Katrina?"

The sound of a door opening downstairs made us both jump. Katrina moved to walk away.

"What have you done wrong, Katrina?"

She glanced downstairs and then along the landing. Eventually, her eyes rested back on me. Then she grinned. Her mouth stretched wide, showing her yellow, crooked teeth. Her lips split and immediately took on a reddish appearance. I realised they were bleeding, little slits of bone-dry skin cracking open. It looked painful, but Katrina didn't appear to notice. I hadn't been expecting her to say what she had.

"I knew they wouldn't let you leave."

Staring at her in return, I hunched myself forward on the bed. Slowly, so not to frighten her. I remained silent but nodded my head for her to continue. Her voice became barely audible, a faint whisper.

"They said you and Amelia couldn't move into your new house."

"Who did, Katrina?"

From nowhere, she spoke clearly, and although it was at a normal level, it felt as though she'd screamed the next words at me, such was the contrast from her previous mutterings.

"The others, silly. They said they needed to stop you moving out..." Katrina paused, as if for dramatic effect. "...until they are ready."

"Ready for—"

The sound of footsteps below startled me. I glared at Katrina, but she was already backing away. She had one parting sentence before she left.

"I'm never allowed to talk to you again."

Lying on my bed, staring at the ceiling, I tried to take in exactly what Katrina had just said. 'Special pills'? Had they really drugged her into an induced sleep? If she'd been so 'naughty', I guessed she must have told the truth that she'd led me into the woods, rather than my initial notion that she'd just happened to see me. Would she have told them she'd taken me to the grave-like mound of earth? They might have even worked that out for themselves. Then again, surely they would have spoken about that, covered themselves against any wrongdoing? It had to be an imaginary story inside Katrina's head to give her some comfort in the absence of her father. Or the family may have informed her that's where he'd been buried, to allow her to grieve.

But then there was the other stuff. Why had 'they needed to stop me and Amelia moving into our new home'? I recalled the night when I crept downstairs and heard them talking. 'How long until he accepts us?' and 'How long until he'll want to move into a new house?'. And what had Graham said? 'We just need to hang on a little while longer.'. For what? Exactly what were they waiting for? And, when whatever took place, what would happen to me?

Springing up off the bed, I crept to the bedroom door and gently closed it. Next, I went to my wardrobe and retrieved the burner phone from my sweatshirt pocket. I had visions it wouldn't be there, but felt immense relief when I took it and held down the power button before the screen glowed into life. As I waited for the phone to pick up a signal, I realised that Lisa could be my only ally now.

As I thought about what to type, the phone beat me to it. A new message arrived, sent only twenty minutes before.

Hi, Matt. Hope you find this message okay. Found out Tracy's husband's name. Don remembered it. xx

. . .

Quickly, I responded.

```
Well, what is it?
```

I paced the room, gazing at the little screen, urging Lisa to reply. I only had to wait a few minutes.

```
Patience, Matt. His name was Ryan Palmer.
She used to be Tracy Palmer. Don said he
had moved in with the family. Will tell
you more in the office tomorrow xx
```

I heard movement downstairs. Hurriedly, I paced back to the wardrobe. Just as I was going to hold the power button down, another text arrived from Lisa.

```
Apparently, he just left one day. Hasn't
been seen since xx
```

33

THE FOLLOWING DAY, I drove myself and Amelia into the office. We didn't have any client visits lined up, but I'd hatched a plan with Lisa after I'd hastily replied to her text message the night before. Amelia told me she preferred it when we drove into work, anyway, citing the busy trains made her feel uncomfortable and claustrophobic.

We had plenty of work on, and thankfully Amelia immersed herself into it every day. If there was one thing about her, she was very professional and went about her job meticulously. Just as well for me, as I could barely bring myself to boot up my laptop anymore.

Lisa had made it abundantly clear that she had a migraine as soon as she arrived in the office. Around mid-morning, Tracy gave her a couple of pills from her hand-bag, and Lisa kept up the pretence by swallowing them with a glass of water supplied by Amelia. She later told me I'd nearly blown her cover by continually asking how she felt.

Just after lunch, she told Mike that she needed to go

home as her headache was getting worse rather than improving. She'd made sure the office was quiet when she made the announcement, leaving nobody in doubt of how poorly she felt.

Fortunately, Mike proposed that somebody give her a lift home as she didn't look well enough to travel on the underground alone. He indicated I would be the ideal candidate. Amelia and Tracy looked at one another before Amelia suggested she came along too. I said it wasn't necessary, and besides, she had so many contacts to get through, people whom we hadn't yet followed up with from Cheshire. Mike agreed that it wouldn't take two people to get Lisa home safely. Amazingly, my plan had worked.

As soon as we were in the car, Lisa let out a tremendous sigh of relief and couldn't help herself from laughing.

"Jesus. I couldn't keep up that charade for another minute. I've got a genuine headache from pretending to have a headache."

We both laughed as we left the car park and set off to Lisa's house.

"Thanks for playing along. It was the only thing I could think of so we could talk alone," I said, once we'd contained ourselves.

As I drove, Lisa told me she'd discreetly asked Don about Tracy, and what he knew of her past. She said she'd made it look like making idle chat rather than anything important. Don had volunteered the information without question anyway.

Apparently, Tracy had been with the company the longest of the three secretaries. Previously she'd been a nurse; specifically, one who administered medication. Her ex-husband, Ryan Palmer, had been a doctor at the same hospital she worked at – it was where they'd met soon after she joined. Don believed that Ryan had a top job, some senior consultant, or similar. When Lisa asked what had happened to him, Don explained that Tracy never really divulged the information. He said that nobody asked too much after Tracy had asked for privacy and told them it wasn't something she liked to talk, or even think about. Lisa said that Don had thought the whole situation to be a little strange, but he respected Tracy's decision.

"So, that's how she knows so much about drugs; what to administer and in what quantity," I said once Lisa had finished.

"What are you talking about?"

I explained about going into Katrina's room and catching her just before she took a load of pills. Then I told her about recent events when I'd hidden the drugs and bribed Katrina with the chocolate. Finally, I told Lisa about Katrina coming out of her room after three days of induced sleep after she'd spotted me in the woods.

"What woods?" Lisa turned to me in the car. "You're talking in riddles?"

She left me with no choice. I explained everything to Lisa. From my first encounter seeing Katrina on the edge of the woods all the way through to her leading me to her imaginary unmarked grave. I told her about the family's strange behaviour, the unexpected Christmas presents from Amelia and the subsequent postponement of our moving house.

"Fucking hell," she said when I'd finished. "How have you stayed there so long?"

At first I didn't know what to say. After I'd laid all the cards on the table, it felt unimaginable that I'd put myself through all that without once thinking of getting out. But it had all happened gradually, crept up on me, and I had never fitted all the pieces of the jigsaw together. There was also one other mitigating reason.

"I love Amelia, Lisa. Or, should I say, I loved her. I fell head over heels, from the very first time I saw her when she interviewed me. In those early days, she swept me off my feet."

I thought of all the long weekends in my flat in North London. Only getting out of bed to eat or drink. The way she used to dress, the heads that turned in the office. After all the years of me jumping from bed to bed, I'd eventually thought I'd met my soulmate; the one person I'd wanted to spend the rest of my life with.

"And now?"

I glanced over at Lisa. She looked wounded, and I realised what I'd just said must have upset her. I put my hand on her knee.

"Hey, I'm sorry. That was in the past. She's changed." I paused. "No, the circumstances changed. As soon as I met her family, and moved in, that's when it all changed. But it was too late, I was in it all too deep. I also wanted it to work." I looked at her again. "You surely understand that?"

Lisa smiled and returned my gesture by squeezing my knee.

"Hey, ignore me. You're right. You are married to Amelia, and we all knew in the office that you were smitten with her when you started with the company. Just one thing…"

She looked deadly serious.

"…you didn't use me, did you? You know, in Cheshire?"

"Hell no," I exclaimed. "It isn't like that at all."

Although I realised why Lisa had asked the questions

she did, the last thing I wanted was for the conversation to be about me and her. The whole idea had been to find the truth about the Reid family and what they needed from me.

We drove the rest of the journey, mostly in silence, both lost in our own thoughts. Eventually, after following the intermittent instructions from Lisa, we arrived outside her house. It was a modest terrace house, but I knew it would still be expensive in the suburbs of West London though I didn't want to pry about her financial situation, especially now her divorce had gone through. It felt awkward, sitting there together. Neither of us knew what to say. Eventually, Lisa broke the ice.

"Fancy a coffee?"

I looked at my watch, knowing Amelia would be clocking the journey to the minute.

"Sure," I said, smiling. "That would be lovely."

Amelia and I drove home without speaking a word. Earlier, I'd stayed at Lisa's for thirty minutes. We'd planned what to do next and to keep in touch via the burner phones. As I'd arrived at the front door to leave, Lisa reached for my hand. We kissed; a long passionate kiss that left me wanting more. During the drive back to the office, I got through half a tube of mints whilst contemplating if my future might lie with Lisa – once my predicament was finally over. But first, I had to know more. Much more.

The following morning I noticed the overnight frost had finally eased and given way to a milder southerly wind. Although Graham had removed my favourite rusty bench, I still took my coffee outside for a moment of peace. I would begrudgingly traipse around the garden, lost in my thoughts. That morning would be different though. When the police car pulled up at the end of the drive, it immediately snapped me out of my trance.

As soon as two police officers stepped from their vehicle, the front door swung open behind me. I momentarily glanced over my shoulder and saw Melissa standing there. She held a piece of toast in her hand.

"Hello," said one of the officers. "We're looking for a Mr Walker."

"That's me," I said. "Is everything okay?"

The policewoman looked at her colleague, who remained a few feet behind her. He stood still; his fingers interlocked in front of him. She turned back to me.

"Can we go inside, please, sir?"

I led them into the kitchen. Melissa followed us. Amelia and Tracy immediately stopped what they were doing at the table and looked from the police to me, and back again.

"Matthew?" Amelia asked. I shrugged my shoulders in her direction. The policewoman broke the silence.

"Would you like to sit down, Mr Walker?"

"It's okay, no, I'm fine thanks. What's this about?"

"We have been informed by our colleagues in Birmingham of some unexpected news, Mr Walker."

"Matthew. Please call me Matthew."

"Okay. Matthew. We have some bad news, I'm afraid." She took her notepad out and flicked through it before stopping at a particular page. "Are you aware that you had an aunt?"

"An aunt? I don't have an aunt."

I looked towards Amelia. She stood rooted to the spot.

It wasn't until later that I realised she hadn't offered to move closer to me, to comfort me.

"Mr Walker, I mean, Matthew. Your mother," she looked at her notebook again. "Your mother, June Walker, had an older sister. A Mrs Edith Weeks."

I shook my head. My mum had never mentioned a sister.

"You must be mistaken. My—"

"I'm afraid it's not a mistake," the policewoman continued. "Your aunt, Edith Weeks, died last week."

Her face took on an even more distressed expression.

"Matthew, I'm so sorry to inform you, but your aunt has been brutally murdered."

PART IV

34

HOLDING onto the back of the chair, I listened to the policewoman's calm, monotonal voice describing exactly what had happened, though sparing the gruesome detail. A full investigation was underway, but at this stage, they had very little evidence to go on. She went on to explain that my aunt was a spinster and had built up a considerable amount of money. The line that drew the largest intake of breath from the room came when she explained that Edith Weeks had left her entire estate to me.

Before they left, the policewoman, a WPC Nina Murrow, gave me her direct contact details before handing me a letter. It was from Edith's solicitor, explaining everything. She recommended I contact him immediately to get everything sorted, and the paperwork signed off.

Amelia proposed that I shouldn't go to work that day. She said it must have come as a tremendous shock and I needed time to get my head around everything that the police had just told me. Even if Amelia hadn't suggested it, I think I would have come to the same conclusion. She and Tracy left soon after to take the train to the office. Melissa made me a sweet cup of tea, suggesting it was good for shock.

As soon as I'd finished my drink, I told Melissa that I needed to be alone and would be in my room. Reluctantly, she agreed, but told me to call her if I required anything.

After lying on the bed trying to take in what had happened, I took the burner phone from my wardrobe and immediately input Nina Murrow's name and number into the contact list. Following that, I called Lisa. I knew Amelia and Tracy wouldn't have arrived at the office yet, even if Lisa was already there. She answered after only one ring.

"Matt?"

I kept my voice very low.

"Lisa, where are you?"

"Walking to the office. Where are you?"

I explained the early morning visit from the police and the subsequent news about a long-lost aunt. I had to repeat a few things as Lisa couldn't hear me against the backdrop of the busy London traffic. I didn't take my eyes off the bedroom door handle, ready to hang up at the slightest movement.

"Shit," she said when I'd finished. "Hang on. Does this make you a very rich man?"

In all the confusion and inconceivable news of a relative I'd never heard of, the fact that I could now be considerably better off hadn't registered with me. I realised I didn't know how much Edith Weeks had been worth, but what had PC Murrow said, 'a considerable amount of money'? The only thing that had constantly swirled around my mind was why my parents had never told me I had an aunt, or why she had left all her possessions to me. Maybe I would never get an answer to that now.

"To be honest, I don't know. I've no idea of the actual amount of money involved. I need to contact the solicitor."

The traffic noise subsided on the phone line and Lisa said she'd just reached the office. She kept her voice down too.

"Do you want me to do anything?"

I'd been thinking all night about Lisa's detective work and the subsequent information about Tracy and her doctor husband.

"Is Don in the office today?"

"I think so, yeah. I'm sure he said he's in all week. I'll get him on his own and try to find out more about what we discussed yesterday."

"Thanks, Lisa."

I'd figured if we could find out what hospital Tracy and Ryan had worked in; we might find out the dates they employed them. It was a long shot, but I thought if I could discover more about their past, it might lead to me learning more about Ryan Palmer's background.

After I'd spoken to Lisa, I called the solicitor who was in charge of my aunt's estate. His secretary passed on my number and said she would get him to call me back within the hour. I waited in my room, not wanting to face Melissa and make idle chat. True to his word, the solicitor returned my call forty minutes later.

"Mr Walker. Thank you for getting in touch."

We went through the formalities, the condolences and

the procedures. I wanted him to cut to the chase, tell me exactly what I'd be inheriting. There had been no mention of amounts of money or property in the original letter, and I hadn't been expecting anything like the figure the solicitor finally divulged.

After clearing his throat, I could hear a rustle of papers on the other end of the phone. At last, he spoke.

"Mr Walker, are you sitting down?"

I wandered around the village in a daze. As soon as the phone call had ended – with instructions to sign off all the paperwork as soon as it arrived – I went downstairs and told Melissa I needed some fresh air. She'd attempted to probe me and enquired if I'd heard any more from the solicitor, but I just shook my head and headed outside. I heard her call after me as I walked along the driveway. I nonchalantly waved my hand above my head, not understanding what she'd just said.

Soon, I found myself walking through the woods again. It hadn't been a conscious decision; I'd just followed my nose whilst my head swam with all kinds of theories. I encountered the same makeshift footpath where I'd tried to keep up with Katrina only the week before.

Once I knew I was in the vicinity of where Katrina had left the track, I found some trodden down bracken off to the left. Realising this was pure chance, I dug several stones out of the ground with the heel of my shoe and piled them into an untidy mound to the left of the path. I tried to make it as natural looking as I could whilst acting as my marker if I ever needed to visit the site again.

Staring at the makeshift cross, I recalled the first time

I'd found Katrina in her bedroom. Her wired appearance and unsettling behaviour. I remembered her saying, 'You should leave our house. They don't think you like us.' It suddenly dawned on me that maybe Katrina wasn't just giving out childish advice then but more of a warning? Had it been the same for her father, Ryan Palmer? Did he have to leave the house? I didn't believe that the cross in front of me symbolised a grave, but I still shivered involuntarily at the prospect.

The phone vibrating in my pocket made me jump. The last thing I'd picked up before leaving the bedroom had been the burner phone. If Lisa tried to contact me, it would be much easier to talk away from the house. She spoke as soon as I pressed the accept button.

"Matt, can you talk?"

"Yeah, I'm out in the woods. What is it?"

"I arranged a meeting with Don, you know, to get him on his own. After we'd talked a bit of business, I casually asked him if he knew what hospital Tracy worked at."

"Yes, go on."

"It was the University College of London. So, I called the hospital, said I was a relative of Ryan Palmer and it was the first time I'd been back in the country for years."

Lisa went onto tell me they had put her through to the personnel department but they couldn't divulge too much information, saying it breached data protection.

"So, I changed tack. Said that I had been out for a meal two or three times with Ryan and one of his colleagues but couldn't recall his friend's name. Again she blanked me until I started putting on this sob story I needed closure and desperately needed to speak to someone, especially as Ryan had no family. I begged, saying his colleague would be my only hope. The woman in personnel asked me to hold the line before coming back a few minutes later."

"And?" I was becoming agitated at the drawn-out story.

"Hang on! I'm getting there."

"Sorry."

"Well, she said she had spoken to someone else in personnel who knew who I was talking about. I couldn't believe my luck."

"Shit, well done, Lisa."

"I'll text you his name and number as soon as I've hung up."

I added the name and number to my contacts and called it straight away. His name was Lee Blackmore and Lisa had even found out that he did the same job as Ryan had; a consultant in vascular surgery – whatever the fuck that was.

My luck was changing. Lee answered immediately. The conversation wasn't easy, but I somehow blagged my way through it, explaining that I was the brother-in-law of Ryan Palmer. I made out Ryan's wife had given me his name as someone who knew him well. At first he was sceptical. He explained that the family had wanted nothing to do with him after he had tried to help find Ryan and found it peculiar that they would contact him now. I realised how it must have resonated and told him that Tracy had let his name slip, and had not meant for me to get in touch with him. But I said I needed to see him urgently. Eventually, he came round and agreed to meet me in a bar near the hospital. He sounded just as intrigued as I was.

We met the very next day.

35

"WELL?" Graham asked.

Right on cue, Graham had turned up at the house before I'd even returned from my walk. Melissa had called him as soon as the police had left. He had paced around me all day, politely asking how I was, if I needed tea or coffee, and even suggesting that he bought some beer from the shop for later that evening. Holding a position of power over him at last, I made him fetch and carry for me all afternoon. I caught him grimacing under his breath, but he still looked after me like a servant.

We all sat down to eat shortly after Tracy and Amelia had returned from work. Katrina joined us for the second time since her drug-induced sleep, and she had been on her best behaviour, speaking only when spoken to. Nobody mentioned the visit from the police and subsequent letter from a solicitor during the entire meal, but as soon as we had finished, Graham's impatience finally got the better of him.

"Sorry, Graham?" I responded, loving watching him

have to work so hard to glean any inkling of information from me.

"You know, Matt, you know."

The others stared at me in silence. It sickened me they appeared to be enjoying the whole scenario. Melissa even smiled in anticipation of any news. I'd just lost a relative to a hideous crime, and all they cared about was what the solicitor had said.

"Oh, the solicitor?"

"Yes!" Graham looked as though he was going to burst. I noticed a gleam of sweat across his forehead and his cheeks were rosy pink. A vein stuck out in his neck and I could swear I could see it throb as the blood pumped around him.

"Nothing to tell," I responded, sitting back in my chair smirking. "I've got to make an appointment to see him."

Their collective faces dropped in unison. Amelia spoke next.

"What, he didn't give you any idea of an amount?"

I leant forward, propping myself onto the table by my elbows. I knew Melissa hated it when people did that. I looked Amelia in the eye. The sarcasm dripped from my mouth as I spoke.

"Oh, I see. Expecting some kind of figure then, darling?"

She backtracked immediately, my response catching her out completely.

"Erm, no. Why should I?" Just as quickly, she composed herself again. "It's just when the police said she'd left you her entire estate—"

"'Her' Amelia. Who is 'her'? Do you mean my long-lost aunt, Edith Weeks, by any chance?"

I scraped my chair back on purpose, again knowing that grated on the family.

"Has it not occurred to any of you that Edith Weeks has been brutally murdered?"

The next morning, I phoned Mike. I asked if it would be okay if I took another day off as I had a couple of things to sort out. He was fine about it and told me to take as much time as I needed. He even suggested that a break from work might do me some good anyway; my recent performance troubled him.

Amelia hadn't been so accommodating to me taking another day off and asked what I had to do that was so important. I made up a story about having to go into London to visit a branch of the solicitors dealing with my aunt's estate. She couldn't argue with me, and I knew she couldn't ask to accompany me. It was the perfect excuse to visit Lee Blackmore without interruption.

As soon as Amelia and Tracy disappeared to the train station, I went to my room to check if Lisa had left any messages. She had left one, but only to wish me good luck with my meeting. I'd texted her the night before to keep her in the loop. She asked me to call immediately afterwards. I put the burner phone into my coat pocket, pleased that I had Lisa on my side.

Melissa wished me good luck as I left for the station before lunch. Just like Graham, she looked ill at ease trying to be so polite when it was obvious she just wanted to know the details.

Walking down the driveway, something made me turn and look back towards the house. Again, Katrina wore the same white dress and appeared like an apparition in the upstairs window. She stared expressionless towards me; her hair sticking up at all angles and her darkened eyes like empty sockets set in her skull. Just as I turned to continue walking away, she grinned at me. It must have been the angle, but her teeth appeared to be missing, showing a black chasm rather than the usual yellow arrangement. Then she really freaked me out. She lifted her arm and made a cut-throat gesture with her bony finger across her neck. Back and forth she slit her neck, continually glaring at me with that toothless grin. I shuddered and hunched the collar of my coat up tight around my neck. Spinning away from the disconcerting image, I hurried along the driveway, away from Katrina and the house.

The bar that Lee Blackmore had chosen was only a stone's throw from the hospital. A typical, old-fashioned London pub with green leather seating circling the perimeter of the main lounge. Several bar stools were already taken when I arrived, and I had to squeeze in between two guys who were drinking dark beer and talking about the previous night's football.

After I'd ordered my pint, I realised I didn't know what Lee looked like, and we'd not told each other what we'd be wearing or how to recognise each other. I found a space on the leather seats, leaving plenty of room on either side of me. I appeared to be the only person in the pub on my own, so I figured he would easily spot me.

Sure enough, five minutes later the door opened, momentarily letting the sounds of the busy London streets seep into the pub. The closing of the door behind him immediately acted as a sound barrier and the hum of people talking inside took over again. Lee Blackmore carried a newspaper under his arm and he scanned the pub, leaving me in no doubt it was him. As soon as I stood he made his way over.

"You must be Matt?"

Lee wasn't what I'd been expecting. We form a picture of people in our heads from the sound of their voice on the phone. I'd imagined a small, squat person with fair hair and maybe a beard or moustache. Instead, he must have been at least six foot tall, wiry in physique and, once he'd removed his baseball cap, I saw his dark brown hair swept over from one side. I could describe Lee as conventionally good looking.

After fetching him a drink, I perched myself down on a small stool on the opposite side of a tiny round table. Suddenly, I felt awkward, not knowing how or where to start, even though I'd played the conversation around my head a thousand times before. Lee broke the ice.

"So, you're related to Tracy Palmer?"

"Known as Tracy Reid again now, but yes, she's my sister-in-law."

After the preliminaries were over, I was keen to get down to facts.

"You knew Ryan well then?"

"Very well, yes. We shared a house soon after he started working at the hospital. He wasn't in a good place when he got the job. His first wife had died of cancer. She was young, mid-twenties."

"Shit, that sucks," I said as Lee stopped to take a sip of his beer.

"Yeah, it really cut him up. It surprised me he'd wanted to go back to work so soon. His ex had died a few months before he came to this hospital. They had lived somewhere in the midlands, near Nottingham, I believe. Anyway, after a while, he told me that his ex-wife had lost her parents a couple of years before. They'd passed within a few months of each other, her mum soon after her dad. Apparently, she died of a broken heart, if you believe in that. Anyway, his ex was an only child, and they left her everything. A few hundred grand he mentioned."

"So, you were surprised that he even went back to work?"

"Well, the timing more than anything. If I'd lost my wife so young, and I had a fair amount of money, I doubt I'd go looking for work so soon. Maybe it was his escape mechanism though, something else to focus on."

Although interesting, the conversation wasn't getting me anywhere with how Tracy fitted in. I hoped my impatience wasn't obvious.

"And when did Tracy come along?"

Lee took another long swig of his beer. I'd hardly touched mine and noticed he was already well ahead of me.

"That was the next strange thing. It must have only been two or three months after Ryan started that this Tracy chatted to him and showed so much interest. They went out for a drink or two and she would be forever flirting with him…"

I tried to picture Tracy flirting with anyone, but the image would not compute.

"…and they soon started dating properly. I sat down with him a few times and asked if he was sure he was doing the right thing. But he seemed smitten with her. I remember her coming round to the house, her hair and make-up, her revealing dresses—"

"Tracy?" I interrupted. "You sure we're talking about the same person?"

"Well, that's the thing. Within a few months, Ryan told me they were getting married. I couldn't believe it. It was like a whirlwind romance. And then after they married, he went to live at her mum's place and whenever I saw Tracy meet him after work, she had completely changed. Her hair, her appearance. She wore dowdy clothes and little make-up. It was like she was an entirely different person."

For the next five minutes, I sat and stared at Lee in silence. Everything he said about Ryan Palmer, he could so easily have been saying about me. Ryan used to come to work and try to get Lee on his own, to talk to him about something. But every time they met, Tracy would appear, never leaving Ryan alone.

"And when we met, knowing it would be impossible for Tracy to be there because of workload or something, her bloody brother-in-law would turn up. What was his name...?"

"Graham, by any chance?"

"Yes. Excuse my language, but he was a right twat. There was something about him."

Lee went on to tell me that Ryan took more and more time off work. He'd had a couple of written warnings, and even when he turned up, his heart wasn't in it. Lee explained that you always had to be on the ball in their profession, otherwise it would only lead to an inevitable sacking.

"Finally, he just stopped coming to work altogether. I tried and tried to call him, but could never get him to respond to my messages. I didn't know where he lived – they lived – so there was very little I could do but keep trying to ring him. Then, one day at work, Tracy asked if she could have a word with me."

I sat forward, intent not to miss a single word he said.

"She said Ryan had gone. I didn't know what she meant at first, but she said one night, when she returned home from work, he had gone, vanished. I asked if he'd left a note or anything, but she just said a suitcase was missing and a few items of his clothing."

"Did you believe her?"

"She said he'd been depressed, something I couldn't dispute, so I went along with it."

"And did he ever contact you again, you know, after he'd left?"

"No, nothing. We'd been so close. It just made little sense."

"And you said you'd tried to help?"

"Yes. I told Tracy at work I would help try to trace him, print off posters, visit local train stations or anything else she could suggest. But she told me it was private, and they wanted to keep it between themselves. She said it was because they were such a close family."

"So, you didn't visit the family home?"

"No. It gutted me, to be honest. Me and Ryan were good friends, and it all finished, just like that." Lee clicked his fingers to emphasise his point.

"And Tracy?"

"She handed her notice in during the next few days. After the day she'd explained about Ryan going missing, I never saw her again."

We chatted for a little while longer. I pointed out why I had been so keen to meet him and told him exactly what I'd like him to do next to help me out – if he consented, of course. He appeared to be in shock at my revelations and volunteered his support at once. In an attempt to lighten the mood, he sarcastically offered me his condolences that I'd married into that family. I liked his sense of humour at least.

Before I left, I ensured he had my phone number stored. I'd already added him to my burner phone and, because I'd told him about Lisa, I suggested he made a note of her number too. As soon as I finished my beer, I stood to leave and shook Lee's hand to thank him for his time.

"Great to meet you too," Lee replied, before appearing to become lost in thought for a few seconds. "You know what? Now I think about it, there was something strange about the whole setup."

"What do you mean?"

"Well, I might have misunderstood the situation, but I always felt as though Ryan desperately wanted to leave that family."

I forced a smile, knowing exactly what he meant. But Lee hadn't finished.

"But somehow, or for some unbeknown reason, he just couldn't get away."

36

LEE's last remark had sent my thoughts into turmoil.

The entire story he'd conveyed to me had *so* many similarities to my own. Approached by a girl, swept off my feet, agreed to marry and then move in with the family. The fact that Ryan had also come into money, albeit before he and Tracy met, struck yet another chord with my personal situation. Could it all be coincidental, really?

I stumbled out of the bar, and although I'd hardly touched my beer, I felt drunk on adrenalin. At first I didn't see him. I just wanted to be alone, and I'd become lost in my own little world. But as soon as I saw him, I yearned to cross the road, walk right up to Graham and punch his fucking lights out. However, it didn't appear as though he'd spotted me. He'd followed me to the pub – by now, nothing surprised me – but he hadn't been paying attention as I left. I ducked behind a small group of people and then hid behind a refuse bin – much to the bewilderment of passers-by – and I studied him. He kept looking at his watch before eventually looking over towards the pub. He must have decided enough was enough, and he started making his way across the road. I decided I had no further time for him, not then at least. Instead, I needed to be alone, to think, to act. I knew I'd found myself in a dire situation, and I was up to my neck in it.

Ignoring Graham, I put my head down, hunched up my collar and marched towards the closest tube station. Only when I reached the top of the flight of stairs did I allow myself to look around. I was just in time to see Graham disappear into the pub. Did he know Lee? Were they in on it together? Surely not. Lee seemed so genuine.

Despite the cold, late January air outside, the underground felt hot and stuffy. My body perspired as though I had a temperature. I racked my brain for what to do next. It even crossed my mind not to return to the house at all, but to run instead; run as far away as possible. I could still seek the solicitor in Birmingham, get what was rightfully mine, and disappear to the other side of the world. I remembered that the Reid family didn't know how much money was involved, but they were cunning. Even if I ran, they would track me down. I'd left the letter from the solicitor on my bedside table; there would be no chance that Amelia hadn't already passed it around the family. I guessed that Graham might have even contacted the solicitor himself to ask for further details. Besides, I would need clothes, my personal belongings, and most of all, my passport.

Without concentrating or paying any attention to my route, I left the tube and exited the station closest to work. As soon as I got outside, I went directly to the café around the corner from the office. Taking our usual table at the back of the shop, I texted Lisa on her temporary phone.

True to form, she appeared in the café doorway about twenty minutes later.

After grabbing herself a coffee, she hurried over to join me. There weren't many people in at that time of day, but I still felt relieved that the low hum of chat would drown out anything we had to say to one another.

I spent the next five minutes telling Lisa all about my meeting, and subsequent conversation, with Lee Blackmore. She sat there, listening intently, with her hands wrapped around her drink. Next, I told her about Graham waiting outside and how he'd gone into the pub, no doubt to interrogate Lee and find out exactly what he'd told me.

"Holy shit. Do you think they killed Ryan?"

"I don't know what to think. It all fits into place, but wouldn't the police have been involved?"

Lisa stared into her drink as if the answer might leap out and explain everything. After a few moments, she replied.

"But why would the police have been informed at all? Anybody can leave home without telling the authorities. Tracy could have told the hospital that Ryan just left one day. That's what they told Lee, wasn't it?"

She was right. If Ryan had left home, there would be no need for the Reid family to inform anybody. Once he'd married Tracy, all of his money would have been shared with her. Without bringing attention to themselves, she had access to everything. According to Lee, Ryan had no other family. Tracy had got what she wanted; as had the family.

"So, what do I do now?"

Again, Lisa looked deep into her cup of frothy cappuccino.

"You've still got Lee's number haven't you?"

I scrolled through my recent contacts, before showing Lisa the screen. She told me exactly what to say, and I pressed the 'call' button. Lee answered on the third ring. I put the phone onto speaker and Lisa leant right across the table to hear.

I'd asked if Graham had found him in the pub and, if he had, what had he asked. Lee told me he'd instantly recognised Graham as soon as he walked in. Lee had immediately put his baseball cap back on and kept his head down. Graham approached a few guys in the pub, before eventually tapping Lee on the shoulder. He said his heart was doing palpitations and he hadn't dared look up in case Graham recognised him. Instead, he continued to look at his newspaper whilst Graham spoke to the top of his cap. He asked Lee if he'd seen anybody matching my description and if he'd seen who I'd been talking to. Lee dismissed him, saying he'd been drinking his pint whilst reading the paper. He said he had seen nobody. Graham tutted, mumbled something under his breath, then asked a couple more guys before finally leaving.

After we'd chatted a little longer, I hung up and turned to face Lisa. Something caught my eye outside, but when I looked, nothing was there. I turned my attention back to Lisa.

"So, Graham is none the wiser about our meeting," I concluded. "He didn't recognise Lee either."

"No, so he still doesn't know why you were in the pub. You should go home, act normal. I doubt Graham will mention seeing you, so you don't acknowledge seeing him. Play them at their own game."

"And then? I can't fucking stay there forever. Fuck knows what they'll do to me."

Lisa reached across the table and held my hand. It felt so good to be with her.

"Listen to me. Play along with them. Until you get the money from your aunt, they still need you to be on their side. If this is what it's all about, you need to gather proof. Find something incriminating in that house."

Lisa went back to work, and I made my way home. She'd been right. The Reid family needed me more than I needed them, for the time being at least. I would not run, not yet. I had to stall getting hold of the money, or at least not let on once I'd got it. And by now, I desperately wanted to find out more.

When I walked in, I found Graham and Melissa standing in the kitchen. Graham looked sheepish.

"Hi, Graham. Been anywhere nice today?"

He glanced at Melissa before turning his attention to me.

"No, Matthew. I've been here all afternoon."

You lying bastard.

"What about you? Where have you been?"

"Oh, into town. Had to sign something at the solicitor's office."

Melissa stopped what she was doing.

"Have you found anything out, Matthew?"

"Not yet, no."

They shot each other a look before Melissa tried to turn on the charm once more.

"Well, I'm sure it will be a pleasant surprise."

"Yes, I'm sure it will."

The mobile phone vibrating in my coat pocket broke the silence. A text message.

Shit, it's the burner.

"Are you going to answer that?" Graham asked inquisitively.

"Well, no. It will be work. Best leave it. I'm supposed to be taking time off."

"But your work phone is in your bedroom," Melissa corrected me. "I saw it on your bed when I put fresh towels in your room earlier."

Fuck. Think.

"Oh yeah. It's my other phone. The one I've had for ages. I've kept it to keep in touch with a couple of old mates."

Going red didn't help my cause. I removed the phone from my pocket to prove it was an old-style mobile. However, it may as well have been a brick for all they knew about technology.

"Looks new to me," Graham said, leaning forward to get a better look. "What does your mate want?"

Turning the screen to face me, I made out one of my friends from the wedding had been asking me if I'd wanted to meet for a beer sometime. If Graham snatched it from me, he'd have seen 'keep strong, I'm always here for you', followed by several kisses from Lisa. I quickly returned it to my pocket.

Graham and Melissa couldn't have looked less convinced if they'd tried.

After scrambling around, I eventually found a new hiding place for the phone underneath a loose floorboard in the bedroom. Trying to settle my nerves, I lay on the bed contemplating my next move. The letter from the solicitor was still on my bedside table, but they had moved it. I'd purposefully turned it, face down, and placed it under the latest paperback I'd been pretending to read most nights. Now, it lay on top of the book, face up. No more proof required that it had been around the family for all eyes to see.

I must have dozed off, and Amelia kissing me on the cheek an hour later, woke me. She said dinner was ready, and that she had some news for me from work. The way she said it made my heart beat fast. It sounded like good news for her, but bad news for somebody else. Her conniving little smile rammed home my fears.

We ate in silence, although Tracy and Amelia kept smiling at one another when they thought nobody else was watching.

I couldn't stand the suspense any longer and as soon as the last knife and fork had been laid down on a plate, I asked Amelia what had happened. I tried to keep it light-hearted, as though it wasn't a big deal. Somehow, I knew it was.

"Well, you'll never guess who Mike let go from work today?"

"Let go? Do you mean sacked?"

"I guess you could call it that, yes."

She let her words hang, knowing the silence would stifle me.

"Well?"

"After Lisa went out this afternoon, to goodness knows where," she smiled at Tracy before continuing, "Mike asked her to accompany him into a meeting room as soon as she returned."

My mind immediately drifted to our meeting in the café, when I thought I'd seen something – or somebody – outside the window.

Amelia changed her tone, adding dramatic effect to her announcement.

"After she'd packed her desk and somebody escorted

her from the building, we couldn't believe it when Mike told us he'd sacked Lisa for gross misconduct."

I knew I had to remain calm on the exterior. Inside, I was seething.

"Wow, what has she done?"

"Well, apparently, she's been sleeping with somebody in the office." She looked at Tracy again. "We've no idea who it could be, but someone had tipped Mike off."

Shit. They know.

"When he asked her about it, he said she broke down in tears and didn't deny it. He said her performance has been going downhill recently anyway, presumably because of her affair. It was the perfect excuse for him to act."

"Oh, right," I stumbled for words. "I wonder who it could be?"

Amelia didn't address me, but she looked directly into my eyes as she spoke.

"That's what we've been trying to work out all the way home. Haven't we, Tracy?"

37

THEY KNOW. They really do know.

Had she found the burner phone and read the subsequent messages? Was it the packet of condoms that Amelia had discovered? Did Graham see something in Cheshire? Had somebody been following us to the café or even know what we'd discussed the day I took Lisa home from work with a headache?

Whatever, or however, they knew. Also, Amelia and Tracy didn't hide the fact that they were behind Lisa's sacking. The way they looked at each other across the dinner table, enjoying their little secrets. And then there were the emails that had been deleted and reinstated on my laptop. All to get me into trouble with Mike; to plant the first seeds of doubt that I wasn't up to the job either. Did they have the same plans for me as they did for Lisa? Had they been behind Chris's demise? I didn't even have to answer my own questions.

Later that evening, I told Amelia that I needed to take the remainder of the week off. I'd deliberately waited until we were in bed so she wouldn't have the rest of the family to fall back on. She wasn't happy.

"But what else do you need to do? You went to see the solicitor today, amongst other things…" There it was again, another underhanded accusation that she knew more than she was letting on. "…so, who else do you need to visit?"

"I just need some time to reflect. This has all come as a tremendous shock to me, even if it hasn't to you."

My comment lit the fuse paper and Amelia's face immediately twisted to irritation. A vein throbbed in her temple as blood rushed to her head. She did not attempt to keep her voice down.

"And what the hell is that supposed to mean?"

I kept my voice level, knowing that my calmness would wind her up even more.

"Well, none of you seemed particularly bothered about a murder, just concerned with what might be in it for you."

There was a knock on the door before Amelia could reply. She got out of bed and opened it slightly, positioning herself so I couldn't see who was outside. She looked back at me before opening the door and going out onto the landing. I glimpsed a sight of Melissa and Tracy before Amelia closed the door behind her. They spoke softly and I couldn't hear a word that was being said. After a few minutes, Amelia reappeared. Her mood had altered like the flick of a light switch.

She went to the bathroom and brushed her teeth, before returning to the room and climbing into bed. She rolled over, with her back to me, and switched off her bedside lamp.

"Everything okay?" I asked, still feeling good about myself. She whispered her reply.

"Oh yes. Everything is going to be just fine."

The next day I walked with Amelia and Tracy to the train station. I'd been worried that at least one of them would take the day off work to keep their eye on me. I'd wanted to follow them onto the platform to make sure they both got on the train but you needed a ticket to get through the barrier. I had no choice but to leave them as they queued for a coffee outside the station.

After Amelia had switched off her light the night before, I'd gone into the bathroom to pretend to brush my teeth. I took my phone with me and went onto Google Maps and input Graham's address; the one that Bob had given me a few weeks earlier, and I'd had etched on my brain ever since. I'd decided I needed to see where he lived once and for all. I doubted it would give me any clues about what might happen, but my curiosity, and Lisa, told me to at least look.

After I left Amelia and Tracy, I scampered out of the station car park and fired up Google Maps once more. Graham's address was still the last landmark I'd put in, and after a few seconds, the app informed me I was an eleven-minute walk away. I took a beanie hat out of my backpack and pulled my scarf up higher so it covered my mouth. Only my nose and eyes were visible. It was a crude attempt at some kind of disguise, but I wanted to remain as inconspicuous as possible. I thought I should be okay anyway as I'd left Graham back at the house with Melissa and Katrina.

Following the directions on my phone, I made light work of the projected time and soon found myself on the street where Graham lived. It was a modest affair, with terraced houses flanking both sides. Between every other property was an alleyway, allowing access to the rear of the houses.

After finding a few houses with numbers on their doors, I realised my side of the road was for even numbers and the odds were on the opposite side. Bob had said Graham lived at number forty-three. So, I made my way on the even side, crouching slightly behind the relentless row of parked cars, the random thought of how it must be a nightmare trying to find a space to leave your vehicle after a day at work popping into my head.

Looking across the road, I saw number thirty-five, thirty-seven, then a house with no number before forty-one and forty-three. There it was, Graham's house, a small, two-up, two-down terrace. His little red car was parked directly outside. The door was painted bright green, and the windows looked fairly new compared to his neighbours. It looked in decent condition, at least from the outside.

A pedestrian stared at me as I stood back to let him pass. He glanced at me and then at the houses opposite where I'd been staring. I couldn't think of anything to say, and I backtracked slightly until he had walked on, out of sight. I didn't know what to do or what else I could achieve by looking at the front of a house.

I hunched my scarf higher until it covered my nose then crossed the road until I was outside his next-door neighbour's. Taking one last look around, I scuttled down the alleyway between number forty-one and Graham's, finding an immediate respite from the strong wind that howled along the street.

Creeping along the alley, I reached the end where you would turn left into his neighbour's garden, and right into Graham's. The back gardens were long and narrow. They must have stretched at least a hundred feet. Number forty-one looked immaculate. Mostly laid to lawn, with flowerbeds, two small glasshouses, and the very end set out to raised vegetable beds. Graham's wasn't so well maintained. A scruffy patch of grass immediately behind his house gave way to something more like scrubland where vegetables might have once grown. The scene was complete with a shed that looked as though a good storm would put it out of its misery. Just like the Reids' house, gardening was not at the top of their hobbies.

Turning back to the house, I noticed the newish windows from the front were also in place at the rear. The back door looked new too, with frosted glass blocking any view into the property. There was one window down-stairs, and I would need to stand on tiptoe to see inside.

Creeping as quietly as I could, I stood underneath and pulled myself up so I could see in. It was the kitchen window, but net curtains, that I hadn't previously noticed, obscured anything. Pushing my face against the glass, I shielded my eyes with my free hand to peer inside. The sight of the person walking past the kitchen door almost made me topple over backwards.

Who the fuck is that?

I stepped back and crouched down, my heart leaping in my chest. I knew whoever it was, hadn't seen me. They had just walked by without looking up. But there was somebody inside Graham's house, and he was up at the Reids' home.

With my mind doing somersaults, I retraced my steps and backtracked along the alleyway. When I reached the end, I stuck my head out and looked both ways. The wind blasted along the street, but fortunately, all seemed just as quiet as when I'd first arrived. The cold January weather meant anybody with sense was indoors, keeping warm.

Crossing the road, I hastened my pace to get away.

Just as I approached the end of the street, I heard footsteps coming from around the corner. Something made me duck behind the nearest car, fearing that Graham might be on his way home. I crouched even lower as the footsteps got louder. Soon, I could see the shoes on the other side of the car as I peered underneath. As the person hurried along one side of the car, I crawled in the opposite direction on the far side. Once I was at the back of the car, I eased myself up into a more upright position. I had to do a double-take before I realised who had just walked past me. Tracy.

How the hell had she got here when I'd watched her get on the train?

But I hadn't watched her get on the train; I'd left them in the queue for the kiosk. Tracy didn't get on the train. I crouched back down, making sure she wouldn't see me if she spun around. As soon as she was opposite Graham's house, she turned, looking up and down the street for any oncoming vehicles.

Needing to see more, I bent my knees to elevate my eyeline above the continual row of parked cars. Tracy was outside number forty-three. I could barely contain my curiosity once she knocked on the front door.

38

EVEN THOUGH I wore several layers of clothing, I became convinced that I would see my heart beating through my coat. I crawled around the car, trying to get as good a view as possible.

Slowly, the front door opened. Tracy acknowledged whoever stood on the other side and reached into her large shoulder bag. She removed something. It looked like a large white envelope, which she offered to the person inside.

I tried to focus on who was at the door. It must have been the same individual who I'd just seen walk along the hallway whilst I stood on tiptoe at the window.

But the front door was only slightly ajar, no doubt protecting whoever it was from the gale-force wind which now gusted along the narrow street.

As Tracy passed the envelope, I saw an outstretched arm reach for it. Moments later, another envelope was passed in the opposite direction and Tracy quickly put it into her bag. Although it was difficult to be sure, it looked like a female's hand; too petite to be a male. Tracy stood speaking for a few minutes before she took a step backwards and glanced up and down the street. Then, the person from inside the house took a tentative step outside her front door. She followed Tracy's lead and checked up and down the street. It wasn't until she glanced in my direction that I recognised her.

What the fuck, what the fuck…

I stumbled backwards, banging heavily into the car behind me. It immediately set off the alarm, an incessant din of repetitive car horn blasting. Just before I ran, I saw Tracy looking up towards the flashing indicator lights. The other person quickly stepped back inside and slammed the door closed behind her. I'm sure they hadn't seen me, or at least recognised me, not from that distance, with my face so well obscured. I'd also run behind the parked cars, crouched down, bent double.

Soon after, I found myself in a park, a few streets away. I wasn't sure how much more my heart could take. What kind of mess had I got myself into?

There was a deep row of trees at the back of the park, somewhere to lie low until I could think of my next move. The wind howled at the branches above me, but I felt safe there; out of sight at least, and the last place anybody would come looking for me if either of the women had recognised me.

Taking the burner phone from my pocket, I first called Lee Blackmore. I told him what had just happened and reiterated that he acted with haste. He knew exactly what I was talking about after our meeting in the pub. Next, I sent Lisa a text to see if she could talk. She called me within seconds. I told her where I was and asked if she could meet me there. Lisa sounded scared, as if the whole situation could get out of control, but she still agreed. I hung up, walked a little deeper into the trees, and waited.

Playing back the scene which had just unfolded in front of my eyes, I tried to comprehend what that woman could possibly be doing in Graham's house. It just didn't make sense.

A figure walking at the other end of the park caught my attention. It was Lisa. Stepping to the edge of the trees, I called her phone and told her to look up to her right. She hung up as soon as she saw me and hurried across the playing fields. Once inside the safe haven of the trees, Lisa hugged me. She looked close to tears.

It was the first time we'd spoken since they'd sacked her the day before.

"What happened, Lisa? What do they know?"

"I've no idea. Mike said somebody had tipped him off that I was seeing someone at work. He said they thought they knew who it was, but I didn't have to tell him if I didn't want to."

"They know, Lisa. The family. All of them."

She shook her head, not wanting to believe any of this was happening.

"So, what happens now?"

I told her I'd just seen Tracy hand over something to somebody in Graham's house.

"It looked like a large envelope…" I trailed off, realisation suddenly hitting me like a fast-moving train.

"What is it?"

"The envelope was large, A4 and white, just like one that had been delivered to the Reid house one morning when I waited for the post. Tracy took one from the person in return."

"So?"

"I remember I tried to see inside it, you know, when

you hold a letter up to the light, you can sometimes see inside it? But Amelia grabbed it from me, like it contained top secret information or something. Later that night, I heard them all talking in the living room, like some secret pact again. Right at the end, Graham raised his voice."

I stopped, making sure I got my facts right. Lisa became impatient.

"Well, what did he say?"

"He said something like, 'do you think he could see what was inside the envelope'." I looked Lisa in the eye. "And there was something else."

I explained that I'd thought I recognised the handwriting. Something hidden deep inside my psyche. Once I'd seen the woman take the envelope from Tracy, I knew exactly where I'd recognised the writing from.

Lisa sat agog as I explained everything. Once she'd stopped asking questions, I told her I'd called Lee before meeting her today and what we had discussed. Lisa agreed to get in touch with him straight away and wait for me to contact them.

As we stepped out of the trees together, she asked me what my next plans were.

"I'm going back to number forty-three. I *have* to know what she's doing there."

Approaching the front door, I half wished I'd taken Lisa's advice and gone with her instead. She'd said it was too dangerous to go on my own, but I knew it could be my only opportunity without Graham being around.

Looking up and down the street, I gently knocked on the front door. I didn't want to alarm her before she'd even opened it.

"Who is it?"

"Delivery. I've got a parcel for you."

"Okay, just leave it outside please."

Shit.

"It needs a signature, madam."

Imagining her panic, I heard a bolt slide open from inside the door. Quickly followed by another. Finally, the handle turned, and the door opened. I immediately jammed my foot inside, knowing very well that she would close it as soon as she saw me. That is exactly what she tried, but I pushed my way in, falling into the hallway with my back to her. She squealed.

"Please, don't hurt me——"

But she stopped in her tracks as soon as I regained my footing, turned to face her and removed my hat and scarf. At first, I thought she was going to scream, but she just stood there, her mouth wide open, unable to take in who had just forced their way into her house.

"Hello, Julia," I said, as calmly as I could. "I think we have some talking to do, don't you?"

Following her into the small lounge, we sat opposite, both in small armchairs; the only two seats in the room. The house felt cold, and Julia looked more gaunt than I remembered. She wore an oversized cardigan which she kept pulling tight across her front. The silence hung between us, building on the already palpable tension in the room. The memories of our night together, after the conference, all came tumbling back to me. I spoke first.

"So, are you going to tell me how you know Graham?"

Julia crossed and uncrossed her arms. She sat so close to the edge of her seat I thought she might fall off. Not taking her eyes off the threadbare carpet at her feet, she eventually replied.

"I'm his wife."

"His wife!" Suddenly I felt a lot more afraid. I had thought she would be a friend of the family, somebody who knew them, but Graham's wife – holy shit. At last, Julia lifted her gaze from the carpet, maybe gaining confidence from my sudden mood swing.

"Yes. His wife. Who did you think I was, the cleaner?"

I realised I was sat next to the front window. The window that looked directly out onto the street. I suddenly felt extremely vulnerable and shifted myself so my back was to the road; believing that at least if somebody walked by they wouldn't instantly recognise me. Somebody being Graham, of course.

"But, that night, the conference…"

I played back our meeting. She had approached me on our stand at the conference, and then again at the hotel bar the same night. She'd listened to my woes, but she must have already known all about me – but how? I recalled her telling me of a job she knew of at Opacy; she even knew what agent to contact about it. Julia had known exactly who she was setting up for the role.

"…you already knew who I was, didn't you, Julia?"

Her expression told me the answer before she even replied.

"But how?"

Julia surprised me by opening up and filling in the details with no further prompting. She said they had known I'd been looking for work and that I'd already applied for two positions. Amelia and Tracy were well connected in the property market and they even knew Grieg at Hammond Appointments. They already had my

CV before I met with Julia. The whole thing had been pre-arranged.

"And your husband. You told me he could be violent, 'somebody I wouldn't want to mess with'. How much does he know?"

She stood and walked over to the fireplace. I wish it had been lit, so at least it would have added some warmth to the place. Julia faced the wall above the mantlepiece as she spoke.

"We just knew you would be the one——"

I stood too.

"The one for what?" Julia turned, probably scared of what I might do. Maybe her usual reaction when questioned by a man?

"The perfect match," she continued. "You and Amelia."

"It was all a setup? How did you know I'd apply for the job, fall for Amelia?"

"We just did, okay?" Julia went back to her seat and sat down. She beckoned for me to do the same. She looked crestfallen.

I didn't interrupt her again. I'm not sure I could have found the words anyway. I just tried to take it all in; every single word. Julia explained everything. She even told me that Chris had been let go because he couldn't offer them anything anymore. He had been set up too, and they'd hoped that one day he and Tracy might get together.

They loved me too when I started.

Julia pointed out that he had money, a substantial amount from an inheritance, but he just wouldn't take Tracy up on her many advances. The family had no way of getting hold of it. Finally, they set him up to fail at work, so Mike had no alternative but to fire him. He'd had a lucky escape.

Unlike Ryan Palmer.

Afterwards, she explained more about her own sorry life. It felt as though our meeting had been the perfect opportunity for her to pour her heart out; she didn't hold back. At one stage, I asked why she hadn't left, run away, but she revealed there was nowhere for her to go. The family knew she had no money, no job. They had done nothing wrong, as far as she knew, so she just did as she was told. They told her little, just asked for her to help when requested to do so. Julia had lost the will to do anything about her own situation.

Once she had finished, she excused herself. I didn't feel she would try to run; she had long given up on trying to escape. A few minutes later, she returned with an envelope and told me to take it. I stuffed it inside the top of my jeans and concealed the rest underneath my coat.

As I stood to leave, a desperate urge to hug Julia swept over me. Even though she was part of the Reid family, I knew she had become as trapped as I had. Once I took a step towards her, she held out her hand to stop me. The single shake of her head told me everything I needed to know.

That's when we heard the key turn in the front door.

39

"Shit, that's him," Julia whispered.

Fortunately, she had re-bolted the door behind me after I'd arrived. It bought us a few moments to think.

"Quick, go out the back door and hide in the alleyway. As soon as you hear the front door slam shut, run back out onto the street, turn right, and get away."

"Okay, thanks, Julia."

She attempted her first smile since I'd arrived. The corners of her mouth quivered as she desperately tried to turn them upwards. Julia's body language conveyed a sense of deep melancholy and yearning. I so wanted to help her escape too.

The exaggeration of keys rattling in the door and Graham's raised voice alerted me to my current predicament. Bending down, I hurried out of the back door, which Julia closed silently behind me. I waited in the alleyway between the two properties as instructed. As soon as I heard the front door slam, I made my way tentatively to the end and peered around the corner. Right on cue, I heard

Graham's raised voice from inside the house. Although I felt the urge to help Julia, I knew I had to get away for my own safety. Julia would have been in this situation a thousand times before; she would know how to handle it – I hoped.

Katrina was sat in the top window when I arrived home. I waved, wanting to keep her on my side. Katrina liked me, even though the family had never wanted us to become friends. She returned my wave, albeit whilst looking back over her shoulder.

Melissa was at the dining room table. Papers took up the entire surface. I couldn't see what was on them, but I could just make out that some had red pen markings and others had notes written in blue. I gripped the front of my coat, suddenly aware of the envelope tucked into my jeans. Melissa quickly scrambled the papers into a rough pile before turning them face down.

"Hello, Matthew," Melissa said, looking up from the table. "Been anywhere nice?"

Her question dripped with sarcasm. Did she know? Had Graham or Julia somehow got a message to her as soon as I'd left their house? It was impossible though – unless the Reid family owned a mobile phone. I had to keep my wits about me.

"Once around the village, once around the playing fields. It's nice to get some fresh air, Melissa."

She smiled, before looking back at the pile of papers in front of her. I was pleased she didn't want to engage in conversation. It felt as though we were well past that stage now.

I ran upstairs, two steps at a time, and shut the bedroom door firmly behind me. Whisking off my coat, I retrieved the envelope tucked into my jeans and sat on the edge of the bed to open it.

Julia had stuffed it full of paperwork, looking very similar to the pile Melissa had just collected on the table downstairs; full of notes in red and blue ink. The first page was a curriculum vitae; somebody called Gareth Firth. I skim read it. Gareth lived in Kent, thirty-six years old, single. Glancing at his work experience, I noticed he had been mostly involved in property. A staple in the top left-hand corner held a second sheet attached. That page contained a family tree. The square in the middle contained Gareth's name, from which it grew outwards, like a spider's web of squares. Each square had a name, a title; 'parent', 'uncle', 'grandfather', and then a particular flow of squares ended, the final one circled in red. There were notes next to it. 'Grandmother. Rich.' Then a red cross with the words, 'too many siblings. Four out of ten.' The notes were in Julia's handwriting.

I picked up the next two sheets of paper stapled together. Another CV. Mr John Appleton. Twenty-nine. Single. Current occupation, estate agent. I flicked over to page two. Another family tree. I followed it to the final red cross. 'Uncle Peter. Very rich. Unfortunately, fit and in good health. Possible. Six out of ten'.

And so it went on. Always single, all living within commutable distance to London and all working in property. Every single one of them had notes scrawled across their family trees, and every one had a mark out of ten. Julia's handwriting was everywhere.

This is what Tracy must have meant when she let slip about collecting information. What had she said? 'Without the internet, we wouldn't be able to gather all this...'.

Picking up the pace, I skipped through the next dozen

attached sheets. Were they all to find a replacement for Chris? Then I noticed they all had a date near the top. Flicking through the ones I'd already read, the dates varied from two years previously, until around eighteen or twenty months ago. That would have been the time I had applied for the role at Opacy. Had Julia given me this particular envelope on purpose?

Starting to panic, I frantically started going through the pile on the bed next to me. I tore a couple of sheets in my haste. My hands were shaking and I could feel the coldness of sweat across my shoulder blades. And there it was.

My name leapt out at me from the sheet like a jack-in-the-box.

'Matthew Walker. Single. Thirty-six. Current occupation, property manager. North London'.

Fuck, fuck, fuck.

I tore the top sheet from the bottom one. Again my name leapt out at me from the centre square of the family tree. The immediate two squares above mine were, 'Daniel Walker. Father. Deceased', and 'Joan Walker. Mother. Deceased'. My family tree had much more of Julia's handwriting on it. There was obvious excitement involved in this search. There were also far fewer squares; far fewer names.

Again I followed the flow to the inevitable red circle. Although the name inside didn't surprise me, it still came as a shock to see it printed in black and white.

'Edith Weeks. Aunt'. I read the scribbled notes next to the square. 'Not married! No siblings. Only sister, Joan Walker. Can't trace any other relative. Need Graham to investigate – urgent! Nine out of ten'.

I read it and re-read it. Over and over. They knew all about my family before I'd even joined the company. Did they really recruit me knowing that I might come into money one day? Did Amelia come on so strong, just to entice me into the family? And now my aunt had been murdered. What had Graham said the night I overheard them in the downstairs room; 'we just need to hang on a little while longer'?

Graham had gone off for a few days at a time before. He'd left the conference in Cheshire a day early, too. That isn't far from Birmingham, or wherever my aunty lived. Is that where he kept disappearing to? Holy shit, had Graham killed her?

Then I remembered Mike telling me they had two or three candidates for Chris's replacement, but Tracy and Amelia had narrowed it down to one favourite. Who was going to get their claws into that poor bastard? And Tracy coming on to Ryan soon after he joined the hospital. I recalled the story that Lee had conveyed to me. His wife had died. She was extremely well off. Tracy came onto the scene soon after, and Ryan had since disappeared. Then Julia telling me about Tracy and Chris. Fucking hell, they're the family from hell.

Retrieving the burner phone from my coat pocket, I sent Lisa a string of messages. She sent several replies, mostly with shocked emojis or profanities; sometimes both. Her last message told me to get out of the house. She said Amelia would be home soon. I realised I hadn't seen Tracy since leaving Julia's house earlier. Had she gone to work or could she be in the house somewhere?

Lisa was right, I had to get out. However, there were some loose ends I desperately wanted to tie up before I ran. I decided to leave it until the next morning. By then, I hoped Lee would have come back to me.

I collected all the papers and shoved them back into the envelope. I put them at the bottom of my overnight bag in the wardrobe, ready to take with me the next day, along with some clothes and my passport. Next, I lifted the loose floorboard on my side of the bed, switched off the burner phone and put it in its familiar hiding place. Just as I was replacing the floorboard, my bedroom door swung open. Spinning round, I saw Katrina standing on the landing. She was looking directly at my hands.

"It's loose, Katrina. It squeaks when I stand on it." I made a squeaking noise, and she giggled, showing off her yellow teeth. But she didn't speak.

"Was there something, Katrina?"

"There's another bedroom. Did you know?"

The way she randomly changed subject still caught me off guard. Shaking my head, I replied.

"Sorry? What bedroom?"

"The one you're going to be staying in," she replied, before sticking her thumb in her mouth and wandering off down the corridor.

What the fuck is she talking about?

Later that night, I attempted to make small talk with the family. I hoped my nervousness didn't show, but I found it impossible to read their thoughts. Graham had arrived in time for dinner – I thought of poor Julia, hoping she was okay. Had he threatened her, had he hit her? – but I had to focus on the present. One more night, I kept telling myself, just one more night.

It was in the middle of that final night when I felt the sharp scratch on my arm. I'd been fast asleep and woke suddenly to the pain inside my left elbow. It happened so fast, my eyes in and out of focus, the bodies in front of me all a blur.

First I saw Tracy, she was holding the needle in my arm, squeezing in the clear liquid. Then I saw Graham. He leant across me, his arms outstretched, ready to pin me down at my first movement. Finally, I saw Amelia. She sat on the bed next to me, her side of the bed; the bed we'd shared for the past few months.

I drifted in and out of consciousness. I thought of me and Amelia. The day of the interview, her long black hair; so shiny. Her prominent cheekbones. The dark crimson lipstick. The darkest brown eyes I'd ever seen. I felt myself smiling.

Amelia coughed, a pretend cough, to wake me from my daze. She leant directly over me and bent down to kiss me on the lips. I swore I could taste strawberries, but how could I? I smiled at her kiss.

She leant back and picked something up off the bed. Everything became blurred again, like we were under-water together, desperately trying to keep our eyes open to see. Amelia spoke, grabbing my attention once more. She held something white up in front of me and shook her head in despair. Her smile had disappeared, replaced by anger.

Amelia waved the paper back and forth in front of my eyes. It was a sheet of paper from my overnight bag; the sheet of paper containing my family tree.

40

THE BREEZE from the open window caused the net curtains to billow inwards. I tried desperately to open my eyes, but my eyelids felt as though they'd been weighed down with lead shots. My head throbbed and my lips felt parched. Every time I licked them, they felt chapped; the skin broken. A sudden movement at the end of the bed made my body tense.

"It's okay. It's only me."

Amelia slowly made her way around to my end of the bed. She sat on the edge. I flinched as she raised her hand above my head, but she just brushed the hair off my forehead and gently ran her fingers from the front to back.

"Shh now. I'm not going to hurt you."

I attempted to open my mouth, but my lips had become congealed.

"Wait," said Amelia. She reached over to the bedside table and retrieved a glass of water. Gently, she placed her hand behind my head, helping me to tilt it forward slightly. She then placed the glass between my lips and tipped a tiny amount of water into my mouth. It was the best drink I'd ever had in my life. To my immediate disbelief, she held the glass away from me.

Like a magic potion, I suddenly felt more awake, and a pang of anger rose from somewhere deep inside. I tried to snap forward, to grab the glass from her, but I instantly realised my hands were tied to the metal bedposts. They'd bound my wrists in leather straps and lengths of thin rope fastened them to the corner bedposts. I pulled and pulled, but it soon became apparent how futile it was. The cord was long, giving my arms movement, but they had tied it extremely well, in complicated knots. Amelia continued to hold the glass of water tantalisingly out of my reach. I tried to speak.

"Give it…" but my throat was too dry. It came out as a mumbled grunt. Amelia smiled.

"Stop struggling, there's no escape." She paused, looking out of the window and then back at me. It was daylight outside; I realised I didn't know how long I'd been there. I looked around the room. Like all the others in the house, it was sparsely furnished. An old wooden wardrobe at the far end, and a chair propped against it. I could see little else of interest.

"Now, listen, Matt…" She allowed me another tiny sip of water. "…do you agree to be good?"

I would have given anything to break free from the restraints, grab Amelia by the throat, and throw her head-first through the window. Instead, I nodded gently.

"Excellent. Listen carefully. If you do as you are told, I'll allow you to drink all of this water." She placed it on the bedside table. My eyes followed the glass as though it held all the essential ingredients to keep me alive.

"We know all about you. But you know that already, don't you? We have tried so desperately for you to fit in, for you to become one of our family. If you had accepted us, we would be living in our lovely new home now. We could be planning our future, even thinking of starting our own family. Your parents would have been so proud."

You bitch.

I recalled the time – a few days after Harrogate – and our conversation. Amelia had surprised me when she'd said, 'It can't be easy for you without your parents, or any other family for that matter.'. I'd questioned how she knew about my personal history, and she'd insisted that I'd told her when I was drunk in the hotel. I'd doubted myself then, but now I knew she had lied.

She looked out of the window again, the cool breeze catching her hair. She looked miles away, deep in thought at what might have been.

With my temper rising, I attempted to speak again, this time successfully forming the words and snapping her attention back to me.

"Fuck your family, Amelia."

She slapped me across the face. Hard. She then took the glass of water to the window and poured half of the contents away. Amazingly, by the time she sat back down next to me, her calm exterior had returned.

"And there is your problem, Matthew. It's all about you, isn't it? Drink enough alcohol until you forget things. Do your job until you become bored with it. Start seeing a girl until you get fed up with her. Move onto the next, fuck them, and then move onto the next. We're trophies to you, aren't we? Jobs are just jobs. Houses are just places to sleep. You've never grown up." She leaned so close that I could feel her breath as she spoke. "Well, now is your very last chance."

She stood and paced the room, contemplating her next words. She appeared to stall for time, trying desperately to keep her emotions under control. Eventually, she stopped striding up and down and returned to her place on the bed next to me. My head still throbbed and my stomach rumbled for food. She must have heard.

"Hungry?" she smiled. "Be a good boy, and I'll bring you food and water."

"What do you want?" I asked. My words came out as a croak and I felt my tongue sticking to the roof of my mouth. How long had I been there?

"Okay, this is what will happen. Believe me, this is your last chance." She shifted on the bed, making herself comfortable. "Tomorrow, your solicitor is coming down from Birmingham." She paused for thought. "Oh yes. You lied again the day you told me you were going into London to visit a branch of your solicitors, didn't you?" She shook her head from side to side as if to exaggerate her disappointment in me. "And Lisa. What is that all about? Graham had his suspicions in Cheshire. The way you looked at each other. We're not silly. Besides, if you're going to use condoms, at least have the decency not to leave a packet lying around with three missing." She smiled at me, loving every second of their detective work. "That good was she?"

Again, she drifted off and stared out of the window. I'm sure I saw tears well in her eyes, but soon she snapped herself out of the trance before concentrating on me.

"Where was I? Oh yes. Your solicitor is bringing all the paperwork in connection with your aunt's estate. Graham has arranged everything. We have told him you have been taken ill, but you desperately want to sign off all the documents so you can get the money transferred into our account."

Our account? Fucking bitch.

"At first he was uncertain, but we have agreed to cover all his costs and said we did not know when you would be well enough to travel. When Graham told him you had lost your job and needed the money, he seemed to come round."

"What did you say?" I croaked. Although it hurt to talk, I couldn't help but interrupt. "I've lost my job?"

"Oh yes, Matt. I spoke to Mike yesterday in the office. He has been concerned about your work anyway. You know, after your screw-up with those customers and your emails—"

Bitch.

"The emails you fucking planted you—"

"Now, now. Calm down. If you don't play ball, you'll regret it forever."

She stroked my hair again, loving the power she held over me.

"As I was saying. After the email debacle, Mike then somehow found out it was you who'd been sleeping with Lisa. Well, it gave him no choice. He didn't hesitate with his decision."

"How dare you…"

I knew it was futile to argue. She had all the facts. To be honest, it wasn't losing the job that bothered me, just the way they had manipulated me. They were treating me like a puppet, each taking turns to pull on the strings. My eyes scanned the bedroom.

"How long have I been here?"

"Only a couple of days. Don't worry, you're fine. Tracy knows exactly how much to give you."

I glanced down at my arm, expecting to see an intravenous drip hanging out, but there was just a piece of cotton wool held on by a plaster. Amelia followed my eyes.

"Oh, we've removed that for now. That was to help you sleep. For the next twenty-four hours, we'll give you tablets. We need you to be a little more focused for a while." She laughed. "Besides, we don't want you looking like a pincushion for the solicitor, do we?"

A wave of tiredness washed over me.

"What do you want me to do?"

"Okay. Your solicitor arrives tomorrow morning at ten o'clock. We will only give you a mild dosage between now and then to keep you sleepy. Before he arrives, I will help you shower and dress, and try to make you look a little better."

Her face took on a much more serious tone. She leaned closer still and emphasised every single syllable.

"Now, this is where your behaviour is critical. You will be nice to him, polite. You will give nothing away about what is going on. You will tell him you are unwell, Tracy will tell you exactly what you are suffering from. If he asks questions about your illness, let Tracy speak for you. If he asks anything about losing your job, I will answer. Do you understand?"

All I could do was nod my head. I had to think, but I was far too tired to come up with anything on the spot.

Amelia reached for the water and again tilted my head forward. She allowed me several sips.

"Good." She laid my head gently back onto the pillow. I could feel myself drifting in and out of sleep. Amelia kissed me. Whatever I thought about her, it still felt good. My eyes opened again.

"What will happen to me after the money has reached *our* account?"

She stood from the bed, not taking her eyes off me. Suddenly she looked sad, despondent. Did she have *some* feelings for me after all? Deep down, I knew I'd held feelings for her. But that was in the past.

"If you are good tomorrow, do exactly what I've just

said, then there is no reason you can't move away and start afresh. We know you will never accept us as a family. That is now futile. But, we have done nothing wrong—"

Another rush of adrenaline hit me hard.

"You've done nothing wrong? Ha! You took me on, knowing full well I was coming into money. The family trees, the selected CVs. My aunt was brutally murdered so things could move faster for you—"

"Oh no. You've got it all wrong. You have no proof of any family trees. And your aunt's murder was nothing to do with us. It's all pure coincidence. You can go running to the police, but I think we both know they'll just laugh at you. There's no evidence, they've already explained that to you."

Amelia left the room, a wry smile on her face as she went. She was right about the CVs and the family trees. I also had no evidence about who murdered my aunt. The police had got nowhere. What chance did I stand?

Sometime later – I had no concept what day it was – somebody walked into the room and woke me. Just as before, my head was groggy and I struggled to open my eyes. It was like the world's worse hangover, yet I hadn't had a drink for days. I forced my mouth open, my lips once again resisting whilst sticking together. My eyes tried to focus on who it was standing next to me. The wild hair was the first thing I noticed.

"Katrina," I said, my throat feeling as though it had a razor blade lodged somewhere inside.

She just grinned. Her hands were behind her back, and she rocked from side to side. I propped myself up onto my elbows, as far as the rope would allow. Every single bone and muscle in my body groaned with the slightest movement.

"What do you want, Katrina?" I didn't have the time or inclination for her crazy games. Suddenly, I realised the family would have no idea she'd come into my makeshift room; they would never have allowed that.

"I've brought you a present."

"That's nice. Is it a drink?"

I lay back down, staring at the ceiling. Silence ensued.

"Don't you want to know what it is?"

I've just fucking asked you.

"Yes. What is it, Katrina?"

"This," she said, moving one of her arms from behind her back. I turned my head to face her.

Her hair stood at all angles and her teeth looked as though she'd applied another layer of yellow to her enamel since I'd last seen her. But it wasn't her appearance that held my attention.

It was what she had in her hand.

41

FORGETTING my own hands had been bound to the bed, I attempted to lunge forward, desperately wanting the burner phone that Katrina brandished in front of me.

"Please, Katrina," I begged, as I lay back down disconsolately.

She tapped on the keys, pretending to send a text, humming as she did. I decided my best chance would be to humour her.

"Who you sending that to?"

"Father," she said, not taking her eyes off the phone.

"What are you saying?"

She paused for a moment before replying.

"That I miss him."

Katrina's faced dropped, and her appearance altered dramatically. She looked full of sadness. I propped myself back up onto one elbow.

"You know what would make him so proud, Katrina?"

She finally looked up at me, at last showing signs of interest.

"If you were to help catch whoever hurt your father, it would make him so proud of his little girl."

"Huh, huh," she said, tapping on the phone again.

"And do you know how you can help, Katrina?"

"No."

"Well, listen. If you pass me that phone, I can make some calls. Then, between you and me, we can find out who hurt him. Does that sound good?"

"Uh-huh."

Oh, please give me strength.

She kept tapping, and I lay back down on my back, exasperated with trying to communicate with her. Somewhere downstairs a door slammed shut. I heard footsteps. Glancing over at Katrina, she was in a world of her own, staring at the phone, apparently oblivious to the noise below. I closed my eyes, sighing heavily, and waited for the footsteps to begin the ascent up the stairs.

"But you're tied up," Katrina giggled. "You can't reach the buttons."

I propped myself back up, knowing any window of awareness was very short-lived where Katrina was concerned.

"But I can if somebody gives me the phone. It's like magic."

I knew Katrina would not have the strength, or the attention span, to untie the tethers holding me to the bedposts.

"Can I have it please, Katrina? You would be like a police detective."

She giggled, holding her hand across her mouth.

As the footsteps grew louder, now approaching the top of the stairs, Katrina finally stopped tapping on the screen. She glanced towards the door and then back at me.

Come on, come on.

Scared of frightening her, I lay still, looking at her through begging eyes.

The footsteps creaked as they arrived at the landing. Whoever it was, they were just seconds away.

Please, Katrina, please.

She peeked at the door again. The footsteps had almost reached us.

Give me the fucking phone.

Katrina took one step towards me. She lifted my pillow and pushed the phone underneath. I dropped my head down against it, letting out an enormous sigh. The door opened a split second later.

"Katrina. What on earth are you doing in here?"

It was Tracy. She looked sceptical, eyeing us both. I spoke groggily, faking a tiredness which had momentarily left me. My heart raced as Tracy approached, carrying a glass of water and two huge white tablets. I recalled Amelia saying they would lessen the dosage that night and the following morning, before the visit of my solicitor.

"She was just asking how I felt, Tracy. Nothing more."

Tracy didn't look convinced, but the combination of my acting and Katrina retreating into her childlike state must have made her half believe I could be telling the truth.

"Okay, but run along now, darling. You shouldn't disturb Matthew. He's not well, and he needs rest."

Katrina walked away, following her mother's instructions. We watched her leave. Just as she reached the door, she turned to Tracy.

"Mother."

"Yes, darling."

"I'm going to be a police detective."

I heard her giggling as she skipped along the landing. Tracy shot me a look. I shrugged my shoulders.

Propping myself up, Tracy held the back of my head and went to push the two tablets into my mouth.

"One at a time please, Tracy. They're nearly as big as my head. You wouldn't want me gagging, trying to swallow both at once."

She tutted but did as I asked. After she stuck the first tablet in, I quickly pushed it inside the gap at the back of my teeth; just as I had all those years ago when I pretended to take the pills that my mum gave me. Tracy tipped some water in, and I exaggerated a huge swallow. I thought I'd overdone my acting as she looked at me inscrutably.

The tablets were so big that I had no choice but to swallow the second. At least I'd only taken one, and so it was less than the normal dosage. No doubt I would still be drowsy, but nowhere near as bad as the full knockout punch.

As soon as Tracy left, I held the bedsheets up with my knees, retrieved the tablet with my tongue and spat it out underneath the covers. I reached for the tablet with my foot and pushed it down to the bottom of the bed.

The following morning I woke more alert than I'd been since they had locked me away. Amelia came in carrying a tray. I suddenly needed the toilet, and I put on my best stupefied voice.

"Erm, Amelia. How have I been going to the bathroom, you know, if I've been tied up?"

She looked at me inquisitively, maybe perturbed by how awake I was. I cursed myself.

"You've had a catheter fitted. Tracy is very clever.

Besides, you've eaten very little, so you've not done much."

Lifting the sheets with my knees, I couldn't see anything.

"Oh, she removed it yesterday, before I came into the room to see you. She said you were very groggy. It's nine o'clock now so we need to untie you anyway."

Graham stepped in without saying a word. He didn't even look me in the face. Instead, he walked to the top of the bed and forcefully pulled one of my arms towards the bedpost. I lay rigid, desperately scared that he would find the phone under the pillow. With the cord slackened, he untied the knot before walking around the bed and repeating his actions on the other side. Once he had finished, he gathered the rope and stood directly over me.

"Don't fucking mess this up today." Then he grinned. "You won't, will you?"

He left as abruptly as he'd arrived. I flexed my fingers back and forth and wiggled my wrists to get the blood flowing freely again. Pins and needles quickly followed before my arms went numb. Not at one point did I lift my head off the pillow.

"You look wide awake. Maybe you need another tablet," Amelia said, observing me.

"I feel like shit. Don't worry, I'll play along nicely."

She rested the tray on my lap. It contained a cup of coffee and a boiled egg. She cut the top off with a knife and handed me a teaspoon to eat it with. As soon as she reached over to help me sit more upright, I snapped and said I could manage myself. I could have kicked myself for appearing so bright and alive, but fortunately, she smiled, no doubt realising that I'd be full of anger towards her and her family.

After I'd finished eating, she helped me to the bathroom. I purposefully pushed the pillow down as I clambered slowly out of bed. Amelia didn't take her eyes off me and even watched me go to the toilet before helping me into the shower. The scorching water invigorated me further, but I knew I had to keep up the pretence of feeling like crap.

Once I'd put on a fresh T-shirt and shorts, I gingerly climbed back into bed. Amelia eventually made her way to the door.

"Erm, Amelia."

She tutted.

"What is it? You need to rest."

"I wondered if you could fetch my wallet and passport. I'm sure the solicitor will need my ID, and I want to make sure it's all in order before he arrives."

Amelia looked at me with disdain. This was supposed to be on her terms, not mine. However, she knew I could well be right, and they hadn't thought of that scenario. At least it gave me a few seconds on my own. I knew what I was about to do would be a tremendous gamble, but, by that stage, I knew I had little choice.

The knock on the front door signalled that it must be ten o'clock, and the solicitor had arrived. After she'd fetched my wallet, Amelia had given me my final instructions. I was to sit upright in bed and only speak when spoken to. She told me to act poorly – it concerned her I didn't look as ill as I should. Tracy came to see me shortly afterwards. She too said that two tablets should have made me much groggier, and she made me take another to 'slow me back down'. Again, I pushed it into the space between my back teeth before spitting it out after she'd left.

"Mr Walker. So sorry to disturb you when you're feeling so rotten."

They introduced me to Victor Thorpe, my solicitor. The whole of the family – apart from Katrina – stood behind him at the foot of the bed. Not one of their eyes left mine, watching every single move. I put on my best 'poorly' voice.

"It's okay. I feel exhausted, but I just need this done."

The four of them glanced nervously at each other.

Victor went through the formalities. At least he'd asked for proof of my ID, and I'd needed my wallet and passport. I gave Amelia a sarcastic smile. She didn't reciprocate. After a while, Graham asked if it would take much longer. Victor shot him a look so Tracy stepped forward and said it was only because I was so tired and that Graham was concerned about my health.

Yeah, right.

Melissa let out a gasp when Victor said the seven hundred and twenty thousand pounds should be in my account within days. I saw Graham squeeze his mother-in-law's shoulder. They were positively ready to burst with excitement.

Once he had finished, Graham, Tracy and Melissa saw him out, whilst Amelia stayed to keep her eye on me. We didn't speak. A few moments later, Tracy returned with Graham who took the ropes out of his pockets and clasped my wrists back in the straps before tying me back up. I begged him not to tie them so tight. He gave Amelia an inquisitive look before she looked at Tracy, and they both nodded in unison.

"I suppose it doesn't have to be so tight, Graham. Leave some more slack on the string so he can at least move his arms around. He still won't be going anywhere."

He grinned maliciously as he tied me back up. The

family were content now, the last pieces of the jigsaw all fitting into place. I just lay there with my head firmly against the pillow. As soon as they left the room, I heard Graham say something to Amelia, and they both laughed as they made their way along the corridor.

Tracy took four tablets out of a container, which I glared at wide-eyed. She pushed one in my mouth, and I immediately lodged it between my back teeth. As she bent to pick up the water, I coughed and allowed the pill to drop on the bed. Fortunately, it landed next to my hip, and I could shift my weight to cover it. Tracy was oblivious as she gave me a sip of water. The second one I had to swallow. After she pushed the third in my mouth, I again lodged it before drinking some water and pretending to gulp. I held the fourth under my tongue until she had left. I let out a huge gasp as I lifted my knees and spat both tablets out and under the sheets.

I lay still for a few minutes, listening intently until I heard the faint sound of chatter from downstairs. As soon as I'd discerned each person's voice, I wriggled my hands back and forth. Graham had followed Amelia's instructions and allowed me much more slack with the restraints. It provided enough manoeuvrability to reach underneath the pillow.

The first thing I found was the phone. I'd been dreading that Tracy would want to rearrange my pillows, but fortunately, she'd left me to rest, confident after she'd administered four huge tablets. As I clutched the phone, a wave of relief washed over me.

Next, I repeated my action with the other hand. But this time, I was reaching for the knife.

42

AFTER GRIPPING the knife tentatively between my fingertips, I gradually pulled it into my hand, inch by inch. One false move and I knew it would be out of my reach. Once I'd manoeuvred it into my palm, I gripped it tight, desperate not to let go.

When Amelia had been to fetch my wallet and pass-port earlier, I'd snatched the blade off the breakfast tray and pushed it underneath the pillow. After she'd returned, my heart went into overdrive as she collected the tray and rearranged the contents. I couldn't believe my luck when she appeared unaware of the missing cutlery.

I was already sweating, and I took a few moments to compose myself. Listening intently for any sound at all beyond the closed door, I slowly twisted the knife around in my hand so I could grip the handle and expose the blade. Next, I lifted my arm up and over the edge of the pillow. It was tricky, and the dampness of my palm didn't help, but eventually, I slid free and I could see the knife to the right of my head.

Again I had to twirl it around so it was at the correct

317

angle to reach the rope between my wrist and the bedpost. The blade looked almost blunt and at first, I could only slide it against the taut fibre. But, with a little more twisting and rotating, the cord made contact with the sharpest part of the knife; the serrated edge. It gripped into the nylon and I wriggled my wrist back and forth, trying to make some impression.

Sweat poured from my forehead and my mouth soon became parched. I relaxed for a minute, but without letting the blade move from its resting position. I tried again, the blunt teeth making a cutting noise above my head. Finally, I heard the twang of the first fibre cutting loose. The twine wasn't thick, but it was strong. However, the angle of my arm above my head allowed me to pull it tight.

Twenty or thirty minutes must have passed, and eventually, I could see the thread fray out of the corner of my eye. With all of my will, I pulled tight on my arm and wriggled my wrist to get as much traction as possible. Another twang encouraged me, then another. I could see I was almost through.

My teeth hurt where I clamped them together, and the bedsheets had become drenched in my sweat. One last effort. The knife gripped hard into the cord and I could hardly move it, but I wriggled and strained until, at last, the restraint gave way.

With sheer relief, my arm broke free, and I accidentally released the grip on the knife. I watched, as if in slow motion, as it twisted and twirled through the air. I tried to catch it, but only my fingertips made contact, sending it spiralling over the edge of the bed before finally crashing to the floorboards. It sounded ten times louder than the noise it produced, echoing around the barren room. I lay perfectly still, listening. And then I heard the inevitable footsteps coming up the stairs, at least two at a time.

With barely having a chance to think, I quickly pulled the sheet up to my neck to cover the sodden bed linen, before pushing my arm under the pillow, grabbing the end of the broken cord, which was still attached to the bedpost, and pulling it taut.

The bedroom door swung open, and Graham almost tumbled over himself, such was his haste to get to me. He looked me up and down, and then at the two bedposts. My heart pounded in my chest, and I repeated a silent prayer over and over in my head.

"We heard a noise," he said, looking around the floor. Fortunately, he had walked along the opposite side of the bed to where the knife had fallen. I tried not to overact this time.

"I might have been dreaming. I feel like shit. I think I've been hallucinating."

Graham studied my face. If he needed any evidence that I could have been telling the truth, he would have seen my matted hair and the sweat trickling from my forehead.

He leaned forward, his hand reaching towards me.

Is he going to strangle me?

Convinced he was moving to grab my throat, I lay there in terror, but he stopped just short and pulled back the bedsheets. His face contorted.

"Hell, Matthew, you stink. And you're soaked through."

I followed his eyes. The T-shirt I wore was drenched. The sheet beneath me looked as though I'd wet myself, and sweat stretched to the edge of the mattress.

"I'll send Amelia up. She needs to change you and the—"

"No!" I shouted, a little too enthusiastically. "Well, I mean, no, thanks. Please let me rest, Graham. These drugs, they make you feel like you're dying. Please," I begged.

He studied me again. Then he leant over to check the string on the bedposts.

Oh fuck.

Looking at the knots, he satisfied himself that they were still intact. Finally, he stood up and pulled the blankets back over me.

"Get some sleep then. Just a couple more days…"

"And then what?," I said, exaggerating my grogginess. "What happens after they transfer the money?"

He gave himself time to think before replying. As he spoke, a wry smile crept across his face.

"Let's wait and see, shall we?"

As soon as Graham had gone, I rolled over and unfastened the wrist strap. With one arm clear, I could sit more upright and I rubbed the other cord up and down the bedpost. At first, I thought it was futile, but I found a notch in the metal around the back, and could soon make headway. This time, I made quick work of the tie and once I was free, I picked the knife up off the floor and placed it next to the phone under the pillow. I lay back down, exhausted. I needed to rest and keep my emotions under control. I had to think and work out my next move.

I estimated it must be close to lunchtime, although I guessed I would be undisturbed until the afternoon at the earliest. The drugs they thought I had taken would presumably knock me out for at least that long. I had a window of two or three hours at most to plan my escape.

Think, Matt, think.

Grabbing the phone, I held it underneath my pillow and pressed the power button. Waiting until the muffled tone of the welcome message had ended, I took the phone out and saw that I had twelve missed calls and umpteen text messages. Most were from Lisa, and a few were from Lee. I played back the messages, pushing the phone hard against my ear to stifle any sound from escaping. Next, I read through the messages. It seemed all was in order, but they were both desperate to contact me; not only through frantic worry for my whereabouts but also wondering what to do next.

I replied once, copying them both into my message. I began by strictly instructing them not to respond to my message until I contacted them again later. Then, I told them where they needed to go and what to do – I would meet them there. I added at the end that they should contact the police if they hadn't heard from me by six o'clock.

Turning the phone back off, I looked around the bedroom, hoping to find some inspiration on how I could escape. Looking at my attire, I knew it would be difficult to leave in only a T-shirt and a pair of pyjama shorts. The very least I needed was a pair of shoes; especially where I was planning to go.

I knelt up on the bed to decipher exactly where I was in the house. The curtains were closed, and the window too far away without me walking across the floor. Would they hear? I had no choice. Whatever I decided, I would have to move across the floorboards at some point.

Placing one pillow onto the floor, I gently spun my legs over the edge of the bed and tentatively put my foot down onto the soft cushion. Picking up the other pillow, I placed it in front of the other and slowly stepped onto that. The floorboards remained silent underneath, and I repeated my actions until I reached the window. It was the only window in the room, and I gently parted the curtains before peering through the gap. The window faced the woods. I must be in the bedroom furthest along the landing; past both Katrina's and Tracy's rooms and the end of the turret extension.

As quietly as I could, I tried the latch holding the sash window in place. It turned easily. I could feel the draft coming through every gap. The window felt bone dry, and the wood appeared splintered in several places.

Looking back at the closed door, I placed the palms of my hands on the lower frame of the bottom pane. Almost too frightened to try it, I tentatively attempted to push it upwards. Again, I was in luck. It moved easily. There was already a gap at the bottom of a few centimetres; this had to be my way out.

Searching the room once more, I noticed the old wooden wardrobe on the far side. Painstakingly, I slid my feet on the pillows, making slow progress, conscious that any sound would have the family rushing up the stairs.

After what felt like forever, I eventually reached the wardrobe. It had a metal key in the single lock, holding the two doors together. Carefully, I gripped it between my finger and thumb. I gritted my teeth as it resisted and strained against being turned. Even though it hardly made a sound, to my ears, it resonated like it was being piped through a thousand-watt amplifier.

Once it clicked into place, the door swung forward. I caught it just in time before it spun on its hinges and clattered against the side of the wardrobe. Holding on, I stopped to allow my heartbeat to return to somewhere resembling normal.

The cupboard contained old clothes, hung on padded coat hangers. I hadn't seen hangers like those since I was a child. They were men's clothes, old-fashioned. Two shirts with no collars, waistcoats and three old woollen suits. Grabbing one of the shirts and a pair of trousers from underneath a matching jacket, I held them against me. They were too big, but they would have to do. At the bottom of the wardrobe were three pairs of shoes. Again, old-fashioned brogues, no doubt each pair to match a corresponding suit. I carefully retrieved a pair before guiding the open door to rest against the outer side of the cupboard.

There was an old wooden chair next to the wardrobe. Picking it up, I slid my way to the bedroom door and as quietly as I could, tilted the chair back, and guided the top rung underneath the door handle. I had no intention of testing it, but I hoped it would hold whoever out for long enough. Retracing my steps, I skated silently, and slowly, back to the bed, heaving an enormous sigh of relief when I eventually made it.

Dressing, I found the shirt fitted okay, but the trousers were too big at the waist. Fortunately, they had a belt attached, and I pulled it to its tightest setting. Finally, I put on the shoes. They were at least two sizes too big, exaggerated by my lack of socks, but again, I pulled the laces as tight as they would go. I must have looked a right state, but it was all I had. I even allowed myself an ironic smile.

The sound of the living room door opening downstairs soon brought me back down to earth.

43

FUCK!

I slid myself off the bed and dangled my feet above the pillows on the floor. Sitting as still as I could, I grabbed the phone and knife and put one into each of the trouser pockets. Straining to hear, I could just make out doors banging below. Whoever it was must have been walking from the lounge to the kitchen, or vice versa. But there were no sounds of footsteps on the stairs.

Desperately trying to hold myself together, I stood gingerly onto the pillows and dragged myself upright. Just as before, I slid my way across to the window. I paused again when I reached it, listening for any noise below. Nothing.

With the window still slightly ajar, I placed both of my hands underneath the bottom pane. The wood crumbled between my fingers and it took a while to find a good grip. The window frame was rotten, and I wondered how it even held the glass in place.

Bending my middle and keeping my back straight, I slowly stood up, praying that the window moved with me.

At first, it didn't move, but as I straightened, it gave with a jolt. A loud jolt.

Oh shit, no.

Standing motionless, with my hands still in position, I listened again. There were stifled noises somewhere below me, distinctive talking and then a raised voice.

Quickly, I bent my midriff again and pulled the window as I stood. It moved farther, but this time even louder than before. The bottom window complained as it rubbed and gripped against the top frame. Instantaneously, I heard louder voices. The door must have opened downstairs.

With one last heave, I pulled the bottom frame as high as it would go and cold air engulfed the room. Taking one last look behind me, I swung one leg over the windowsill, before turning half circle and bending my body down, ready to slide through the gap. As I lifted my other leg up and over, I heard footsteps bounding up the stairs, beyond the closed door.

Quick, Matt, quick.

The ground below looked a long way off, but at least the grass gave me hope of a softer landing. Holding onto the ledge, I lowered myself down. I saw the bedroom door handle turn, then furiously wobble, as the chair wedged itself tighter underneath.

"Stand back!" shouted Graham from the other side.

I leapt at the same time as I heard the loud thud above me. The force of my impact made my knees give way, and I fell in a crumpled heap to the floor. For a few seconds, I lay motionless, certain the pain would hit me. But nothing. I'd somehow escaped uninjured. I heard Graham shouting, and I glanced upwards. He was leaning out of the window.

"Bastard!" he yelled, before pushing himself back off the window ledge. "Get out of my way!"

Sprinting across the lawn, I turned immediately left, knowing that the coal bunker had to be around that side of the house. From there, I knew my way into the woods; the quickest path.

My shoes slipped, and I tried to make fists with my toes to hold them in place. Taking the phone and knife from my pockets, I gripped them as I ran as quickly as my legs would carry me. I didn't look back; instead, keeping my head down, almost diving into the trees, and feeling some kind of sanctuary as soon as I reached the woods.

I zig-zagged off the makeshift footpath, forcing myself as deep into the undergrowth as I could. The trees were evergreen and close together, providing some kind of hideout. As soon as I felt semi-comfortable, I stopped running, aware that the sound could be more of a give-away than any possible sighting. Trying to regulate my breathing, I watched and listened.

At first I couldn't hear or see anything, although the thick woodland made it almost impossible to distinguish much. Then, somewhere in the distance, I heard muffled voices. The distinctive boom of Graham's tones echoed around the woods, but I still couldn't make out if it was Tracy or Amelia who responded to him; maybe both. At least they sounded some distance from me.

Crouching down, I pressed the power button on the phone and waited impatiently for it to start up. The opening message was the last thing I wanted to see – 'Low Power. Charge Your Device'. Only one bar appeared in the top right-hand corner, and that flashed on and off.

Shit.

As instructed, Lisa hadn't sent any more messages, so I found her last one and clicked on reply.

. . .

```
Where are you?
```

My eyes darted around me as I waited for her response. There were still faint female voices somewhere in the distance, but I could no longer hear Graham. The phone vibrated in my hand.

```
In the woods. Where r u?
```

Think.

```
Where in the woods? You need to get out!
```

I waited as patiently as my heart would allow.

```
You know where! At the grave. Lee is
digging. Why?
```

My fingers shook as I typed.

```
Get away! Now! They're here!
```

Come on, come on.

. . .

`Who?`

Another message followed before I could even respond.

`Oh fuck. I can hear voices.`

I stood up, trying to find my bearings. I'd gone so far off the track I didn't know where the unmarked grave could be. If anything happened to Lisa or Lee – or both – it would be my fault.

I'd told them both about the grave and my crude pile of stones to mark the spot and where to leave the footpath. The day I'd met Lee in the pub, I'd explained it all. And then when I'd seen Lisa under the trees, I told her too. They had been in touch with each other, as per my instructions, and my last text from the bedroom had been to meet me there. What I hadn't expected was Lee to take a shovel and start fucking digging.

Before I moved again, I dialled 999.

"Emergency, which service do you require? Fire, Police or—"

Shit, no. Not now.

I looked at the phone – blank. Holding down the power button, the phone flickered into life before immediately cutting out to an empty screen.

Bollocks.

Shoving it back into my pocket, I slowly stepped forward; my eyes and ears peeled for sound. Tentatively, I crept forward, out of the dense undergrowth but still in the shadows of the trees. The only sound I heard was the soft crunching of ferns underneath my feet or the occasional twig snapping but they were damp, and the noise minimal.

Step by step, I made my way to where I thought the makeshift footpath must be. I knew it meandered through the centre, so I kept walking, and watching, until I finally saw the flattened track. My bearings told me to turn left, and whilst keeping a few metres to the side, I followed the path towards the unmarked grave.

At first, all remained quiet, eerily quiet, and it amazed me that when I heard any other sound, it calmed my nerves. But then I heard footsteps. Lunging into the undergrowth to my left, I crouched and waited. The steps were getting closer, but I couldn't distinguish from what direction.

My eyes darted up and down the path, desperately not wanting to see anybody but intrigued by who it could be in equal measure. The tap on my shoulder nearly made me jump from my skin.

"What the—"

But Lisa quickly put her hand over my mouth, stifling any further sounds. I tumbled backwards, unable to keep my feet. She crouched down beside me; she looked petrified.

"What is it?" I whispered.

"They've got, Lee, I'm sure of it."

"Who has?"

"Graham, them. I ran when I heard voices, but he wouldn't come. He kept digging."

I embraced her, holding her tight. Her body shuddered as sobs escaped. Putting my arms on her shoulders, I looked Lisa in the eye.

"When I asked before, did you and Lee make the phone call?"

She looked confused.

"Shit, I don't even know what day it is, but before they locked me away, I asked you to phone the police. Did you?"

She nodded, attempting to wipe the tears away that ran down her cheeks.

"And?"

"It's true. The detective rang me back earlier. They followed up on your idea. I told them everything you told me to say. Graham killed your aunt. They also want to investigate the disappearance of Ryan too. It's why Lee went digging. He went wild."

I'd asked them to contact the police, WPC Nina Murrow. I'd given Lisa the number from my phone. She had kept in touch with the local West Midlands constabulary. Before then, the police had had no luck trying to find a murderer. Whoever had done it hadn't left a single trace — or so they thought.

"So, what are the police doing now?"

"I texted her about thirty minutes ago. I didn't want to call. I've no idea who can hear me in here. They are on their way. Apparently, there is another path up here, from a village down the other side."

"Good, well done, Lisa…"

The sound of footsteps, and another noise, like something being dragged, made me trail off. I crouched low, pulling Lisa down with me. Then Graham's voice sounded — too close.

"We need to get rid of them," he instructed.

"How, where?" It was Amelia.

A pause.

"We don't have time to get them back to the house.

We must bury them here, in the woods. If it's somewhere off the beaten track, they won't find them for ages. Nobody will know, and without a body, there is no crime."

I stared at Lisa. She shook from head to toe. I gripped her tight, knowing she could give our whereabouts away with a single sound. Just along the path, we heard footsteps treading on the thick undergrowth. Whoever it was, they'd left the main track. Graham spoke again, this time even closer.

"Both of you, go to the house and pack. Get Katrina ready, but sedate her. Tell your mother we have to leave in one hour."

"What about you?" Amelia asked.

"I'll bury the body and bones here. That idiot Lee has done the hard work by digging up Ryan. Then I'll cover the other grave with branches and ferns. Matthew knows where it is, and that stupid bitch he's got in with. It's the first place the police will check. It will stall them when they find nothing but a mound of earth. It gives us a chance to get away."

Tracy and Amelia appeared on the path, only a few metres away. We watched them embrace. They spoke, but I couldn't work out what either of them said. They parted. Amelia going towards the grave and Tracy retreating to the house. I suddenly realised that could be the very last time I'd see my wife.

Lisa and I couldn't let go of each other. We sat, crouched on our knees, watching the main path through the woods, barely daring to breathe.

Then, Graham appeared behind us.

44

FORTUNATELY, he hadn't spotted us. He was dragging Lee's body through the dense ferns of the forest floor. Such was his concentration, he only had eyes for the task in front of him. He shuffled backwards, deeper and deeper into the undergrowth; a shovel tucked tightly under his arm. If we'd made the slightest sound or movement, he would have heard us straight away. Although we sat as still as statues, I became convinced he would hear my heart beating in my chest or the tiny whimpering sounds that escaped Lisa's mouth each time she exhaled. Eventually, he dragged the body far enough away that he was no longer in sight.

"What about Ryan?" I whispered in Lisa's ear. She shrugged her shoulders.

"You heard Graham? He said the police would find nothing. Do you think Katrina made it up all along or has he already removed the bones?" She shuddered at her question. We both already knew the answer.

The sound of the spade hitting the ground reverberated around us. It sliced in and out of the soil. Now and then, Graham would grunt, cursing under his breath. I finally let go of Lisa and made a hand gesture that we should head towards the track. It would put further distance between us and Graham, and allow me to find my bearings. I planned on running in the opposite direction from the house, towards the initial unmarked grave of Ryan and beyond towards the village. I had no intention of going back towards the house; I hoped I'd never see it again. Or the occupants.

Tiptoeing our way, I held onto Lisa's hand. One trip or subsequent squeal would alert Graham. After what felt like an eternity, we found ourselves back on the trail. Looking both ways to ensure nobody could see us, we retreated cautiously, one gentle step in front of the other.

As soon as I believed we'd put enough distance between us and Graham, and we'd be able to quicken our pace, I turned to face Lisa. She smiled awkwardly and, reading my intentions, gave a slight nod of her head. We broke into a trot, still holding hands; it gave us both an unspoken boost to know we at least had each other.

Allowing myself a quick glance over my shoulder, we hastened our speed further. We were too far away now for Graham to hear us, even if we accidentally stood on a fallen branch or tripped on a protruding root. The path followed a curve to the left and memory told me we were not far away from the grave. Slowing down, I pulled gently on Lisa's hand. She looked at me, unsure of my intentions.

"Why are we stopping?"

We slowed to a walk, and I pulled Lisa into the undergrowth next to my pile of stones.

"I need to see for myself."

After a few more minutes, we'd made our way to the

grave. It had been dug and refilled, fresh soil now on top forming a new mound.

"Give me your phone, Lisa."

Not taking her eyes off the grave, she fumbled in her pocket. A solitary tear ran down her cheek in recognition of what she saw. She passed me the mobile, which I immediately powered up. A beep told me an answer-phone message had been left, and I quickly called to listen. I smiled as I hung up.

"They're on their way. The police. They're coming up from the village. We need to follow the path to the top of the hill. Apparently, you can see from there." I gripped her hand. "We're going to be safe."

We turned in unison. I've no idea how neither of us heard her. How the hell had Katrina crept up without a sound?

"Shit, Katrina," I said, holding onto my heart. "I didn't see you."

Katrina just stared at us. She stood only two metres away. I'd got used to her hair, sticking up in all directions, but that day it had taken on a whole extra dimension. She looked like a cartoon character when they stick their fingers into an electrical socket. Her complexion appeared ghostly white, almost translucent. When she opened her mouth, her lips were blood orange, exagger-ated against the yellowing teeth.

"Hello, Katrina," Lisa took a step forward. "Matthew has told me all about you."

Katrina didn't move. Lisa took another step towards her.

"If you come with us, we can buy you something from the shop. Would you like——?"

"Shut up, bitch!" Katrina bellowed at Lisa. Her voice

echoed around the trees above. Lisa stepped back to join me.

Oh fuck. He'll hear.

"Hey, now, Katrina. We're just being friendly…"

Katrina's stare redirected from Lisa and trained in on me. She appeared to be looking from somewhere deep inside her head, and not from her eyes at all. Her voice had gone gruff, deep. It was as though she'd become possessed.

"Where is my father?"

I followed her eyes. She looked at the new mound of earth behind us. I realised immediately what she was thinking.

"Oh no, Katrina. No, no. This wasn't us," I pointed at the grave. "This was Graham. He's dug up your father. He's in the woods now."

"Liar!" she screamed. Her tone put the fear of God in me. I felt Lisa shaking.

"It's true, Katrina." Lisa tried again. "I can show you."

I shot Lisa a look.

"No. No way. I'll show you, Katrina."

We'd been so caught up with Katrina and trying our level best to keep her calm, that we didn't hear Graham approach from the pathway.

"Show her what exactly, Matthew?" He carried the shovel over his shoulder. His forehead gleamed with sweat, and his matted hair stuck up at angles. Katrina turned to face him and repeated her question.

"Where's Father?"

Graham crouched down, so he was face to face with her. He lay the shovel on the ground. I wished I could have just grabbed it and taken his head clean off.

"Your father is safe, Katrina. He's safe and asleep."

"You. Killed. Him." Her voice rose on each word. And then she spoke evenly again, slowly. "I know. I watched you kill my father. A long time ago."

Graham tried to reach out to her.

"No, no. I didn't hurt him, Katrina. He hurt himself. You see, he was sad, and he didn't like our family."

He looked up at me.

"And this man doesn't like our family either."

Katrina watched me too. I shook my head and mouthed it wasn't true. Graham stood again.

"Now, run along, Katrina. Find your mother. She's at the house."

"No. The police have taken mother. And Amelia. I watched from the woods."

I glanced at Lisa. Could it be true?

Katrina backed away. I spoke to her as she stepped backwards, still looking at the grave.

"Get help, Katrina."

Graham took a stride towards us. Lisa and I stepped back in unison.

"Stand back, Katrina," Graham said calmly. "We can still be together. You and me."

Katrina took a few more steps away. She appeared to be going into a trance again. I shouted at her, desperately trying to get her attention.

"Your father is in the woods. This man killed him, Katrina. This man is—"

"Shut your mouth!" Graham lunged for me, but I was just quick enough to sidestep his main surge. His huge hand caught my face though, and a sharp pain seared along my cheek. I immediately felt blood.

He turned, now crouching, ready to pounce again. He looked like a demented animal, wounded, yet still with enough strength to kill. Lisa stepped between us.

"Get out of my way, bitch!" he yelled and lunged forward again. He caught Lisa square on, knocking her flying backwards. She landed with a thud and her head snapped back as she hit the ground.

"You bastard! Leave her out of it!" I swung at Graham, missing by a mile. He smiled at me.

Checking Lisa was still, he crept towards me. He looked like a giant and his hands appeared to have grown larger still. I knew if he got hold of me, that would be it.

Each time he tried to grab me, I swerved back and forth. If I had one advantage, it was speed. But I knew I could only keep this up for so long. I took a glance at Lisa, flat-out on the floor. I could see her breathing, but she looked out cold. Then, out of the corner of my eye, I saw Katrina. She'd picked up the shovel.

I stepped back, knowing I had to keep Graham's attention on me.

"They know, Graham."

He answered as he kept his step in line with mine.

"Who knows what?"

"The police. They know. They've found your car, on CCTV—"

"You're lying. You don't—"

"We told them your number plate. You know, your shiny new car? You made a mistake, Graham."

"Bullshit." He was becoming animated, losing control.

"You parked too close to my aunt's house, didn't you? The police found it, on camera, on the night you murdered my aunt."

"Still no proof I did it. I've visited a few times be—"

"Oh, but this time they saw you approaching the house. I'm guessing you didn't leave your car before. They asked neighbours you see, neighbours who also have security cameras. They're amazing little things, Graham. You know, technology and the internet."

His face screwed tighter. Veins popped up on his forehead and the side of his neck. I wasn't finished.

"And we've got copies of family trees. Curriculum vitae. All of which have Tracy's and Melissa's handwriting on them. And do you know who else's handwriting is on them, Graham?"

His eyes widened.

"What the fuck are you saying?"

I lowered my voice for effect.

"Your wife, Graham. Your lovely—"

He lunged forward with all his force, connecting with my legs and bringing me to the ground in one swoop. As we landed, the first thing I noticed was the twigs of the makeshift cross that lay dormant on the ground next to us. Graham's face was only inches from mine, his eyes dilated, blood vessels looking as though they would pop at any second. I'd never seen such hatred etched across anybody's face before.

As he retracted his arm and clenched his hand into an enormous fist, I closed my eyes and waited for the inevitable. But he didn't strike me. In fact, he stopped mid-swing. With one last stare into my eyes, he collapsed, slow motion-like, to my side.

I looked up. Katrina leant over him with the shovel, poised to strike again. But there was no need. She'd hit him with such force that she'd killed him with a single blow.

As I pulled myself free, Lisa groaned in the distance. I rushed over to her, helping her groggily to sit upright. She looked dazed, but only that.

We both watched Katrina. She dropped the shovel and fell to her knees at the side of the new mound of earth. As calm as I'd ever seen her, she picked up the two pieces of wood and slowly wove the green wool round and round until she had formed another crude cross. She pushed it into the ground, her shoulders jerking as she silently sobbed for her missing father.

Meanwhile, Graham lay motionless by her side. By now, a steady stream of blood had escaped from the back of his head. I watched, mesmerised, as it slowly meandered its way through the freshly dug soil of the unmarked grave.

THE FAMILY TRILOGY

Part Two - Available Now

MOTHER

Can Matt finally move on from his living nightmare?

Afterall, he is still family

Available in both eBook and Print Versions

REVIEWS

Enjoy this book? You can make a big difference

Honest reviews of my books help bring them to the attention of other readers.

If you've enjoyed this novel I would be very grateful if you could spend just a few minutes leaving a review (it can be as short as you like).

Thank you very much.

ABOUT THE AUTHOR

Sign up to Jack's newsletter at the link below…

www.jackstainton.com/newsletter

Jack Stainton is an emerging author of psychological thrillers. His first book, 'A Guest to Die For', has received critical acclaim, on both sides of the Atlantic.

Now living in Devon, England, with his wife and two crazy cats, Jack's perfect day is sitting in his favourite café, drinking copious amounts of coffee, whilst writing his next book.

He's now living a lifetime ambition.

This is Jack's second novel.

facebook.com/jackstaintonbooks
twitter.com/jack_stainton
instagram.com/jackstaintonbooks

A GUEST TO DIE FOR

Jack Stainton's debut Psychological Thriller

Available online in both eBook and Print Versions

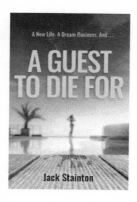

...I bought the book and read it in two sittings. Very good, lots of twists and red herrings.

This does exactly what a thriller should; it keeps you guessing until the end...

Excellent book full of twists and turns. The characters are brilliant... The ending was totally unexpected...

Sucking you in with a dreamy hope of a better start, the fear of what might happen next will keep you turning the pages!

A fantastic, gripping debut!